Song of Kosovo

Also by Chris Gudgeon

Fiction

Greetings from the Vodka Sea

Non-Fiction

*Ghost Trackers: The Unreal World of Ghosts,
Ghost-Hunting and the Paranormal*

Stan Rogers: Northwest Passage

The Naked Truth: The Untold Story of Sex in Canada

Luck of the Draw: True Tales of Lottery Winners and Losers

*Consider the Fish: Fishing for Canada from
Campbell River to Petty Harbour*

Out of This World: The Natural History of Milton Acorn

*Beyond the Mask: The Ian Young Goaltending Method, Book
II (with Ian Young)*

*An Unfinished Conversation:
The Life and Music of Stan Rogers*

Behind the Mask: The Ian Young Goaltending Method

(with Ian Young)

Humour

*You're Not as Good as You Think You Are:
A Demotivational Guide (with "Sugar" Ray Carboyle)*

Chris Gudgeon

Song of
Kosovo

A NOVEL

Edited by Bethany Gibson.
Jacket and page design by Julie Scriver.
Printed in Canada.
10 9 8 7 6 5 4 3 2 1

Library and Archives Canada Cataloguing in Publication

Gudgeon, Chris, 1959-
Song of Kosovo / Chris Gudgeon.

Issued also in electronic format.
ISBN 978-0-86492-679-1

1. Kosovo War, 1998-1999 — Fiction. I. Title.

PS8613.U44S66 2012   C813.54   C2012-902937-8

Goose Lane Editions acknowledges the generous support of the Canada Council for the Arts,
the Government of Canada through the Canada Book Fund (CBF), and the Government of
New Brunswick through the Department of Culture, Tourism, and Healthy Living.

Goose Lane Editions
500 Beaverbrook Court, Suite 330
Fredericton, New Brunswick
CANADA E3B 5X4
www.gooselane.com

In loving memory
Paul
Barb
Jess

Historical sense and poetic sense should not, in the end, be contradictory, for if poetry is the little myth we make, history is the big myth we live, and in our living, constantly remake.
— Robert Penn Warren

PRELUDE

IT WAS THE SUMMER of 2001, and through an odd set of circumstances I found myself in a barren office building in the ancient and melancholy city of Priština, capital of what is now recognized (by most people outside the Serbian sphere) as the Republic of Kosovo. The office building was literally in the shadow of the Sahat Kullan, the rococo clock tower that dated back to the waning days of the Ottoman Empire, and I spent many collective hours watching French soldiers from KFOR beetling over the tower — they had taken it upon themselves to replace the clock's rusted mechanical works with a state-of-the art electrical system — when I should have been collating and archiving a mountain of mildewed files. I had come to Priština, a youngish man seeking some kind of calculated adventure, and was swept up instead in the chalky underworld of the office functionary.

Our job was simple. Working with a small team of translators and admin staff, we were to organize tens of thousands of documents that had been collected by the advancing Kosovo Force — KFOR for short — the NATO peacekeepers charged with restoring order within Kosovo while making sure that the integrity of the proto-country's borders remained intact.

It could have been mind-numbingly dull work, but given my training as a social historian, and my natural inclination toward task-centred solitude, I dissolved into a minor dreamlike joy. My days took on a tidal rhythm: mornings and afternoons quietly huddled in my work cubicle, surrounded by a Berlin Wall of files; domestic solitude in the evenings, alone in a Spartan flat a few hundred metres from the office. I came, in time, to see myself as a kind of detective approaching every piece of paper as a potential clue to helping me understand the endless mystery that was, and remains, the Balkans.

Still, it was a tough slog. There were endless lists of names, haphazardly collected so that any sense of context was lost (was it a list of prisoners or dinner guests? Were they the names of schoolchildren who'd received their immunizations or members of one of those sports clubs that seem to permeate every level of Balkan society?). There were minutes of this meeting and that (one day, I came upon a treasure trove of documents from the Priština Horticultural Society, seventy-eight years of motions, bylaws, amendments, citations minutely detailed). There were invoices ("thirty-six hundred kilos of ground beef"; "twenty-seven hundred knitted hats") and memos ("Notice to staff: the rolling electrical blackouts will continue until the end of February. In the meantime, please avoid use of kerosene heaters within the premises.") There were seas of affidavits and legal briefs, great rolling rivers of draft manifestos and legislative amendments. There were fragments of sentences, which could have been the beginnings of great literary works or the remnants of shopping lists — one could never be sure.

It was amidst this cultural exuviae that I found the *Song of Kosovo*, although the real credit for the discovery should go to Octavian Rădescu, the Romanian polyglot who headed our translation team. I don't know exactly where or when he found the document, I just know that at some point rather later in my tenure I would sometimes be drawn out of my blinkered reverie by the sound of Rădescu, bivouacked in the cubicle next to mine, laughing discreetly or muttering a mild Romanian oath — "*O Doamne!*" — over and over again. Eventually, I took the bait and asked him what he was reading.

"*Pjesma o Kosovu,*" he said, in flawless Serbian. "*Song of Kosovo.*"

It wasn't exactly the title of the document, I came to understand: Rădescu had christened it in the manner of the Serbian epic song-poems he personally revered and considered literature of the highest order.

Thereafter, whenever we were bored or slap-happy from inhaling a toxic mixture of dust mites and Serbic conjugates, Rădescu would read passages of the document, impossibly translating from Serbian to Romanian to English as he went. Ostensibly, it was some kind of affidavit or brief, addressed to a certain Nexhmije Gjinushi (who had for a short time worked, I eventually verified, for the UÇK — the Kosovar Albanian nationalist liberation organization — which had begun compiling evidence of war crimes before the final shots in the conflict were fired). But in terms of its content and tone, the *Song of Kosovo* was like no legal brief I had ever encountered. Even by the standards of jurisprudence, it was long and somewhat rambling, and told a story almost too unbelievable to be true. Then again, as Rădescu never hesitated to remind me, Serbia was a country where the unbelievable was a matter of course, where mere months previously, for example, a wheelbarrow full of *dinars* could not buy a loaf of bread.

So, *Pjesma o Kosovu* joined my narrow list of obsessions for the duration of that Serbian summer. I spent hours in my flat with the manuscript laid out on the plywood box that served as both my kitchen table and desk, methodically (and poorly) translating the document from Serbian Cyrillic into something akin to English. It seemed a never-ending pursuit. My output rarely exceeded half a page a day, the progress impeded not only by a morass of idiom and syntax, but by my near-pathological attraction to the trivia, which led me to verify, or at least attempt to verify, even the smallest of details.

Near the end of my term, I found myself in an unpleasant circumstance for any reader. I had not finished translating *Song of Kosovo* and, given that I was barely a quarter of the way through, was unlikely to ever make my way to the end. I must confess that for a time I considered stealing the document (concealing it under my cloak and escaping under the cover of night, perhaps, although I did not then, nor have I ever owned such a garment), a pointless strategy given that everyone in the office regularly took files home, with no formal process for tracking the comings and goings of documents. Still, the drama intrigued me; I plotted out the caper but, in the end, abandoned it. It would have been such a small crime in a universe of state-sanctioned pathology and random atrocities, but I could not bring myself to do it. So I went instead to Ilmari Kunnis, the perpetually agitated Finn who headed our unit, and asked him directly. Kunnis was hungry looking, insectile, and not given to pleasant conversation. In particular, he was short-tempered, a general disposition worsened by the fact that, thanks to KFOR regulations, our office was the only designated non-smoking building in all of Eastern Europe. Frankly, I was terrified of this impatient cricket. Still, I held the file up for him to see and asked directly if I could take it with me.

He paused a long time, then finally asked, "Why?"

I could only shrug, and offer meekly, "A going-away present?"

Kunnis took the file from my hand and flipped through it tersely. After a few minutes, he shook his head. "Take it. Fuck. I don't care. Then he added with uncharacteristic softness: "You are a strange man, my friend."

I turned to go, my prize in hand, but he grabbed my elbow. "While you're at it, Chris, take some of these with you, too." He pointed his thumb at the stack of files beside his desk, a pile that rose, literally, from the floor to almost the fluorescent lights in the ceiling. "Do us a favour, Canada: take them all. I'll carry them to your flat myself!"

And that was that.

For several years I carried the document in the bottom of my briefcase wherever my travels took me — Turkey, Greece, Afghanistan, Pakistan, the Sudan — always intending to finish my rough translation but never quite finding the time to do so.

Until now. Finding myself rather more domesticated than I have been in a decade, I decided turn my attention once again to *Песма о Косову*. With a more focused approach, I endeavoured to translate the document and render it something rather more readable than my previous half-efforts — with no intention beyond the personal desire to bring a protracted and at times hypnotic read to a final conclusion. That other people started to show interest in the document is not an unpleasant surprise; every serious reader takes some pleasure in uncovering a hidden gem, regardless of its lustre. That my translation found its way to a publisher in a remote corner of the country I hadn't called home for several decades, however, is nothing short of miraculous. A wonder, to my mind, only exceeded by Goose Lane's offer to publish *Song of Kosovo*. After wading through a minor morass of moral and legal concerns, we were finally able to reach an acceptable agreement. The result is the volume you now hold in your hands.

A few caveats up front. First, the backdrop of the story — the dissolution of the former Yugoslavia and the resulting death throes — can be difficult to follow. It was one compact country, roughly the size of Michigan, held together by Tito's velvet fist. But when it fell, it did not shatter like glass but spattered more like liquid mercury into a group of formless, ever-changing globs.

At issue were not so much concerns of statehood but rather a kind of religio-ethnic sovereignty. In almost every region of the Balkans you will find enclaves of Catholic Croats, Orthodox Serbs, and Muslim Albanians, along with various other groups. So as one state tried to slip away from the Yugoslavian sphere, the localized tensions within the state intensified. As Croatia tried to wean itself, for example, the minority Serbs feared that their personal identities and connections to the larger Serbian community would be taken away. In Serbia itself, the Albanian majority in Kosovo worried about its future in a larger Serbian state. The result was a series of wars that raged in pockets across Tito's former country for much of the second half of the 1990s. From these pangs emerged Croatia, Slovenia, the Federal Republic of Yugoslavia, the Croatian Republic of Herzeg-Bosnia, Serbia and Montenegro, Macedonia, Republika Srpska, the Autonomous Province of Western Bosnia, the Republic of Serbian Krajina, the Republic of Bosnia and Herzegovina, the Republic of Kosovo . . .

As of this writing, some of these states still exist.

For my part, and despite my more obsessive inclinations, I tended to ignore this shifting political backdrop as I worked my way through the document, other than to recognize that it was a region accustomed to ongoing and eternal flux.

Then there is the matter of the folk hero Miloš Obilić, and again, some context may be useful. While I don't claim at all to be an expert on Serbian culture, this much I know: Serbian history — and by that I mean the place where memory and myth converge — begins and ends with Obilić. His mother, it is said, was a fairy queen, his father, a dragon. As a child, he was heralded for his prodigious feats of strength and daring, a born warrior who drew his physical power, so the story goes, from being weaned on mare's milk. As an adult, he joined the knightly Order of the Dragon, boonsman and blood brother to such legendary Serbian heroes as Milan Toplica and Ivan Kosančić, battling Turks and rescuing maidens, never forswearing the Serbian virtues of village, tradition, chivalry, and the selective chastity of courtly love.

Obilić is best known for his role in the Battle of Kosovo, the pivotal, albeit highly mythologized, moment of Serbian history. In the spring of 1389, Sultan Murad I, ruler of the Ottoman Empire, marched forty thousand troops across the Nišava Valley, deep into Serbian territory. The army was only nominally Muslim, with some five thousand Janissaries, the sultan's own personal guard made up of new recruits, twenty-five hundred mounted cavalry, hordes of *Akıncıs* — the advance terrorist squad — and several thousand peasants, press-ganged mostly, sustaining themselves, no doubt, with visions of plunder, one eye constantly on the lookout for a means of escape.

It was a formidable force, augmented by a core of turn-coat Serbs that included arch-nobles like Zavida Kraljević, Konstantin Dejanović, and perhaps even John VII Palaeologus

— the ambitious but ill-fated Greek who headed the Byzantine Empire for a tumultuous five months — all of whom threw their substantial resources into Murad's camp in hopes of advancing their own political aims.

Prince Lazar was leader of the Serbian troops, and his force was somewhat more homogeneous, made up of some five thousand of his own troops, at least as many Bosnian Serbs under the lead of Lazar's son-in-law, the shifty Vuk Branković, along with mercenaries and sympathizers from Poland, Hungary, and Croatia.

Lazar's somewhat Serbian army confronted Murad's slightly Muslim forces on the Field of Blackbirds, a low plain and critical crossroads for the Balkans. There was some skulduggery at the start of the battle, as Obilić found his loyalty questioned by Branković (a man of dubious integrity himself, who would ultimately pull his forces from the field when it became clear that the day was lost). Furious, Obilić swore an oath on his father's grave: he would personally kill Sultan Murad, or die trying.

Obilić led the charge and fought valiantly despite the intervention of a witch, who cursed Ždral, Obilić's mythic horse, leaving it vulnerable to the Turks' arrows, and who revealed to the enemy Obilić's most cherished secret: that he hid the keys to his armour in his vast moustache.

In the end, Obilić would fulfil his rash promise. Lying amidst the dead and dying in the aftermath of the battle, he waited patiently for the arrival of the sultan. Medieval warfare was a brutal craft; swords and short knives were designed to penetrate, gouge, and shred. Men rarely died quickly. The life leaked out of them, slowly, amid the stench of shit and entrails. The dying wept like babies and cursed like men.

It was far from a decisive battle. The casualties were heavy on each side, and as Murad sat on his horse, offering a prayer or considering his next move, a corpse rose from the purgatorial heap and lunged forward. Obilić's light sword struck the sultan directly in the heart, and he buried it to the cross before Murad's Janissaries could react. An instant later, Obilić was dead, decapitated with a single stroke. They didn't stop with the head, the sultan's men. They cut Obilić's body to ribbons, fed most of him to the dogs, and paraded his head and massive genitals on top of spiked standards. But no matter. The deed was done. Murad had fallen and Serbia's promise had been fulfilled.

Of course, as Obilić's story underscores, any discussion of the political or historic context of *Song of Kosovo* also begs a larger (in artistic terms) question: how "true" is this story? That is, what elements of this story embrace a verifiable, measurable, and shared reality, and what elements are fabrications, the work of a semi-deranged mind, a prankster, or a literary poseur? In the end, I am afraid, it is impossible to say. The Albanian warlord Korbi Artë, for example, who holds Zavida's life in the balance: did he exist? My research tells me that it is possible he did. In various documents there are indirect references to a man (or men; it's possible that the Korbi Artë of history is a composite figure) with a similar name and sharing his penchant for brutality. He had a reputation for cold-hearted calculation and slaughter, this Korbi Artë — he was directly responsible for the murder of, perhaps, as many as thirty-seven hundred men, women, and children — and had seemed to come from nowhere to take effective control of the hills and backcountry of south central Kosovo. The fact that any definitive trace of him has disappeared from public record since the end of the Kosovo war is meaningless. Hundreds, if not thousands, of others rendered themselves invisible in the aftermath of the conflict. Korbi Artë's case is not exceptional.

More intriguing is the case of Zavida Zanković himself. I have established with a fairly high level of certainty that a man of this name lived and worked in Belgrade during a period that roughly corresponds with that described in the manuscript. And while I cannot find any direct documentation that suggests that a Serb named Zavida Zanković was being held for trial by Albanian authorities near the end of the war, I have found nothing that refutes it. In the end, though, both the Christian and surnames are fairly common throughout Serbic Europe, and the most likely candidates appear to have disappeared in the general Balkan Diaspora, which reached a peak in the late 1990s (but has been ongoing since, at least, the demise of the Austro-Hungarian Empire). In any case, we cannot rule out the possibility that, while the circumstances occurred as described, the names were changed to protect the safety of everyone involved.

For my part, I take my cue from Rădescu's arbitrary title of the work. Like the epic songs of Serbia's remarkable literary prehistory, it is less a rendering of events as they occurred in some kind of historic context. More, a representation of those kinds of events that only take place outside of time and history. This is not a story of Serbia or Kosovo or about Serbia or Kosovo or from Serbia or Kosovo, but can only be understood as something that exists above and slightly to the left of these temporal states. Of course, it almost goes without saying that history is ever nothing but fiction of the highest order.

Finally, I must apologize for the roughness of this translation. It is a difficult task, translation — Umberto Eco calls it "the art of failure" — and I am not studied in it. Still, I do find myself indebted to a vast team of academics who assisted me along the way. Particular thanks are due to Dr. Georges Bogolmov of the Department of Slavic Studies at Carleton University in Ottawa, Canada, Sandra Urschel of the New York's Pratt Institute, and of course, the entire staff from the Department of Philology, Univerzitet u Beogradu.

Puno Hvala!

I would be remiss as well if I did not acknowledge the generous support of the National Council of the Arts and the Deutsche Forschungsgemeinschaft. Without the generous efforts of all of the aforementioned, this work would have never seen the light of day.

CG
Aix-en-Provence

Песма о Косову

1

THE SONG BEGINS SIMPLY. First with silence. Then with a soft melody, played on a *guzal* or *kaval*, rising like smoke in the distance. Soon, a *dajre* will join, setting a deliberate beat, only slightly slower than the pulse of a human heart.

Over time, more instruments will join in, and then voices, as sweet as air.

Eventually, Nexhmije Gjinushi, melodies will intertwine and overlap, rhythms emerge and collapse, and the song will thicken, impenetrable like a fortress or the mind of a lover. It is the song of distance, the song of separation, defined more by the spaces between the notes than the notes themselves. It is the song of death and life. It is the song of separation and completion. The song is specific to this time, this place, these instruments, these players. The song is timeless and sweet and putrific, a song as prehistoric as grass, as ancient as the gods. The song is insistent, a temperamental white noise that drifts in and out like a distant radio signal that you can turn neither on nor off.

In these vacant hours, alone in my comfortable cell (waiting for you, Nexhmije Gjinushi, to bring me your cheerful, hollow help), the song snakes in and out of the shadows, rises and falls like a spring breeze, weaves itself, like history, around you and inside you. Cover your ears, my dear, run, hide. There is no escaping it.

2

YOU'VE ASKED ME TO write down my thoughts, Nexhmije Gjinushi, to provide a full accounting of how I came to be in this place. Leave nothing to the imagination! — that was your decree. You believe it will help me in my impending trial. But we know better, don't we, dear? It's an exercise for us, a ritual: you playing the dutiful counsel and I, the earnest defendant. I will peck my story and you will consult your law books and we will sit in rooms waiting for Korbi Artë's great black boot to come down and squash us both.

Still, we play, biding our time.

"Mother's occupation?"

"Apprentice harpy."

"Father's occupation?"

"Future war criminal."

I'm afraid irony is lost on you, my dear.

"Nationality?" (You have a way of pursing your upper lip whenever you ask me a question that you know I will not answer directly. I find this trait endearing, Counsellor.)

"Hmmm. I don't like labels. I think we should just accept people for who they are, and not for where they come from."

"You're not making this any easier, Mr. Zanković."

"I am not trying to be difficult. *Imagine no direction*. Wasn't it the Buddha who said that?"

"I am quite certain that it was John Lennon, Mr. Zanković, and I am even more positive that a military tribunal will not find the song relevant to this case."

I must say, Nexhmije Gjinushi, you have my deepest sympathies. Your earnestness and dedication will never earn you any friends. More to the point, you are in a tough spot. Although you wear the uniform of the UÇK, I can only assume that, since you are in Korbi Artë's house, he is your master. I will never understand it all completely, the cross-pollination of tribal factions, paramilitaries, police, international advisors, and regular soldiers that make up your army — it's almost as confusing as the Serb ragtag. So, I respect your *desire* to do a good job, but forces, I fear, are conspiring against you.

Admittedly, the complexity of my case would tax a dozen Valtazar Bogišićs, so I can only imagine what it's doing to the mind of my unexpected lawyer. The charges alone are dizzying: fomenting treason, conspiracy to conspire, impersonating a prisoner of war, impersonating an officer of the Ushtria Çlirimtare e Kosovës, consorting with history, providing material support for a terrorist organization, murder in the first degree, genocide, crimes against humanity, et cetera. And even those that should have been the most basic of questions, Nexhmije Gjinushi, are proving difficult to untangle. My citizenship, for example. Was I Kosovar or Serb? I appear to have been wearing an Albanian tunic, typical of this region, at the time of my arrest, and can speak a passable if not overly cultured Gheg. I am, however, factually Serbian, as Korbi Artë himself could easily attest, should he choose to do so.

And in any case, I am the least of Korbi Artë's worries. Why he should find time to bother with me, I do not know. Something to do with history.

And so it goes, back and forth, I and you — my counsel — huddled together in my cosy cell as little Adelina maas and nibbles on the horsehair chair. I cannot help but notice the softness of your cheek, my Kosovo Muse, the slight, deferential slope to your shoulders. When you leave my cell, my dear, the scent of your sweet candy perfume — some designer knock-off no doubt — lingers for hours. I have come to realize — with the utmost respect to my Sweet Angel Tristina — that I am falling into a kind of infatuation with you, Nexhmije Gjinushi, something lyrical and insistent, almost akin to love.

3

BTW: MUCH APPRECIATION to you and NATO for the use of the iBook, Nexhmije Gjinushi. Who could have imagined a computer that fits into a suitcase! The refugees of the world will thank Steve Jobs; he's making diasporas so much more convenient.

You've asked me to write down my story, Counsellor, and I have dutifully begun. It brings me a certain peace or, at the very least, a distraction from the song descending from the hills. Your intent is to develop a body of evidence, and this I understand, my dear. I understand the urgent nature of your request too, Counsellor. Five days is hardly time to prepare for a trial of this complexity. The iBook will help immensely. I will endeavour to put things into some kind of context, but I fear that the shape of events will elude me, and in the process, my genuine bewilderment will be taken for obfuscation (which I can't imagine will please the Court). But I will try.

Exhibit A

My name is Zavida Zanković. While technically a lowly *Razvodnik* in the Provisional Armed Forces of the Federal Republic of Greater Serbia, I have no personal commitment to this or any other cause. Not that I require your sympathy or absolution,

Nexhmije Gjinushi; as a lapsed pretend-Buddhist, I do long for any sort of material afterlife.

Exhibit B

I am a Serbian by birth, having been forged in that future former country, Yugoslavia, and in my twenty-odd years have accumulated almost nothing. The sum total of my possessions to date include a name (and even that I am not longer certain belongs to me), some borrowed clothes, an envelope with documents of dubious value, and a small herd of sheep, which at last count ran somewhat less than two.

I suspect that the fact that I was dressed in a rather Albanic fashion at the time of my arrest has created some confusion. It is not, as it has come to be logically assumed, a deliberate attempt at subterfuge or espionage. It was simply a matter of practicality and — yes — survival. I was found in the dress of a Kosovo farmer because I had been salvaged and supplied by a Kosovo ranchman and heroin runner, the imperial Fisnik Valboni. He, quite literally, gave me the shirt off his back, and through him, I acquired little Adelina, setting me on my current career trajectory.

Exhibit C

This place I think you've heard of, Nexhmije Gjinushi. They call it Kosovo, but it has been called many things over time: Dardania and the Principality of Dukagjini, the Autonomous Province of Kosovo and Metohija, and Socialist Autonomous Province of Kosovo. For a time it was reduced to constituent parts: the Banate of Zeta, the Banate of Morava, the Banate of Vardar Republic of Kosova; and throughout its history it's been malleable, a splutter of clay or, better, a scrap of meat, pulled and torn by varieties of scavengers until it has no permanent form. It's only an idea, this Kosovo, an abstraction. Look on any map, and you'll see, very clearly, in that amorphous space that plugs the hole in the earth where Serbia, Montenegro, Albania, and Macedonia almost meet, a hand-painted sign: UNDER CONSTRUCTION.

Exhibit D

More specifically, I am the reluctant "guest" of Korbi Artë, having arrived at his compound seated on the back of an ancient Russian motor scooter, clinging with one hand to the thin shoulders of Vasile Lupu, Korbi Artë's aide-de-camp, while holding little Adelina (half-stuffed into the front of my jacket, her wet nose nuzzling my Adam's apple) with the other.

The compound sits deep in the Šar Mountains on the very edges of what appears, from my limited vista, to be a more urban settlement. You have a better idea I'm sure, my dear, with your comings and goings. I sometimes imagine where you go at night: to a little condo, no doubt, or a cottage overlooking one of the tiny lakes that pock these mountains.

The compound itself is nondescript. Fortified, yes, but that is not unusual in these parts. You may not know, Nexhmije Gjinushi, that, when I first arrived, Adelina and I were placed in a dark room on the third floor of the smaller of the two houses (both with the vaguely Spanish lines and windows and doorways framed by ornate Moorish arches). It was comfortable enough, I can assure you: a small bed with an overstuffed mattress, a horsehair armchair (which Adelina commandeered), a small desk with an old fashioned ink blotter and a sheaf of green notepaper — and every four hours I was allowed fifteen minutes of "relaxation time" in the slate-floored terrace. And so I waited in my velveteen boredom, sleeping on my dimpled mattress, labouring through days-old editions of *Koha Ditore* (which assured its readers that Slobo had already all but capitulated, even as Serbian shells rumbled in the hills around me), pacing the orange carpet of my room and the black stone floor of the terrace, and playing Pesë Katësh with the elderly Imbrahim Kaceli, who, Vasile Lupu repeatedly assured me, was in fact my bodyguard and not my jailer (although I could not help but notice that the old man moved his hand to his pistol whenever my pacing brought me too close to a doorway).

"Am I a prisoner here, Vasile Lupu?" I would ask with regularity. Vasile Lupu answered all my queries with an earnest patience — Albanians are nothing if not gracious hosts — and the careful diction and the relentlessly trilled "r" that identified him as native Tosk speaker and, therefore, not of this place. A military adviser from Tirana, no doubt, sent, like you, to advance the cause of Greater Albania.

In any case, Vasile Lupu would insist that I was a guest in Korbi Artë's house and was free to go any time I wanted. "Of course," he would add, with a forceful sincerity that made it clear I had no choice in the matter, "For your own safety, it's best you stay put. Besides, I'm betting you'll want to meet Korbi Artë first."

Exhibit E
At 6:30 in the morning on the third day of my stay, Vasile Lupu entered my room accompanied by four paramilitary policemen. After rousing me with a firm shake, he opened a grey envelope and took out a thick paper, which he unfolded methodically.

"I have here, Zavida Zanković, a warrant for your arrest.

You shall be removed from this place immediately and taken to a secure facility to be held until such time that your case can be heard by the proper judicial authorities."

I must admit that I laughed at first, all the time realizing that a joke of this magnitude would have been beyond Vasile Lupu's limited capacity for mirth.

"And the charges?"

"Fomenting Treason, Conspiracy to Conspire, Impersonating a Prisoner of War, Impersonating an Officer of the Ushtria Çlirimtare e Kosovës…"

I felt the anger boiling in me; I quickly composed myself. "What is the meaning of this?" I rose from my bed quickly to underscore my indignation. "Am I not a guest of Korbi Artë? Hasn't he himself invited me — welcomed me — into his home? He'll have your heads."

There was a long quiet pause, and even the police — men, no doubt, almost beyond all shame — looked away. Vasile Lupu stood silently, his shoulders slightly slumped, folding and refolding the document in his hand.

"Korbi Artë" — he began —"signed the order himself."

So there it is, Nexhmije Gjinushi, the evidence pertaining to my arrival at my present circumstances, to the best of my recollection.

I suspect, though, you'll be wanting more — the details *inside* the details. A full accounting of how I came to be in this place, just as you've requested, Nexhmije Gjinushi. And so I will take you now to the exact moment where my journey began.

4

ONE MINUTE I WAS biding my time — a teenager, true — but still clinging to the edges of childhood, not exactly innocent, but rather unaware and unconcerned about the greater world around me. The next I was thrown, violently and quite literally, into the world of adults.

The force lifted me off the toilet seat and drove me head first into the lavatory wall, no difficult feat. Even at thirteen, I was slight and scrawny, a nest of bones; the lavatory was as dark and cramped as every other room in our small house

I think I stayed there for a moment, my face pressed up to the wall, one foot in the WC reflexively struggling for a toehold in the turded porcelain. Father was at it again, experimenting. We were used to the occasional bursts and pops, to small colourful fires that appeared and disappeared spontaneously, to clouds of wretched black smoke that smelled of rotted chicken wandered through our house like displaced ghosts. I believed Dobroslav Zanković to be some kind of wizard or itinerant magician, a man of great power and mystery who spent hours wrapped in the corrugated aluminium shed he'd constructed on the patch of mud and small stones that was our yard, conducting experiments that would, one day, uncover the secrets of existence.

As my senses recovered, I became aware of a metallic tang in the back of my throat. I lifted my hand to my mouth and felt the warm sap, and still slightly confused I looked at my fingers and found them black with oxidizing blood. Few things terrify a young boy more than the sight of his own blood, and yet I could not gain my feet. Every time I extended my leg, Nexhmije Gjinushi, my small foot slipped again in the filth and it was soon wedged in the drain opening.

"Beba! Beba!" I called frantically to my younger brother, Dobra. My shadow in childhood, he was never far off. "Get Mati, quickly. I'm being eaten by the toilet!"

But no response and I imagined that he too was laid out somewhere, bleeding, his head half-embedded in a wall, unconscious or worse.

And now I was certain I would get sucked into the pipes — I'd heard of such things happening — and carried away by the murky Morava River. I could see it, my corpse, washing ashore in the woods between Aleksinac and Beograd, to be torn apart by packs of feral dogs and ravenous, yellow-tusked boars.

"Beba! Beba!" Only nine months my junior, he was what my aunts generously called "simple." Perhaps he could hear me, but in his...simplicity...thought it only a game. Just as likely he was off exploring the mines.

Eventually, I was able to pry my free leg under the washbasin cabinet and, placing both hands on the towel rack, freed my other foot. But now a new horror revealed itself. As I drew the back of my hand across my face to clear the blood away, I felt — what? I want to say nothing, but it seems impossible to feel nothing. I guess it is more accurate to say what I did not feel: my nose. Somewhere between the explosion and the wall, my nose had gone missing.

I raced through the small house in a panic, crying for my

mother, leaving a trail of blood drops and little shit prints behind me. I found her in the kitchen, sitting at the folding charcoal-coloured linoleum table (her most prized possession, purchased from Robna Kuca, Beograd's finest department store).

Mother was a Kosovo Maiden through and through. Do you know the term, Nexhmije Gjinushi? It describes, not an ethnic Albanian as one might think, but the perfect Serbian woman, full of piety, charity, compassion, bitterness, and melancholy. The original Kosovo Maiden is part of the mythology of my peoples, Counsellor, famous for wandering the battlefields of Kosovo in search of her betrothed, the warrior knight Milan Toplica, blood brother to legendary hero Miloš Obilić himself (it is telling, Counsellor, that we remember the name of her fiancée Toplica but not the name of the maiden herself, isn't it?). She lives on today, this Kosovo Maiden, in the hearts and minds of every *baba* and *majka*, in the romantic films on the state-run television channels, through images forged in Serbian epic poems and Uroš Predić's maudlin painting (a fixture in the popular imagination, Counsellor, rivalled only perhaps by the velvet Christ and those poker-playing dogs).

In any case, there was mother, her hair was somewhat askew. Some of the pots and dishes had fallen from the shelves, scattered, no doubt, by the force of the blast. She sipped her tea and her expression, as always, betrayed little. She looked at me and my bloody face with a kind of blasé disdain.

"Let's get your shirt off, Vida," she sighed, tugging my T-shirt up from the bottom, as she mumbled about the difficulties of laundering out bloodstains. Then she began wiping my face with the knot of tissue she kept perpetually wadded in the rolled-up sleeve of her blouse. She rubbed roughly at first, then became more deliberate and select, until she was quite dainty, dabbing at the area around my once-nose.

"What have you done here, Vida?"

"Am I going to die, Mati?

"Yes. Eventually. But for now, we'll need to find your nose."

The whole world was ending! I thought, and only later, covered in blankets and holding a garlic plaster to my face, did I realize that it wasn't the whole world that was ending but just part of my world that had come to an end, as another part had begun.

5

WAS THAT THE FIRST time I ever passed out, Nexhmije Gjinushi? I am not sure. Certainly, it is the first time I ever remember passing out. It remains lucid: the leaden weight in my head, the darkness that absorbed me before gravity took charge. I suppose I was semi-conscious, and while I was aware that I had lost my faculties, and that I was falling down, I was not afraid. Even as I felt my head strike something hard, and only later would I learn that I had crashed into the corner of mother's prized table, breaking off an irreparable chunk and splitting my forehead in the process — I felt no pain and less fear. I was filled, instead, with a kind of elation: rapture? That's the word. It was a religious engulfment, a *connectedness* to rival that experienced by the Holy Martyr Djordje of Našice or any of the legion of tormented Serbian saints (are there saints in your faith, Nexhmije Gjinushi? I can't imagine that there wouldn't be; you Muslims have such rich and active imaginations. There is so much we don't know about one another!).

My rapture did not last long. I soon recovered into the world of blood and feces and a mother torn between tending to her dismantled son and lamenting her broken, beloved linoleum table. But in those lost moments I felt my soul soar like a blackbird over the fields of Kosovo. And the cause of this rapture? Some disengaged synapse jolted into action by the blow to my head? A stress-induced seizure wreaking havoc with my cerebral cortex? A sudden coincidental infusion of the Holy Spirit? Whether caused by forces physical or metaphysical, I cannot say. I just know that I felt wondrous. And that's when it happened. For the first time I saw him. Sitting there in a great throne of vines and leaves, the colour of night, a mighty rock of a man, his black hair entwined with garlands, suited in gleaming silver armour, in his right hand a great steel sword, reflecting light so boldly that it almost blinded me, at his feet, a mound of fresh and bloody corpses.

At first, Miloš Obilić did not speak. He laughed instead, like a rumbling lorry, his breath hitting me like the sweet sting of incense. Then he held his sword out to me.

"Take it, my son..." His words landed somewhere between invitation and command.

He smiled broadly, his great square jaw filling the darkness with teeth.

"Zavida Zanković, take the sword..."

And he held it out to me, a tease, to be certain, for no matter how much I stretched forward to receive the gift from this, my demigod, it always remained a fraction beyond the tips of my fingers.

And then I fell back into the other world. I opened my eyes to find my father bent over me. His sick breath slapped me, rotted by the chronic stomach ulcers that burned him — like an everted heretic — from the inside out. He dabbed, alternately, my bleeding forehead and my bloody former nose, and cooed words of comfort.

"It's okay, Vida. We'll fix you right up, son, we'll fix you right up."

Meanwhile, my four brothers were lined up, enjoying the

spectacle. Beba Dobra covered his face with his hands, trying to suppress his laughter. It was indeed a game to him. My mother towered behind them all, the chunk of broken table in one hand and stack of clean linen strips (prepared in advance, I can only assume, for just such a medical emergency) in the other. She handed Father a clean strip with wordless operating-room efficiency whenever one gauze became too bloody, all the while upbraiding him with the silences between her words.

"You're finished then" — she paused, handing Father a gauze — "working?"

"I'm closing in, Bice. We're almost there this time, I can feel it."

Father waited for her to respond, you could see it in his face, waiting and hoping. Mother slowly tore a strip of cloth, bisecting it cleanly. She handed it to Father.

"So," she said. "You won't be needing the shed anymore?"

Father feigned concentration, dabbing my face intently.

"My workshop, my love, will be fine. My work…" His voice faded to an imperceptible mew.

Father had, to use mother's phrase, "an active mind," not necessarily a good thing in her estimation. While she nominally supported his chemical investigation into the transmutational properties of certain base metals, she remained theoretically opposed to the "active mind" behind these investigations. For her, the phrase implied a certain reckless creativity, more suited to a lunatic or a criminal than a civil engineer with a wife and family and other obligations. But her perfectly spaced silences and chronic disdain were, at that point in our lives, as close as she ever came to criticising him.

"Do I need the doctor?" I asked urgently. "I don't want stitches. Am I going to get stitches?"

"Shhh, Vida, you don't need a doctor."

"Are you sure?"

My brothers instinctively raised their hands, as if protecting themselves, as I questioned Father's medical authority.

"Do you think I don't understand simple medical procedures?"

"Your father was a pre-med student —"

"Exactly, Bice. I was almost a medical student before being accepted into the Faculty of Mechanical Engineering, don't forget. It's a simple nasal contusion."

"You need to listen to your father."

"Indeed. See, Bice" — my mother bent down and admired her husband's diagnosis; this was practical science, something she could appreciate — "a simple sinal abrasion that will be best treated with a garlic plaster and a salt water enema. It's alright, my dear, you may touch it."

Mother gingerly touched the tip of bone protruding from my nasal cavity. I could hear the cartilage crunch as my nose retracted slightly. My nose, it seems, had not been blown off by the force of the explosion, as my mother and I assumed, but merely (and I use this word judiciously) crushed by the impact of my face with the wall. My mother considered it a blessing — at least I hadn't lost my teeth. Dentists were scarce and expensive in this remote corner of the Serbian republic; surgeons were in much greater demand, and therefore in higher supply. My Father concurred, deciding indeed that reformed appearance marked me for great things. A revolutionary perhaps — or even martyr.

"The medical term is saddle nose," Father said, proudly pulling the words from some cobwebbed corner of his memory. "It a relatively common condition, characterized by the concave nature of the nasal bone. I'm happy to say you will live, young man. All you need is some bedrest and basic medical treatment. I'll get the rectal bulb and saline solution."

My father stepped back for a moment to appreciate his handiwork; he turned and pulled my mother with him in his orbit. "We won't be but a moment."

I was left, Nexhmije Gjinushi, whimpering softly, thinking how would I get through life without a proper snout, wringing my hands tightly wrapped in the linen bedsheet. My brothers stood before me, caught somewhere between compassion and fraternal Schadenfreude. Jovo, the eldest, stepped forward and put his hand on my shoulder in what I assumed was, for him, a rare moment of empathy. "Don't worry," he said, glancing at my other brothers, now grinning like idiots. "You'll get used to the madness."

6

TO AN UNSERB, it might be difficult to comprehend the significance of Miloš Obilić. Even to an Albanian such as yourself, Nexhmije Gjinushi — raised upwind from the stench of Serbian history, tempered, if I may mix my metaphors, in those Illyrian fires, buried (to continue my barbaric line of thinking) in the Songs of the Frontier Warriors — Obilić must seem an anomaly. Was he an illusion? a phantom? a figment? a vision? I cannot say. That's a question better left to psychologists or politicians (species which proliferate in the current Serbian loam; is it the same in your Albania, Nexhmije Gjinushi?).

What I can say is his guest appearance during my adolescent rapture was, I believed at the time, a signal that I had reached a certain manhood and an honour beyond expression. That he would continue to visit me throughout my brief life is both overwhelming and unwelcome. Who wants their hero, their God, hanging around their neck, intruding in their life at every unexpected turn? Everyone's shit stinks after three days, as we Serbs say, and Obilić's shit is the grandest, warmest, vilest pile of crap of all.

Besides, there is relevance to this testimony. I am not suggesting an insanity plea (although, in a pinch, I am not opposed to such a strategy if you see a value in it, dear Counsellor). My point is simply that, for a Serbian (or Kosovar or Albanian or Macedonian or any of our Balkanoid kinsfolk), History is a living thing that has its own heft and a mind, as it were, of its own. None of us is beyond it.

In any case, there are so many questions I want to ask you, Nexhmije Gjinushi. Last night, as I lay in my comfy cot, my fingers sore from typing, my martyr's nose itching from the cold, Adelina chewing at my shirt sleeve — a little bedtime snack — I imagined us going for coffee somewhere: America, I suspect. A nice place, like one of those Starbucks you see in the magazines, listening to Nirvana or whatnot. And we have a conversation. You tell me about your family, your three sisters (I imagine you have three sisters, Nexhmije Gjinushi, you just seem the type), and your father and mother, who, for the purposes of this imagined conversation, separated when you were still quite young. Your father, I decided, is a successful merchant or perhaps a diplomat. Your mother is remarried, having found herself a wealthy widower, who had made a small fortune in the shipping trade. Do you have a shipping trade in Albania, Nexhmije Gjinushi? No matter. You do now!

And while I do admit that the scent of your cherry perfume hangs in the air like a distant melody, and your skin, as white and soft as Adelina's little paws are black and coarse, hangs in my memory...

This is not an erotic fantasy, Nexhmije Gjinushi. It is just having a conversation, connecting.

So, as Slobodan Milošević's impotent, intermittent thunder rumbled in the distant Šars — it is impossible from this vantage point to tell if the artillery shells are advancing or retreating — I pictured us sipping our double half-caf cappuccinos and talking about your first boyfriend and that teacher you had a crush on in Grade 6...

And that is how I fell asleep.

And when I woke up this morning — too early, I'm afraid; the blackbirds were still asleep — I had only one thought in my mind: my father! You had told me so much about yourself, Nexhmije Gjinushi, and I had given nothing back. My father. You've asked me about him several times, and you must forgive me if I haven't been forthcoming.

It was Father's active mind that had brought us to Crnilo, a sunless little town on the edge of Serbia's coal mining country. My family's coming to this village was not so much by design, but through a sort of accumulation of defeats. It wasn't that Dobroslav Zanković was bad at what he did; he was an intelligent, studious, and innately serious man. It's just that he approached life rather like a wind-up monkey. Long stretches of intense activity, clashing his tin cymbals, which gradually petered out until there seemed not a clang left inside. At that point he retreated to his bed to read salacious detective magazines, thick medieval technical texts (a worn Latin-Serbian dictionary at his side), and eccentric monographs on the lives of Orthodox saints, to listen to Dizzy Gillespie and other illicit American jazz music, to sigh expressively, and to sleep, sleep, sleep.

We'd probably moved fifteen times before we came to Crnilo, where Father had been recruited to oversee the planning of mining operations. It was simple work for a man of his education, experience, and ability. Coal mining was an ancient, risky art and one at which our nation of martyrs was particularly adept. Father's role was not, as he had originally hoped, to ensure that the pits and shafts were designed using the most modern of techniques and theories and constructed for maximum safety but, rather, that the traditions and superstitions that defined the industry were adhered to in a systematic and orderly fashion.

The Yugoslavian Workers Mining Collective (Crnilo) was not the pinnacle of Father's career. At his peak, he'd been overseer of public works in the grand and ancient city of Niš. But for him discarding jobs was a natural process, like a serpent shedding its skin. After Niš, Father moved through a concentric circle of jobs, from manager of a textile plant, to municipal planner for the village of Gornje Nerodimlje, to an ever-diminishing ring of hydroelectric plants and coal mines, shedding each job as his emotional moulting season began. While not exactly a blight on the Zanković name, Crnilo was certainly a step down for the member of a family that had spawned prominent doctors, lawyers, and political figures (Father's own great-uncle Rudric Zanković had plotted with Danilo Ilić during the early years of *Crna Ruka* — the Black Hand. It was said, Nexhmije Gjinushi, that Rudric himself procured the cyanide for Nedeljko Čabrinović, co-conspirator in the assassination of Archduke Ferdinand. Although the cyanide was outdated and ineffective, and Čabrinović's subsequent attempt to avoid capture by drowning himself in the Miljacka River failed — the water at that time of year in Sarajevo was only five inches deep — Rudric is still regarded as a hero in certain hyper-nationalist circles.)

Still, Father wore his silver hard hat (an emblem of his exalted position in the mine) with a certain pride and seemed content, or at least secure in his discontent. Don't get me wrong, Nexhmije Gjinushi, the mine was happy to have an engineer of such distinction, as unproductive and unstable as he was. For his part, Father had a place to live, a job which afforded him the modicum of status he was accustomed to, and freedom to chase down both his demons and the elusive philosopher's stone.

There was one advantage to Father's mood shifts. They allowed me to appreciate the full range of religious experience. While my brothers Jovo, Brati (who was called the Stammerer, although he only stuttered briefly as a small child, and then, only on complicated words with harsh consonants), Djordje, and Beba Dobra all aligned themselves with Mother's unflinching, functional acceptance of the teachings of the Serbian Orthodox Church (which thrived as an unsanctioned necessary evil during the Socialist years, marginalized more for its support of Alexander Karađorđević, exiled Crown Prince of Yugoslavia, than for any ideological reasons), I grew fascinated with the extremes of Father's faith. In the lean hours, with his heart slacked, Father's black mind was drawn to the most mystical reaches of ours, the most mystical of Christian churches. He studied the teachings of Grigorije Molčalnik and the other Hesychasts, who believed grace could only be obtained through absolute withdrawal from the temporal world. And during his good weather days, when his heart was sailing full and by, Father drifted into a cheerful atheism, a jolly Jehovah, magnanimous yet jealous, accepting no god outside himself.

What a topsy-turvy universe my father inhabited! You would expect a man in the depths of depression to stand at the eternal precipice and see nothing but the void. At the same time, it would make sense that a man like Father, when overwhelmed with manic energy, would find God everywhere he looked. But his philosophy was personal, the saints were his saints, their suffering did not exist; it was his suffering, just as the void only existed because he was there to experience it.

We were buffeted, then, from one end of the Holy See to the other. Depending on his mood, Father might deny my brothers and I our saints' days, hold us back from church to lecture us on Epicurus (who worshipped matter only and believed that, if there were gods, they took no interest in the human condition) or banish us to our room to study graphic martyrologies, glumly quizzing us afterwards on the exact nature of their suffering and death.

"Djordje Bogić, a parish priest from Našice, tied to a tree, his ears and nose cut off —"

"By whom?"

"Huh?"

"Tied to a tree by whom, Vida?"

"Tied to a tree by Ustaše members — Beba, hush! — by Ustaše members and a minister of the Latin Church, his ears and nose cut off, his tongue and beard pulled out, disembowelled —"

"His eyes drawn out."

"His tongue and beard pulled out, his eyes drawn out like grape seeds. They disembowelled him next, splitting open his guts like a pig and wrapping his entrails around his neck."

"And?"

"And then and only then — Beba, don't distract me! — they untied him and shot him."

"O holy Hieromartyr Djordje, you lent yourself to the apostles' way of life and succeeded them on their throne. Inspired by God, you cleansed yourself through meditation by practice and prayer; wherefore you became a perfect teacher of truth, fighting for the faith unto the shedding of your blood. Intercede with Christ God that He may save our souls. Amen."

"Amen."

"Poo!"

"Beba!"

"Beba!"

"Poo!"

Of course, Father's divine moods produced some discord in our family. Mother was quietly devout, and while she happily accepted his darkest piety and prayed through even more firmly clenched teeth during the height of blasphemous manias, she never openly questioned or supported him. She was a Kosovo Girl through and through.

Jovo, the eldest of the brothers, took a more proactive approach.

"Look at you, Dobroslav Zanković, in bed like a war widow crying for her lost husband."

At his low ebbs, Father would simply moan and turn to his side, leaving mother to half-heartedly win the day.

"Leave your Father alone when he's working."

"Working? He's weeping in his pillow."

"You don't understand the burden of a brilliant mind, Jovo; it weighs heavy."

Jovo would snort and march off to the forest, to smoke with his friends and drink potent, homemade plum *rakia* he regularly stole from Father's workshop.

Things did not always end so quietly, though, when Father was approaching his high tides. Jovo would upbraid him for his feminate mood swings. Father quaked at the implied challenge to his masculinity.

"You compressed turd, you troll, you diseased node" — Father would by now be standing at his full height, something that impressed us mightily as children but had begun to lose its impact as the teenaged Jovo outgrew him by a head — "you wart on the ass of this house, you excrement, you less than material thing —"

"Slava, *please*..." Mother would say, almost seductively. We boys knew our world was out of whack when Mother was acting as the peacemaker.

"You loathsome carbuncle, you syphilitic pizzle, you swine's whore, you son of Abraham..."

"Fuck you, Dad. Fuck you..."

Things would continue like that for several minutes, as the man and his full-grown son stood toe-to-toe, staring each other down. Usually the standoff ended with nothing more than a brief grapple and a shove or two, and as a child (I was second youngest, and Jovo was some six years older than me) I remember being both frightened and oddly comforted by these confrontations. There was genuine violence in their tone and words, which often came perilously close to comedy (two ancient birds puffing themselves up in some instinctual show of power); at the same time, there was something about the ritual I found calming.

Eventually, though, the cocks came to blows. Jovo must have been seventeen or eighteen, and Father was in the depths of one of his deepest depressions. He had put himself to bed a week earlier and emerged only occasionally in a pair of ragged briefs to use the lavatory or simply stand at the front window shaking his head, as if he could not stand the sight of the world he had been born into. On perhaps the third day of this exercise, Jovo could take it no longer.

"What kind of man are you, skulking around the house in your underpants? Get dressed, Princess, you're embarrassing all of us."

Jovo shook as he spoke. It was the first time I realized how humiliated he was by Father's antics; Jovo took Father's behaviour personally.

I watched my father stand silently staring out the window,

his expression never changing. In retrospect, he was swaying a little more than usual and may have perhaps been more drunk than we were accustomed to. That may explain what he did next, for without saying a word he turned and cracked my brother in the side of the head with his fist.

Jovo staggered slightly but recovered soon enough and swung wildly back. He missed more or less, then the two of them fell together, each one trying to wrestle the other to the floor. It progressed like a real fight between real people in the real world and not like some cowboy fight in an American movie. No one stood helpful as the other man positioned his jaw for the perfect haymaker; no one took a fist square to the chin, only to bounce back up again unharmed; no one (and mother was particularly thankful about this) smashed a chair over the other guy's head, to watch it disintegrate on contact. There was lots of grunting and pushing and frantic attempts to twist the adversary to the floor. There were punches, to be sure, more hurtful than painful, though, made from close quarters, that glanced off a chin or a tooth or landed with such little impact that they likely hurt the hitter's knuckles more than they made an impression on the hittee.

It was over within three minutes, as most real fights are. Both of them exhausted quickly, just like fighters in real life, taking a moment to recover their breaths and retreat to their corners: Father, back to bed; Jovo, out the front door and not to be seen again by any of us for several cold months.

7

AND THEN IT WAS SPRING in Crnilo again, Nexhmije Gjinushi; the blackbirds had begun to nest, and Father's dark fog had enshrouded us all. He'd been staying in his bed for days, eating very little except for large lumps of hard cheese and bitter chocolate and drinking litres of potato wine. He kept the curtains closed to his room day and night. He defecated in a cardboard box in the corner of the room, like a cat. Mother had taken to sleeping on the couch.

One night I brought him a bowl of hot stew (Mother, never underestimating the power of her cooking, believed that Father would get better if only he ate "a decent meal") only to find the bed was empty. He'd crawled, it seemed, out the window and had disappeared into the darkness. My mother quickly organized a search party with a half a dozen of the neighbours, who'd come, I suspect, to depend on Father's antics to spice up their flavourless lives. I was in a group that searched along the river from one end of town to the other and deep into the forest. We had no luck at all (although we did uncover a young man and woman, making love against a tree. So rich was their passion that, even as the flashlight illuminated his backside, they didn't miss a stroke).

It was nearly four o'clock in the morning when Father was discovered.

My brother Brati was part of the team that found him. They were assigned the railway track that ran roughly parallel to the river, although it followed a rather less serpentine route. Brati came to love telling and retelling the tale of how the mayor, Simeon Uroš, quite drunk himself, had literally, on his way to take a piss, stumbled over Father. The details got more extravagant over time, but it is possible that the mayor actually did piss a little on Father's leg before realizing that the mound of earth was actually a living being. Father had apparently drunk himself into a stupor and lain down on the railway tracks to wait for the train to come and do what he could not. Fortunately, he'd put too much faith in the Jugoslovenske Železnice, the state railway company; he should have known that, in Yugoslavia, the trains never ran on time.

Had the discord stayed in the family, Nexhmije Gjinushi, perhaps my little life story would have taken a different turn. Unfortunately, there was no closet big enough for Father's skeletons, and it was inevitable that in the flux of humours his behaviour would spill into the real world.

Most of the incidents were relatively harmless. There was the time, for example, he showed up at the Church of the St. Andrej, pacing anxiously at the back, until he could contain himself no longer. Father Grygor was barely into the first antiphon — "Hear my prayer, O Lord; let my cry for help come to you. Do not hide your face from me when I am in distress. Turn your ear to me; when I call, answer me quickly" — when my father marched to the front of the church.

He paused, and the congregation stilled, the only sound the constant ak-aking of black-lunged miners cracking like gunfire in the distance.

"My sermon today," Father finally announced, "is from the Gospel of Barnabas. Of course, you've never heard of this ancient and venerated book, the Holy Church having suppressed it a thousand years ago..."

From my pew in the back I could see Father Grygor slump forward slightly, his long beard sag, as if his whole body was caving in on itself. But only for a second. Then he stood straight, graciously stepped back, and with a sweep of his hand announced that the "learned Dr. Zanković" would now favour the congregation with a lesson. While the very picture of Orthodoxy, Father Grygor, like all great priests, was part showman and recognized good theatre when he saw it. He must have known that no matter how impious Father's lecture might be, it was sure to be the talk of the parish for the next month or so and would ensure that there would be no empty pews for the foreseeable future.

Indeed, Father's sermon was as impassioned as it was polemical, citing heated passages by this forgotten apostle (who asserted that Christ was an inspired messenger, an earthbound man whose wisdom paved the way for the revelations of Mohammed, the true Messiah). While many of the lesser bumpkins stormed out of the church in a show of protest (only to slink back later before the Great Entrance of the chalice and *diskos* to partake in the Holy Communion), most people appreciated the show. There was scattered applause as he finished, and the good priest thanked my father warmly.

Not all of Father's theatrics were so well received. Perhaps the lowest ebb was the time he arrived in the village square, an armful of books swaddled to his chest. The summer had ended, leaves were getting ready to roll over and die, and the mushrooms, those edible cancers, were sprouting up throughout the forests that surrounded Crnilo, the last vegetative outburst before winter. As he walked toward us I could see Father's breath steam, little puffs, like a slightly asthmatic locomotive.

Father dumped the books in a heap then disappeared, only to reappear moments later, still puffing, with another literary load. Beba Dobra was beside me, his hand clenched at his chest, as if in the midst of a joyful prayer, his fingers and favourite yellow sweater smudged black from omnipresent coal dust that sugar-coated our town. Beba could not contain his delight as Father approached. My brother stood at the head of the small crowd that had begun to gather in the square, curious to see what Father had up his sleeve. Beba called to Father and waved. Father looked up without acknowledging his son, then shuffled off again.

"Oh, Tata's doing something funny, Vida!"

"Yes, Beba. Tata's definitely up to something."

Again, Father returned with an armful of books, which he dutifully added to the pile. He made the trip several more times, and soon there was quite a stack representing perhaps half of all the books he had in his workshop. Some of the other villagers got into the act, throwing their own contributions onto the growing pyre, still waiting for Father's next unpredictable turn.

He did not disappoint.

He soon had a pile almost as tall as Beba and myself. After walking around it several times, contemplating it carefully, adjusting a textbook here and paperback there, he disappeared once more.

He did not come back. We waited five, ten minutes. Nothing. Another five. Still no sign of Father. Some of the villagers gave u and wandered off to their next distraction. Perhaps, others thought, this was the end of the show? Perhaps, today there was only a limited performance piece, the creation of a book sculpture that must be analyzed and critiqued on its own merits? Was it a statement, one man wondered, about the nature of literature, how it was both obvious and invisible in a culture like ours? Or perhaps, thought another, Father was saying art — all art — is at its core an object and could only be appreciated as such. We tend to view books as individual works of literature, disconnected; Father was suggesting, the amateur art critic maintained, that all books were one book, and should be contemplated as a whole. Book was all, a single concept; the words, the stories, the ideas the books contained — these were irrelevant.

But then Father appeared from around the corner. Walking deliberately, his housecoat open at the waist, careful not to spill any of the liquid from the near-overflowing soup tin he was carrying. It was a large can, family-sized, and Father reminded me of the tightrope walker I'd once seen when the sad Kazakhstan Circus, with its jaundiced hippopotamus and drunken, rotten-toothed clown, had visited our town. The traditional dancers, of course, and tightrope walker were the only things worth seeing. And now, here was Father, step over step, one foot at time, his free hand held out like a wing to protect his balance — an aerial artist. Father did not spill a drop.

"It's honey, I think," said one man.

"Honey, that's absurd!" said another. "It's vodka. Why else would he be so careful?"

"No. It's petrol. I can smell it from here." It was Miodrag Petković, my former schoolmaster.

Petrol. The word ran quickly through our pack. And as Father reached the book pile and began to judiciously pour the petrol on the heap, a cluck of recognition could be heard. Ah, a book burning! Here was something even the yokels could appreciate.

And so he circled the books, measuring the drops with the

same concentration a painter might give to his canvas. Then he was off one last time.

With the promise of a good fire the crowd no longer minded the wait. When we saw him turn the corner this time, the rabble quickly hushed, polite and attentive, ready for Father's performance.

"Go, Tata, go!"

"Beba, shhh!"

Father walked as before, step over step, his full focus on the precious soup can, now refilled, and that imaginary tightrope wire. He came to a halt beside the books and, with a dramatic thrust, removed a lighter from his shirt pocket.

He stood silently for a moment, for greater effect, then flicking his thumb, ignited the lighter while dumping the entire contents of the soup can over his head. The air was suddenly thick with the smell of petrol, but I was not yet afraid. Perhaps it was because I was too young to grasp the full impact of Father's intent. Mostly, though, the entire piece was simply so well executed (the flick of the thumb, the sharp turn of the wrist as he poured the petrol over his head); I was mesmerized.

Someone cried, Dobroslav, no! And still I did not understand.

A couple of the more thoughtful men — Miodrag Petković and the postmaster, Dositej Obradović — slowly advanced toward Father, whispering his name. But the moment anyone took a step toward him, Father brandished the lighter and moved it several inches closer to his head.

"Weehaa!" Beba cried in delight. This was surely the greatest show he'd ever seen.

I took his hand.

"We should go, Beba." He looked at me as if I was the lunatic, and when I tugged he planted himself like a stone. "It's almost dinner, brother. We should go."

Did I know what was coming, Nexhmije Gjinushi?

Not exactly.

But by now I understood that something wasn't right; the crowd had grown fearful. They were no longer enjoying the show. Someone picked me up and began carrying me out of the square. My fingers dug into the fat of this strange neck, and I buried my face in dirty hair that stunk of American aftershave and garlic. But a second drama had opened; someone had made the mistake of trying to pick up Beba Dobra. In the long list of do's and don'ts when it came to my brother, uninvited human contact was prominent. As some well-meaning fellow had scooped up Beba to carry him away from the unfolding scene, my brother went nuts. He began screaming and kicking and biting and flailing his arms as if he was being cradled by Death himself. He was not a small boy; although nine months younger than me, he was already several inches taller and outweighed me considerably. I was nothing but sinew and bone, but thanks to a lifetime of isometric seizures, Beba Dobra had the build of a tiny weightlifter.

As several men grappled with Beba, my own abductor turned to help, and I once again saw Father's performance. He was bent now over the pile of books, carefully leaning with his lighter outstretched. Around him, a semi-circle of townsmen had gathered, several of them carrying large red fire buckets full of water or sand, a number holding thick horse blankets. At that moment I understood. Father wasn't just intending to torch the family library; there was greater literature at stake. I began to sob and call my father, although I am certain my words were lost in my bawling.

And so the scene played out before my eyes, despite the best efforts of well-meaning men. Father set the books ablaze then slowly began to circle the pyre, stepping now slowly, foot over foot, no longer like an agile and balanced high-wire artist, but more like an ancient shadow, trying to re-create some prehistoric and well-forgotten folk dance. He stepped side to side, cautiously feeling for his footing, his back almost to the flames as he kept his eyes on his protectors/adversaries. The dry paper and petrol had ignited quickly, and soon the flames flailed like demons, the black smoke rising over the town and drawing even more spectators to the scene.

The wind was egging the fire on now, sometimes blowing the flames close to Father's petrol-drenched clothes, and in my own tears I found myself growing angrier and angrier at him. I was calling his name, but he would not heed me; he would not make eye contact and he would not stop his ridiculous dance. Step over step. Step over step. Even I, as a child, understood how grossly unfair he was being. It was one thing to kill yourself, deprive your sons of a father (even one so out-of-kilter with this world); it was another thing to do it before our very eyes. That was beyond cruel, beyond selfish, almost beyond human, and certainly beyond anything anyone could expect from even the most unreasonable father.

The dance continued. Step over step, the flames sometimes reaching for him, sometimes recoiling to prepare their next advance. And as I watched, a strange sensation overtook me, as if a warm wind was blowing within my chest, soothing me and drawing me away. In that moment, I saw the image of Miloš Obilić appear beside my father, matching him step for step. It had the effect of elevating the moment, Obilić's stern precision raising Father's self-absorbed dance into a ritual observation. Dressed in full battle gear, his sword held steady in front of his chest, his eyes watching me, never veering from mine. Suddenly, the air was filled with the scent of something. Apples! Apples and lemons! It washed away the rank petrol.

Step over step, Father and Obilić danced around the fire, and though I could not see his lips moving, I could hear the old soldier's voice, calling me.

"This dance is your dance, Vida," he said. "This dance is our dance; I pass it on to you, as it has been passed for generations, from father to son to son. Listen, Vida, to the music of the wind, to the *Song of Kosovo*, and dance with me."

A loose book tumbled from the pile and rolled to Obilić's feet, and in that instant, he disappeared. Gone, the smell of apples and lemons. It was all smoke and petrol now, and I watched Father bend over the partially ignited book and pick it up. His fingers carefully avoided the flame. Father stood and contemplated the book for a moment, his eyes intent on the little flame. Then he shut his eyes tightly and inched the book toward his head. His lips moved although no words seemed to be coming forth. Was he praying? Was he reciting some alchemic incantation? Was he talking himself into it? I always only have questions.

I do know that within the next instant, another gust came up, at once blowing the flames away from Father and extinguishing the one book he held in his hand. In that second, Miodrag Petković leapt forward and brought my father to the ground. It was a surprisingly efficient takedown for a man of his age (leading me to decide that the rumours of my doughy former schoolteacher's athletic prowess and his near-selection to the 1964 Yugoslavia Olympic wrestling team were true), and in the moments that followed several more townsmen joined the heap. Soon there was a goose pile of wriggling, grunting men almost as high as the burning book pyre, with Father at the bottom screaming now in a panicked voice: "Let me up! Let me up! I can't breathe!"

When they finally pulled Father from the bottom of the

heap, it was his turn to cry. He wailed like a baby. Four men carried him back home, each holding an appendage, and as they carried him away, he cried and called for me to come to him, comfort him, I suppose. For me, this was the saddest part of all, to see my father reduced to a sobbing girl in front of this, the entire town.

By this time, my gentle abductor had set me down, and I turned my ears away from Father's pleas. Where was Beba?

Beba! Beba!

And there he lay in his own corner of the square. In the excitement and stress, he had succumbed to one of his seizures. I ran to him and saw his face pale, his eyes wide and sightless, but pain-free, his fist clenched so tight that the knuckles were red and seemed ready to burst through his skin. I knelt down and gently turned him from his back to his side. I cradled his head to protect it from the hard ground.

Several men stood by, discussing what to do.

"We must put a pencil in his mouth, so he doesn't swallow his tongue."

"I haven't a pencil. Will a ballpoint pen do?"

"I'm not sure. I suppose it could shatter in his mouth."

"Is an inky mouth worse than a swallowed tongue?"

I thought to correct the well-meaning dolts. It's an old wives' tale. Epileptics do not swallow their tongues. I mean, just try that; just try to swallow your tongue! It's attached, you see; it's attached right there to the bottom of your mouth. It's simple physics, you pillocks, you horses' cocks. What kind of imbecile could think that a boy could swallow his tongue?

I know what you're thinking, Nexhmije Gjinushi: what was the name of the book, the one that fell from the fire?

I've wondered that myself. Many times I've kicked myself for not going to look. In reality, even if I'd thought to do it, it would have probably been too late. Most likely, the book was tossed onto the flames almost at the same moment my father was being carried home to be bound, splayed, to the bed until the dark mood passed. The fire, you see, burned for days. The people of Crnilo, never ones to waste a good fire, all converged on the village square, bringing garbage and unwanted clutter — books, mostly, and broken toys and automobile tires and corrupted Socialist plastic furniture. Everything was tossed on the heap. Our town had not been that clean in a long, long time.

But now my fingers are burning, good Counsellor. It's already late into the evening, and even I, son of my father, need some rest.

8

THE SONG OF KOSOVO has never been transcribed. It cannot be captured on paper. The issues are both technical — no notational system yet devised can capture its complexity — and pragmatic: the song is still unfolding. At any given moment, it is complete yet incomplete. Like time, it reaches forwards and backwards; it has depth and breadth and width and loft. Like heaven, it is perfect in its way and therefore without true beginning or end.

Likewise, the words to the song cannot be recorded. They include every word ever uttered in any language, and converge only in that space between, say, your lips and mine. One of the peculiarities about the *Song of Kosovo*, Nexhmije Gjinushi, is that while each performance is unique in itself, every performance is essentially the same. Regardless of how the melodies shift, the instrumentation changes, or the lyrics are incanted, the tempo or pitch or scale is modified — each iteration of the song is, at most, a minuscule variation on the original.

I am contemplating the music now, as I wait for you to come, although you must excuse my Albanian. I think "contemplating" is the wrong word. I am concentrating, Counsellor, trying to block the song from my mind. It is too distracting, Nexhmije Gjinushi, and would drive a man to drink (have you never wondered why alcoholism is so prevalent in our neck of the woods? It's that damn song! Everyone is trying to get it out of their heads. Personally, I would rather get on with some good smoke, but despite that we are in the midst of a major drug corridor, weed is hard to come by here).

You'll be happy to know, though, that I am not merely wasting my time. Time has not taken a vacation, Counsellor, and with just four days left until the Big Day I continue to record this affidavit. I have even put some thought to our legal strategy. I realize that we have never specifically discussed one, and I am hoping that it will involve more than a simple re-telling of the facts, then throwing me to the mercy of the Court. I'm inclined to believe that this institution's stockpile of mercy may be in short supply. However, I appreciate that our options are limited, so let me suggest we claim some kind of diplomatic immunity or, better, a non-diplomatic unmunity; you see, regardless of my alleged political, religious, or cultural affiliations, the fact of the matter is that I belong to no one, and despite my nominal Serbism (and Mark of the Martyr), I am a deeply irreligious man who holds no affiliation to Islam, Catholicism, Orthodox Christianity, or any of the world's other 4,268 organized faiths. Of course, this doesn't necessarily exclude me from taking a position in the ongoing troubles between our peoples, Nexhmije Gjinushi, or from having a vested interest in the outcome. You know as well as I do that the issues at stake are purely political and have little to do with ancient religious divisions and more with the curious psychological needs of a handful of embittered, aging men (with, albeit, fantastic hair — you never see a bald Balkanoid do you, Nexhmije Gjinushi?), struggling to make their mark on history.

If pressed, my dear, I would categorize myself as a former lapsed Buddhist, having found myself in principle attracted to the general indifference of the religion — is it a religion,

Nexhmije Gjinushi? One can never be sure with those Buddhists. They are hard to pin down, which, of course, is the
major selling point. In this and many other regards, Counsellor,
I am not my father's son. Still, any religious leader whose entire
doctrine can be summarized on a matchbook is all right by
me. The Buddha once said that he taught one thing and one
only: suffering and the end of suffering (technically, of course,
that's two things? In any case, it's marvellously concise and
rather germane, don't you think, and leads me to wonder, as
I am a closet Buddhist, if the Buddha himself was perhaps a
closet Serb?).

If unmunity doesn't fly, Counsellor, we could try another
tack. We can claim that by virtue of my Buddhism (lapsed
Buddhism, to be sure, but that is the sort of technicality
regularly overlooked in Kosovo), I am a neutral and sovereign
entity. Admittedly, Nexhmije Gjinushi, this is the weaker of
two weak arguments. So let me add a third, Counsellor, one
both compelling (on a purely emotional level) and genuine.

The simple fact is that my descent into this geographic
purgatory was undertaken with only the purest of intentions.
It was for Love, you see, my sweet Counsellor. Love! Surely you
can appreciate that, and understand that every step I marched
away from my Red-Haired Angel of the Salivating Dogs was,
as I truly believed at the time, one more step towards her. My
blessing, my beatitude, come and gone so quickly!

But I don't want to get ahead of myself, Nexhmije Gjinushi.
In good time I will tell you how we became lovers, Tristina and
I, but that was years after my family had moved to Beograd,
chased like stray dogs out of Crnilo. There is much more I could
tell about my time in this town, Nexhmije Gjinushi, but I don't
want to mire you in the effluence of my life. For the record, I
have provided you with the most pertinent facts and am left,

out of a sense of filial duty, to clarify the details pertaining to what has come to be termed in the popular press as the Crnilo Mining Disaster.

In truth, Father has been unfairly savaged because of the whole incident, with little thought given to personal costs he paid as a result of the explosion. But that is the nature of the song, I suppose; eventually, everything is sucked into it, reshaped by it, and, finally subsumed by it.

You are correct in thinking, Nexhmije Gjinushi, that it had been a major news story that was widely followed around the world. Across Serbia, the press kept vigil. In the days directly following the blast, the TV offered around-the-clock updates, with the story of hope and potential survival capturing the hearts of a people sinking further into an economic depression and the quagmire of ethnic tension. As the days passed, and the prospect of finding survivors faded, the focus of the press reports changed. Hope gave way to defeat, a theme more familiar to the reporters and their audience, and the story transformed into a kind of proto-Serbic epic, pitting the heroic miners against incompetent and arrogant owners, usurpers of the natural order, who may have been (if reports in the ultra-nationalist press were to be believed) agents of Albanian Turks. In the aftermath of Crnilo, Father was vilified, a modern-day Vuk Branković.

For my part, I cannot separate the incident at the mine from the larger context of my life. In my teenaged rememberings, it all streams together so that the mining story itself is not a separate paragraph in the larger story of my life, but part of the unstoppable march of events that would lead me to the conclusion, if I were a religious man, that there was a God in heaven and He was a total, total bastard.

It started small. Father received a strange package in the mail.

About the size of a deck of cards, it was wrapped in royal blue paper with gold trim. FROM THE OFFICE OF THE PRESIDENT, SOCIALIST FEDERAL REPUBLIC OF YUGOSLAVIA, BEOGRAD.

"What's this...?" Father turned the package over in his hands, shook it gently, held it to his ear. When it comes to the mails, Serbs are by nature a suspicious people. And packages from the government are given special scrutiny.

Somewhat satisfied, Father handed it to Beba Dobra, who tore it open eagerly. Inside was a blue velveteen box, the kind that one might expect to hold some cufflinks or a costume brooch. Beba tried to open the box and in his frustration put it between his teeth and tried to pry it apart; animal force was Beba's solution for almost everything. Father was by now very curious and rescued the box from my brother's sloppy mouth. He undid a small clasp and opened the lid. A sheet of thin paper, folded an impossible number of times to fit into the tiny container, fell out. Father unfolded it.

"'To My Honoured Comrade, Dobroslav Zanković,'" Father read. "'In recognition of your contribution to the economic development of the Socialist Federal Republic of Yugoslavia, in the specific area of Mining, Metallurgy, and Steel Production, I am pleased to present you with the Medal of Merit in Economy, Third Class. In your capacity as Senior Operations Manager...'"

Here Father's voice trailed off. I caught the odd phrase — "allocative efficiency," "production quotas," "central planning committee" — before Father picked up the thread again.

"We have spilled an ocean of blood to create a society dedicated to the harmony of peoples and fraternity of workers, and we shall not allow anyone to touch or to destroy it from without or within. Yours in brotherhood and unity: Borisav Jović; president, Socialist Federal Republic of Yugoslavia."

Father set the letter aside and looked in the box. Carefully, he extracted a small blue ribbon, intersected by three thin gold strips.

He picked the ribbon up and examined it for a moment. "What horseshit!"

He pinned the ribbon to his face with his finger, just under his nose, then scrunched his upper lip to hold it in place. "Look," he said, pointing to his blue moustache. "I'm Commander Tito! No."

He paused and thought for a moment.

"No. I'm Comrade Hitler!" He did a funny German salute, and then began goose-stepping comically around the living room. He grabbed an umbrella from the stand and started to waddle back and forth between the kitchen and hallway. Mother came out now, laughing so hard there were tears in her eyes. "He's Charlie Chaplin!" she explained, and while we were only dimly familiar with the name, and knew nothing of the Little Tramp, we laughed along with her until our stomachs hurt.

Over the next few days, Nexhmije Gjinushi, something curious took hold: Father grew less dismissive. He read the letter from Comrade Jović over and over again, and began to drop his name indiscreetly into his conversations. We might be talking about anything — school work, for example — and Father would suddenly crow: "President Jović thinks the estimates for milk production are uncommonly conservative this year..."

He appeared one day in a tattered military uniform, having assigned himself the rank of field commander, his Medal of Merit in Economy now augmented by several other colourful ribbons and a string of authentic-looking medals that Father must have pried off of some old veteran in exchange for Lord knows what. He talked of Jović in the familiar and hinted broadly that they had served together during the early days of the People's Liberation Army. He began littering his conversation with military jargon, and gave far-reaching economic advice to anyone who would listen. At kitchen tables around our neighbourhood he became a scathing critic of Russian imperialism, advocating the "normalizationing" — he'd become quite adept at Socialist triplespeak — of our relationship with NATO and the West, while savaging the United States, which he called The Great Provocateur. He dismissed America's brand of "slave capitalism," its "culture of appropriation" and its "vengeance-based imperialism" while mocking its inability to win through fixed elections and police terror what for Yugoslavia had come so easily: true democracy, brotherhood, and unity.

"Yes," Jovo groused. "The Democracy of One, elected by the Brotherhood of the Terrified, united by Ignorance of the Hateful."

Along the way, the importance of the Medal of Economic Merit increased exponentially in Father's mind. It was no longer, as he originally intimated, a pro forma citation, issued out of bureaucratic compulsion, but a personal communiqué from Jović himself, who'd somehow gotten wind of Father's experiments and immediately recognized their significance. So Father's new avocations — military tactician, economist, social critic — augmented his alchemic studies, and Yugoslavian Workers Mining Collective (Crnilo) be damned, he spent hours upon hours in his newly restored workshop surrounded by beakers, chemicals, test tubes, and compounds. We could hear him out there till the darkest hours of the night, his medals rattling as he hummed patriotic songs or carried on imaginary conversations with President Jović, discussing politics, science, and the atheistic theology to which they both subscribed.

One morning he emerged just as we were sitting down to our cornbread and jam. He was walking with one hand outstretched, palm-side up, paying careful attention to something in the middle of his hand. He entered the back door. Dark circles shadowed his eyes, yet his face glowed.

"There. I have done it, Comrades."

"Done what, Nana?"

He held his hand out toward us and we circled around. I bent even closer. In the middle of his palm was a small speck. Yellowish.

"Look, my loves: gold. I have done it! I have unlocked the secret of transmutation."

Brati leaned as close as he could. "It's nothing, Father. It's a sliver of dust."

"It could be anything," Jovo piped in. "A chip from a tea cup, an edge shaved from one of your borrowed medals." Jovo eyed Father's decorations with suspicion.

Father would have none of it. He leered more manically, glowed more fervently.

"Gold." His voice was almost a whisper. "Bice, contact the President immediately. I will alert the newspaper and Radio Yugoslavia."

"Tell them to make sure they bring their magnifying glasses."

Only Beba Dobra caught the spirit of the moment. "Are we rich, Father?"

"We are, my son. We are wealthy beyond imagination."

Beba shivered with delight. "Will we buy a television, Father?"

"We will, my son, buy a thousand televisions."

9

THE AUDACIOUS JOY PERSISTED. It seemed Father never slept or even rested. He stayed awake for four straight days, counting stars by night (he was determined to prove they were a finite number), and lecturing Beba and I by day on the intricacies of transmutation.

"The ancients believed that the process of turning base metal into gold, bringing insufficiency to perfection, consisted of four stages. The first, *nigredo*, the blackening or putrefaction that worked as surely on metal as it did on a decomposing body or soul. It is the state of where we are in the world, so far removed from that pre-chaotic golden spark."

Father produced an ornately detailed ink drawing of what I presumed was the beginning of the universe, although it looked rather more like the face of a bearded owl.

"The second stage is *albedo*, the process of burning off the impurities in a metal, a lightening or whitening of the essence, although it could be more correctly thought of as a process that restores the metal's capacity to reflect pure light."

By now, Dobra had lost interest and was adding his own flourishes in red crayon to father's drawing of the dawn of time.

"The third stage, *citrinitas*, sees that reflective capacity completely restored, with the moon the defining metaphor, a wondrous object in its own right, but a reflective glory only, with the capacity to illuminate but not enlighten. For the alchemist to achieve citrinitas, a tempering or seasoning that can be best imagined as the yellowing (this is the literal origin of the word) of the pages of a book, was rare indeed, and suggested as much his own spiritual progression as any achieved alchemic artistry. Finally, *rubedo*. Yellow and now red merging into gold, the perfect, restorative union of the elements, of One with God. Purity re-attained."

"Will I make gold from nothing one day, Father?"

"Don't be stupid, son. Only a great man can contain the power of purity."

And then, the next day, the spell was broken. Father crawled deep inside that black cavern. It took six weeks for him to emerge again, and only after a course of electroshock therapy and a nutritional routine, overseen by my mother, that included regular cups of liquorice tea and colonic, applied twice daily, distilled from Holy Basil, rose petals, and sage.

And so, he ebbed and flowed. There were to be other suicide attempts, to be sure. A plate of poison mushrooms (which turned out to be merely rancid and slightly hallucinogenic); an overdose of laxative; an attempted hanging that almost, inexplicably, succeeded.

And the highs. Comrade Jović was not his only friend, it seemed. Tito too — he had a citation, somewhere, and Professor Einstein, we learned, was an early advocate of Father's genius. To hear Father tell it, it was Dobroslav Zanković and not his (previously) more celebrated uncle who gave the cyanide to Nedeljko Čabrinović; and then St. Slava himself had made contact and the Apostles, who spoke to Father through the scriptures and became quite friendly, ultimately convincing him that he had a new mission in life. He was to become the alchemist of the soul, transforming the base Christians of our town into pure, enlightened atheists.

Can you follow the line of reason? I can't, and I dare say I have become something of an expert on things metaphysic. The chemical logic by which Father ordinarily lived was replaced by a logic of accidental associations and presumptive magnanimity, which culminated in the disaster that shook our community during our final fall in Crnilo.

It was the eve of the Feast of St. Andrej, the third most important day in our parish's calendar. Winter had already announced itself and settled in for a long visit; a layer of thin snow had come to coat the black dust that permeated our town.

It was a Friday evening, as I recall, and my mother had taken me out of my literature class and sent me to go track down Beba Dobra. He'd disappeared, as was his habit. It was just as the winds were picking up and the deep cold was tightening its grip on us. Mother was concerned: Beba wasn't dressed for this weather, and with his various sensitivities, he was always susceptible to illness. "He'll catch his death," Mother said, as she pushed me out the school door and off toward the mines.

Why did he favour these dark places? I cannot say, Nexhmije Gjinushi. But certainly, this is where Beba Dobra spent much of his free time, wandering the endless kilometres of mine shafts wormed into the earth beneath our town. Maybe it was the dirty warmth that attracted him, the permanent dampness that smelled vaguely of decaying wood. Without question, the labyrinth of dark shafts stank of adventure and mystery. There we were: explorers, cavemen, astronauts, mermen, the Mole People. Perhaps, though, it was simply that here was a world that Beba could manage with ease. He seemed to have internalized the entire underground landscape, and could navigate the black passageways as easily as the rest of us could find our way to church. They called him The Canary, the men who worked in these pits, and in his oversized yellow jacket that covered his hands and hooded his head, Beba did appear in the dusty light of the mines to be, if not a giant bird, at least some kind of otherworldly un-mammal.

As usual, I did not find Beba. He found me. Whenever my mother sent me to retrieve my brother, I knew that all I needed to do was enter any random shaft, get myself thoroughly lost, and wait for Beba to show up.

On this particular Friday I did not wait long. I was deep in a seam and had only just sat down on a rock, with a handful of smaller rocks to pitch at the rats. One whiskered fellow, the size of a small bureaucrat, peeked its head around the corner. I took aim.

"Boo!" Beba screamed, leaping out from a shadow. It was part of our ritual. He would sneak up, and I would pretend to be frightened, and then I would tell him he had to come home, and he would say "no" even as he began to lead me to the surface. Sometimes, still, he might take my hand, even though I was in my final year of high school and he well past his sixteenth birthday.

We arrived back in town just as the pageant was starting. At the head of the procession, a gang of serious-looking adolescent boys in white *podrizniks* were carrying a large wooden saltire. Bound to the cross at the wrists and ankles with elegant velvet cords was the beautiful Dušan Mićić, a porcelain man-boy in his early twenties, with flowing yellow hair, like a Latin Christ, and bold green eyes, one of which was lazy and always seemed to veer off into the distance. Dušan, a fixture in the role of St. Andrej for as long as I could remember, had captured the hearts of many of the young women of Crnilo, although, it was darkly whispered, he was disinclined to return their affections. Still, he made a grand martyr: fragile, gracious, fragrant, and only somewhat narcissistic.

The Holy Martyr was followed directly by a small line of petty officials: the mayor and council (who, as Communist Party members, were there as "observers only" and not, the newspaper regularly assured us, as "designated celebrants"); the mine manager, a sombre, mouseish man with the curious Gaelic name of O'Dowd, although he appeared to me more Croat than Celt; a limping, one-armed veteran whom we all just called *Ujak* — Uncle — and who always seemed to be given a prominent position at ceremonies of this type; and our own Father Grygor and his wife (a smiling, red-faced *baba* with a bubbling fountain of bosom and a massive red birthmark that scalded the entire side of her head). The good father himself carried the censer, penduluming frankinscented smoke that immediately made me think of Christmas and all that glorious food.

Several paces behind Father Grygor, Pavel. Plodding with porky little steps, half-wheezing, half-snorting as he moved, an asthmatic pig, Vicar Bishop Pavel, the ninth most senior member of the Serbian Orthodox Church, looked neither right nor left but straight ahead, beyond the church of the Holy Martyr and the hillock it stood on, beyond the modern municipal centre rising in the background, beyond the ancient mosque at the edge of our town, beyond the low mountains in the distance, no doubt beyond Aleksinac, seat of his own diocese, to someplace bigger, better, beyond. My guess: Beograd, centre of the Orthodox universe.

Vicar Bishop Pavel leaned heavily on his crozier, holding the staff so tightly that the tips of his fatted and much-jewelled fingers had turned white, his graceful nails seeming ready to pop off. His Holiness stopped suddenly, directly in front of me and Beba Dobra, so close we could have spit on him. He held his hand to his chest. He staggered for a moment, his great gut seeming to drag toward the earth. His faced turned bright red as he struggled to catch his breath.

The procession moved on, without hesitating, oblivious to the vicar bishop's distress. Only Dušan Mićić, from his high vantage, noticed anything was amiss. The young martyr appeared quite flustered at the sight of the stumbling prelate and made as if to step down from his cross, only to remember those velvet cords and his pre-eminent position.

"Pavel!" Mićić cried, which appeared rather informal, given the circumstances. The puffing, red-faced bishop looked up and nodded at the beautiful martyr and, with a single, familiar glance, seemed to assure the young man that he was well enough. Vicar Bishop Pavel took a tentative step or two, scrunched his eyes tightly, then wheezed forward again.

Beba looked very serious for a moment, pointing at Pavel.

"Poo," he declared, almost wistfully.

"Poo indeed," I replied, so softly only he could hear. "Poo indeed."

Our family, you see, had a history with Vicar Bishop Pavel and history, for Serbs, was never a good thing. He'd appear, this stuffed cassock, at Christmas and Easter and significant Saints' Days, each time somewhat fatter than the last, to impose himself on our dinner and dispense rambling sermons, uncommonly grand and, to my ears, utterly unintelligible. Even Mother was caught napping when Vicar Bishop Pavel spoke.

Of course, the distinguished prelate was much less inclined to indulge Father and his occasional ecclesiastical forays. Several times he'd had sharp words when Father tried to interrupt his service, and once he'd even called for the guards to haul Father away, leaving good Father Grygor tugging nervously on his beard.

"Perhaps you have need for guards in a parish the size of Aleksinac, Holy Father," Grygor finally offered. "But in this modest church, we cannot afford such a courtesy."

But that was neither here nor there. The reason for our family's general disdain for the vicar bishop was his dismissal of Beba Dobra from the Christmas pageant two years previous. Having secured by acclamation the role of third shepherd to the left, Beba had practised every day for a month to perfect his single line ("A star! It's as bright as a thousand diamonds!"), only to have Vicar Bishop Pavel arrive at dress rehearsal and decide that it would be disrespectful for "a boy like Dobroslav" (he got that wrong; there were no boys like Beba Dobra) to speak at a festival honouring the birth of our Lord and Saviour. Father Grygor protested, citing numerous scripture and growing so angry that at one point he dropped the pretence of respect and began calling the distinguished vicar bishop by the diminutive of his given name: Peta. But, perhaps still angered by the unseemly behaviour of the doll assigned to play the Baby Jesus (who had allowed his plastic head to fall off at a critical point in the rehearsal), the vicar bishop would not relent. Only at the last minute was a compromise reached. Beba Dobra was recast as a lamb and assigned one, small line: "Baaaa." He delivered it with gusto and a small sigh.

Father, who was deep in his bed and deeper into his cups by the time we got home that night, did not rouse when told what the vicar bishop had done; he managed only to extend his grimace a little further. Mother, for her part, was so angry that she prayed in silence well into the night. We found her the next morning, Nexhmije Gjinushi, asleep on her knees by the couch, a wad of dried tissues stuck to her fingers, her forehead resting on a fading picture of the Blessed Virgin.

But that was two years ago, and out of my mind as I watched Vicar Bishop Pavel, wheezing heavily but undaunted as he stood before us in the pulpit. He had begun the second hour of his sermon by elaborating on his earlier exegesiological point that the Bible, especially in the eyes of Serbian Orthodox commentators, was both a historical and meta-historical document, when Father appeared in the narthex. He was, of course, completely naked, save for a small text wedged under his arm.

I say "of course" because in the context of the time, it had become accepted in Crnilo that Dobroslav Zanković did not wear clothes. Again, while I cannot explain my father's choice specifically, I can say that it was related to his studies of both the Doukhobor sect of Western Canada, whose most radical members practised mass nudity and arson as a protest against materialism, and the Jainist Digambara monks, who, in an effort to attain full spiritual enlightenment, reject all forms of materialism, including bodily attachment. It is their practice to go naked.

Nudity for Father was both a spiritual statement and the logical conclusion to the imaginary political conversation he'd been having with Comrade Tito. In Father's mind, being an atheist did not mean being aspiritual, while being a socialist did mean rising above Judeo–Christian morals and Western capitalistic values. The simple act of shedding one's clothes, Father believed, was the ultimate expression of brotherhood, unity, and Socialist democracy.

Needless to say, the practice had not caught on.

Still, few people stirred when Father entered the church. And while many of the congregation, expecting a good show,

77

no doubt, roused themselves and strained forward in their pews as Father began to make his way forward to the chancel, Vicar Bishop Pavel took no heed. His nose was deep in his sermon notes.

"In my own personal study... study of moral hermeneutics" — Pavel read with little inflection, puffing and pausing as he went, as if life itself was a vast obstacle — "many of which... were taken, I might add, under the direct supervision of Patriarch German, Archbishop of Peć, Metropolitan of... of Beograd and Karlovci, and Patriarch of all... Serbs, himself a noted Biblical scholar..."

By this point, Father Grygor had spotted Father. The good priest tugged on his beard furiously. He looked around, perhaps searching for a way to divert the imminent collision. Suddenly inspired, Father Grygor stood up, drawing his hands upward to his hips, silently instructing the rest of the congregation to stand as well.

The strategy seemed to work. Father's naked body disappeared in a sea of faithful as the vicar bishop panted on, never lifting his eyes from his prepared text. Perhaps the ruse would have succeeded if someone could have managed to grab Father, by the arm say, and steer him off in another direction. But Father simply rolled on and finally emerged from the cover of crowd mere metres from the pulpit. Still, Vicar Bishop Pavel did not notice him, and may never have looked up from his notes if Dušan Mićić, still bound to his saltire and propped in the ambry, hadn't cried out in alarm. Not words exactly, but an elongated, distressed gurgle and just enough of a noise that Vicar Bishop Pavel lifted his eyes, looking first at the delicate saint and then to the naked Dobroslav Zanković.

The prelate smiled politely, then turned his head slightly, not quite able to take in all this new information at once. Perhaps he thought this was all part of the pageant.

Father took the prelate's confused silence for acquiescence, and strode to the lectern. With Mother beside me now offering a new and almost silent prayer to the Blessed Virgin, Father closed the vast Bible that lay before him and cleared his throat.

"I will be reading today," he announced with the fullest authority, retrieving the small book from under his arm, "from the *Akaranga Sutra*, the most sacred Jainist text. The world," he began, "is afflicted, miserable, difficult to instruct, and without discrimination. In this world full of pain, suffering by their different acts, see the benighted ones cause great pain…"

Father did, truly, have a wonderful speaking voice. It was deep and whole, like that of an American jazz singer, and his tongue rolled over rich consonants in a way that both calmed the listener and underscored that this was a man of culture and learning.

And so the two men, Vicar Bishop Pavel and my own father, stood not three metres apart, the former at the pulpit, his head turned and brow drawn as he gathered his thoughts, the latter at the lectern gesturing emphatically. With every thump of his fist, his middle extremities shook their approbation. To the naive observer — a stranger who had just wandered in from the street, for example — the scene had a rowdy calm, a debate between learned adversaries, hateful at the core, but each honouring the rules of decorum. But most of us understood that Pavel's silence was merely momentary; he was gathering himself, like a great wind. Father Grygor had already made his way to Father's side and, using his mitre, gallantly tried to restore a level of physical decorum. But we could not expect Vicar Bishop Pavel to stay silent for long.

All at once, the fat prelate exploded, throwing both hands in the air and shouting at Father in a coarse and guttural northern dialect. Leaning heavily on his crozier, the vicar bishop began to limp toward Father.

"As I have heard it, I shall tell how the Venerable Ascetic, exerting himself and meditating, after having entered the order in that winter, wandered about, I shall not cover myself with that robe, only in that winter..."

Caught in the middle, Father Grygor was not sure what to do. His strategic use of the mitre had allayed the concerns of some of the more faint-hearted members of the congregation, but as the Holy Father shuffled his way across the chancel, wheezing and spitting rough invectives, Father Grygor must have begun to fear for my father's safety. He dropped the headpiece and took a step toward the vicar bishop, who simply lifted his crozier and knocked his subordinate out of the way.

"...for a year and a month he did not leave off his robe. Since that time the Venerable One, giving up his robe, was naked, world-relinquishing, and wise..."

By now the cream-skinned martyr was calling from his cross, pleading with his servant, the good vicar bishop, to calm himself, as some members of the congregation stood and shouted as well, torn between the desire to restore order and the lure of the looming confrontation.

Father continued — "...then he meditated with his eye fixed on a square space before him of the length of a man, as the many people assembled, shocked at the sight; they struck him and cried..." — as the Vicar Bishop raised his holy crook and brought it crashing down on the head of this lowly, maniacal lamb, with such force that I was surprised it did not break.

Mother elbowed me in the ribs. "Do something!"

Why me? I cannot say. Perhaps I was just in the wrong place at the right time.

I stood and looked around stupidly.

I saw Father, who had struggled to remain on his feet. He had a small cut on his forehead, and he wiped the blood away as he strove to find his place.

"Knowing…" His voice remained strong, and he hesitated only a little. "Knowing the female sex in mixed gathering places, he meditated…"

Again the crozier came thundering down, this time cracking in half with such force that the gilded handle flew into the nave, knocking the postmaster, Dositej Obradović, who'd risen to offer his assistance, flat out. This time Father fell to his knees, and I could see blood flowing from a cut just above his right eye. Vicar Bishop Pavel remained hunched over, from the follow-through, and appeared to be holding his chest, again struggling for breath, and as voices rose from all corners of the church — and none louder than Dušan Mićić, demanding to be unbound and released from historic martyrdom — I pushed my way toward the lectern, torn, in my adolescent angst, between wanting to defend whatever may have been left of my family's honour and sincerely desiring to evaporate from the face of the Earth.

Already, a couple of good men had gone to Father's aid and were helping him to his feet. The vicar bishop, too, had recovered slightly and arched himself back to his full height and girth. His face ashen, his lips as grey as death. A weighty calm fell upon the scene, and for a moment I thought the worst was over. Then Pavel shook himself like a great wet dog and raised his broken crozier once more.

I took three steps — one, two, three — and laid my hand on

the vicar bishop's shoulder, intending to uncrook him. Mind, Nexhmije Gjinushi: I am, and have always been, a lover not a fighter. I had no self-assurance when it came to physical confrontations; I wasn't sure at all what I planned to do. Fate had its own ideas, though, and the moment I touched Vicar Bishop Pavel, he let forth a muffled grunt and collapsed to the floor.

10

MILOŠ OBILIĆ DID NOT APPEAR until much later, Nexhmije Gjinushi. I had half expected to see him in the chancel, raising his great Turkish sword to block the vicar bishop's path or perhaps shrouding Father's fallen body at the lectern.

But no.

Only after the crowd had moved from the church to the town square, after the Muslims, still appreciative of Father's explication of the Barnabas Gospel, had formed a protective circle around my father and I (a needless exercise, since neither of us were in any danger; the vicar bishop was already mourned but not missed), while Croatian worshippers from the Basilica of Blessed Jerome, in the midst of their own celebration when the ruckus arose, had fled the safety of their church and sat on its steps, watching the strange proceedings. Only then did I see Miloš Obilić, perched on top of the dormer that jutted from the spire of St. Andrej's, executing a slow Gnjilanski Cacak — the dance of the bridegroom.

Foot over foot, step over step, careful not to fall.

"This dance is your dance, Vida," I could almost hear him say. "This dance is our dance; I pass it on to you, as it has been passed for generations..."

11

DR. KARAĐORĐEVIĆ, WHO HAD a front pew and attended directly, would later tell me that Vicar Bishop Pavel was dead before he hit the floor. Some called it witchcraft and looked at me as if I possessed the hands of the devil. Most were more forgiving. Father Grygor consoled me, and said that it was the work of God and Pavel's weak heart. Patriarch German himself wrote me a long letter, provided me with absolution and a personal blessing, which my mother keeps to this day (if my brothers are to be believed) pinned inside her brassiere, right next to her heart. Still, Dušan Mićić, who was inconsolable at the scene and had to be taken away on a stretcher, never spoke to me again.

His heart. Surely that was it. A life of holiness and sacrifice, of temperance, and the eschewment of pleasure. No doubt, under the weight of those good works the vicar bishop's heart had just given up on him. He is in a better place, I suppose.

But heart or no heart, it was little consolation. I had laid my hands upon this man, this Messenger of God, and he had immediately been taken. I had Death's Hands, I was certain, and no amount of reassurance — medical, philosophical, ecumenical — could change my young mind.

I could barely sleep that night. My mind was filled with images of dead vicars and howling, translucent Christ's. I drifted in and out of half-dreams and finally collapsed into a long nightmare about Baba Yaga, an ancient hag familiar to children throughout the Slavic world. I was a child again, although dressed in these borrowed rags, with Baba Yaga chasing me through a landscape that was, by turns, a thick black forest and the dank tunnels of a coal mine, riding her magic pestle like a flying broom, looking to capture me, kill me, and crush my bones like a *raskovnik* root to make her tea. Soon, the rains came in my dream and Perun himself, Zeus of the forgotten Serbic pantheon, stood in the clouds, hurling cartoon thunderbolts to the Earth. Whether he was trying to impede the witch's progress or take me out, I could not be sure. And with each bolt he tossed, his giant Moorish slave hammered a fist onto the skin of an enormous yellow *goč*, and the heavens shook with raw thunder that rumbled through my head. The force of the drumming was so strong, so violent, that the bed seemed to shake. As I came to full consciousness I realized that the thunder was real, the bed was shaking, and more than that, the plaster was falling off the walls, the books that lined my room were tumbling from their makeshift shelves.

And the then the tiny window above my bed shattered.

I felt myself lifted from the bed and thrown to the floor, and I could only think that Father was at it again.

I picked myself up and staggered towards the hallway. The sun was high in the sky, and my brothers had already roused and gone out.

As I reached the door, another thunderous explosion shook the whole house, which seemed this time to lift off its very foundation. I leaned against the wall like a drunk and made my way to the kitchen, to find Mother alone and cowering beneath her beautiful table.

"What's he done now?"

Mother did not reply. She cocked her head, listening in the distance. We could hear sirens and voices rising. I could see the fear in her face.

"What is it? The Americans? Did they drop the atom bomb on Moscow?" Instinctively, I fell to my knees and crawled under the table too.

She shook her head.

"I have lived in fear of this moment..."

"What is it Mother? For God's sake, what's going on?"

"It's the Rapture," she said, in a voice almost devoid of emotion.

"What are you on about, Mati?"

"No one knows about that day or hour, not even the angels in heaven, nor the Son, but only the Father..."

"You're freaking me out. There's a simple explanation surely..."

"As it was in the days of Noah, so it will be at the coming of the Son of Man. For in the days before the flood, people were eating and drinking, marrying and giving in marriage, up to the day Noah entered the ark, and they knew nothing about what would happen until the flood came and took them all away..."

"Come, Mati, come —" I took her arm. "Let's go find Father. He's a brilliant man, a genius. He will know what's going on."

"Two men will be in the field; one will be taken and the other left. Two women will be grinding with a hand mill; one will be taken and the other —" Mother suddenly held her hand to her breast. "Beba!" she cried, and now grabbing my arm, she dragged me out from under the table. "Come quickly! We have to be quick!"

"What is it now, Mati?"

"Beba! Beba is in the mine!"

A rain of fine black soot fell and all around us was chaos and destruction. Chunks of concrete lay smoldering in the street, twisted metal skeletons, cracked wooden planks and yellow intact mine tools. Debris was scattered everywhere, on the ground, on rooftops, and dented into cars, hanging tangled in bushes and trees.

"Mati, what's going on?"

She steamed forward, without a word, past the crowds of people milling in the streets, past the low apartment block near the edge of town, its windows shattered, past a row of gypsy huts where men and women were frantically digging around a chunk of concrete the size of a dog, past the thinning forest that circled Crnilo, the trees decorated with brightly coloured pieces of cloth, that struck me as almost Christmassy, until we came across a strange object lying across our path, an object that I at first mistook for a branch, then as some kind of plastic toy. Only after Mother stepped over it carefully, and quickly picked up her pace, did I understand: it was a human arm, its fist clenched in fear or defiance.

As we moved closer to the mine, I saw more pieces of things, many of which I could not define but others almost too grotesque to fathom: a human head, one eye punched out; the torso of a man, planted into the ground like a fence post, his work clothes blown off, but safety helmet still firmly in place; a nearly intact body, the father of Kosta Šarović, a classmate of mine, hanging upside down in a branch, his arms outreached like a proficient gymnast who had just completed a difficult, inverted dismount. Velimir Šarović's dead eyes were cocked in a jaunty manner.

It took me a moment to collect my wits as we entered the mine site. Hundreds of people were milling about, in seeming disorder, and something — *something* was too strange to even comprehend.

The buildings. That was it.

Everything was flattened, as if the entire industrial complex had suddenly decided to lie down and sleep. As I took in the sight, I began to see that the human activity did indeed involve great purpose and a kind of ant-like complexity. Men were moving about in detailed groupings, each dedicated to specific tasks: some carried great hoses; others had picks and shovels; still others, identified by white crosses on their red armbands, were carrying medical supplies. Everyone with a purpose and intensity I had never seen from the people of this town.

And the midst of it all, my father, in work clothes and silver hard hat, holding a walkie-talkie in one hand, shouting orders, consulting, in charge. Could this really be the man who, as recently as a week ago, had lain in bed for forty-eight straight hours weeping? Who no less than a month before had been forcibly removed from the grounds of the Presidential residence in Beograd, insisting, as they hauled him off, that Slobo himself was awaiting his visit? Who three and half months earlier had jumped from the spire of St. Andrej's church only to land, miraculously, unharmed on the roof of the mayor's new Yugo, flattening the contraption like a tin can?

Mother left me and approached Father. They spoke briefly, Father at first dismissing her, then, as if he grasped finally what she was saying, drawing his head back as if he'd just been struck a strong blow.

He and Mother ran to the area that had once identified the mouth of the mine. Once upon a time, not so long ago, the mine entrance had appeared orderly and professional: a series of safety gates surrounded by a chain-link fence, an inviting entrance way, with freshly painted metal doors; a bright metal sign proclaiming THE YUGOSLAVIAN WORKERS MINING COLLECTIVE (CRNILO): WELCOME! — a change area for miners, and a portable commissary where everyone, from the lowliest worker to O'Dowd himself took their meals. Now there was nothing but an open gape in the surface, a twisted mouth spewing chunks of black rock, concrete, and metal pylons.

A crew of men worked frantically to clear the entrance.

Father jumped in, pushing two men aside, and began to dig frantically through the collected detritus with a small trowel. Mother joined him, scraping the black rocks with her bare fingers.

I can't say how long they dug, Nexhmije Gjinushi. Time lost all sense. I know it was dark when they finally removed enough debris to allow a shaft of air to peek through. A sick, smell wafted forth. Instinctively the workers, each now covered in the thin layer of soot from the black rain, averted their heads. And still, they kept digging.

It was dark again by the time they'd cleared a space large enough for someone, a small child perhaps, to climb through.

Father and Mother, exhausted, their faces black from the coal, their fingers shrivelled and curled like talons, were arguing for the first time.

"Bice, no: it's impossible. No one can go in. The gas — who knows? We have no idea."

"He's small enough. Surely he can worm his way through..."

"There may be pockets of air, or one of the auxiliary shafts, he may have found his way to one of those. We can't even be certain he was..."

"The boy's no bigger than the wind itself, he's just a breeze..."

Father made to speak again, furling his eyebrows as if to rebuke his wife. And then he simply stopped. He leaned forward and wrapped his arms around her. She buried her face in his neck and stayed there for a long time. I was used to seeing my father weep, but as I think about it now, recollecting the crumbs of my whole life, I am certain that that was the only time I ever saw my mother cry.

12

THE YUGOSLAVIAN WORKERS MINING COLLECTIVE (Crnilo) did not implicate Father by name, but the official review made it clear who was responsible. The final report of the Crnilo Mining Disaster Committee cited numerous safety violations — inadequate ventilation, outdated electrical and hydration systems, dangerous build-up of coal dust — and identified "systemic failures at the planning level" as the ultimate cause. According to the official report, the incident began deep in the northernmost sub-shaft when a string of heavily laden coal carts broke free from the others. The renegade carts quickly gained speed as they descended back down the shaft and were soon moving in excess of thirty metres per second. Eventually the carts derailed and crashed into the one of the main archway supports.

What caused the initial spark? That question may never be answered. Perhaps it was the friction of the metal carts colliding? Or damage to the electrical wiring? In any case, something ignited the cloud of coal dust raised by the commotion of the runaway carts. The dust itself is extremely volatile, vastly more combustible than a solid lump of coal, and capable of producing violent explosions. In a well-run mine the air is constantly hydrated to weigh the coal dust down, so it settles harmlessly on the ground. Crnilo's sprinklers had not functioned properly since the 1950s, and throughout the mine the air was thick with black dust, a chain of floating bombs waiting to be ignited. The first explosion set off another and another and so on, spirally through the whole underground system.

Eighty-seven people died in the explosion, miners mainly (one family lost nine members, fathers, uncles, brothers, cousins) but also a few of the poor Roma living on the edge of the mine. No family in the town was untouched. In retrospect, though, it's a miracle so few people died, and had the explosions not coincided with a shift change, the death toll could have been much higher.

For his part, Father was quite publicly released of his duties. Given the general interest in the story, Father's dismissal was something of a spectacle. He ceremoniously handed over his silver hard hat like a defeated general, as the photographers clicked (before, and this is the absolute truth, Nexhmije Gjinushi, repeating the entire humiliating episode at the prompting of the videographer from the state news service, who had somehow bungled the shot). In private, O'Dowd offered his condolences and absolved Father, conceding that the safety concerns he had dutifully passed on to the management committee were routinely lost to the perpetual red tape of the central office, in Beograd.

What caused the coal carts to separate and crash in the first place? When would the mine reopen? Who would compensate the families of the men who had lost their lives? And what about the child's yellow sweater? Investigators had found one near the epicentre of the blast, although they had no opinion as to the whereabouts of its owner. It's possible the sweater had simply alighted there, tossed and buffeted, as explosion after explosion forced currents of air to crisscross through the tunnels. As for the sweater's owner, Emerik Ćalušić, leader of the recovery operation, offered faint hope.

"It's possible he escaped through one of the vents," Ćalušić suggested, taking tea amongst the bric-a-brac of my parents' cramped parlour. "Perhaps he struck his head and lost his memory. Such things have happened before."

Neither Mother nor Father responded. Ćalušić lifted the cup to his lips, negotiating underneath his outlandish moustache to take a sip. "I've heard the stories of one boy who went missing in such a way. They found him several months later, in the woods, sleeping with a pack of feral dogs."

"We appreciate you calling, Emerik Ćalušić, but now my wife and I wish to be alone. I am sure you understand."

Ćalušić nodded, beads of tea clinging to his moustache. He took a couple more fast sips, then stood and silently excused himself, pausing for just a moment at the front door to turn his head in my direction, maintaining eye contact with me for a second or two longer than seemed comfortable. Was he looking for the devil in me, Nexhmije Gjinushi? I suspect the answer is yes. The good people of Crnilo could not have helped but make a connection between Vicar Bishop Pavel's remarkable demise and the Biblical rapture that had occurred in the mine. So, while my Father took the official blame for the disaster, Counsellor, in the eyes of the people, I was never beyond suspicion.

Was it a heavy burden to carry? I suppose, in its way. Although some burdens, like the sleep I now feel descending, are so big they carry you. And now, Nexhmije Gjinushi, my eyes are heavy. I must save the changes I've made and shut down the iBook for the night. My warm bed and little Adelina are waiting patiently.

13

BIG LEADERS HAVE SMALL EARS — do you know that expression, dear Counsellor? It's common among my people, you see, and it came to mind as I perused the newspapers you brought me this morning. As I was flipping through, I saw an old photo of the Dayton Peace Accords. There they all are, Clinton, Milošević, Izetbegović, Tuđman, shaking hands and making the future safe. That was five years ago, Nexhmije Gjinushi! Yet these great men were deaf to the Song of Kosovo, impervious to music that has rained down from every hilltop and disco, every burnt home and hungry dog in every corner of every inch of this place for almost every second that has passed since they put pen to paper. Big leaders have small ears!

Of course, the whole notion that peace can be bought with a signature is comical in itself. Peace cannot be achieved on its own, my dear. It's elementary physics. It's a sort of conceptual parasite, which can only exist in the absence of war. Peace pays what war wins — that's another expression of ours. We are a philosophical people, my love, which comes in handy every now and then.

In any case, it was pleasant to see you again this morning, Counsellor, and I welcome the news you bring of the outside world. I do hope you're right in your thinking, Nexhmije

Gjinushi, and that NATO's forces do have Slobo cornered. The copy of *Blic* was instructive, and I must admit that my heart skipped a beat when I saw the pictures of Ušće Tower burning in the nightscape. I could see the tower from my parents' little flat in Beograd; I must have walked past it a thousand times, and I could only think of my poor mother, shaking in the darkness of the blackout, cursing the gods of America who would inflict such damage on her vista. It certainly makes sense that NATO would target this building, for not only is it the tallest skyscraper in the city (second only to the Avala Telecommunications Tower) but the tallest building of its kind in all the Balkans.

To see it in flames — what a powerful image for all Serbs! Although... perhaps the symbolic value was not *all* that NATO intended. Built in the Golden Years of Yugoslavia proper, it was headquarters for the Central Committee of the Savez Komunista Jugoslavije — the League of Communists. I remember visiting Beograd as a child and seeing the tower at night, interior light strategically left on to spell Tito's name. After his demise, Slobo and his SPS boys took it over and turned it into a monument to their own glory. So for most of us, then, the Ušće Tower represents the recent past, and to see it burning, and the dreams of Soviet glory burning with it, was something of a victory for all of us. The greater victory — and this is NATO's fatal mistake, I fear — is that despite being hit by twelve different Tomahawk missiles, it didn't go down. In fact, there was barely a dent in it. Sure, a little fire here and there, some broken glass, but the mighty Serbic boar, the beast, did not collapse. Imagine what this means to a people obsessed with history — with the illusion of structure, Nexhmije Gjinushi. I wouldn't count them out just yet!

Still, I appreciated the newspapers and thank you again for the letter, which I can only categorize as my own personal symbolic defeat. I had hoped that the numerous pieces of correspondence I created over the past months had found their way to Tristina. To get one back like this (Return to Sender: are there three sadder words in the world, Counsellor?) is one of those minor heartbreaks that have come to define my life. I hope that other letters made it through, but am no longer confident. I will, however, include this one in my testimony and will put it in its proper context for you, in an effort to bolster our argument.

In any case, you left in such a hurry this morning, Counsellor, you almost knocked over your tea. I understand that you must be a very busy person, and I hope everything is okay? I must say — and please don't take this the wrong way, my dear — that I thought about you for a long time, until the memory of your perfume had completely dissolved. It's funny; I realized that we have lived in such close proximity for centuries, your people and mine, and yet there remain cultural nuances and unspoken norms that are beyond our mutual comprehensions.

And before you ran off I was just about to tell you a story. A story first set down by — you guessed it! Our friend the Buddha. It concerns a certain guard who patrolled the border between two kingdoms. Every day he would see this same peasant leading his donkey across the border. He let it go at first, but after a while, he became suspicious. "Why is this fellow going back and forth, day after day?" the guard wondered. "Perhaps he is smuggling something?"

So, the guard determined that he would find out what the peasant was up to. That day, he searched the traveller and his donkey thoroughly, but came up empty-handed.

"You can pass," he told the peasant, making a mental note to check the man again the following day.

Well, the next day came, Nexhmije Gjinushi, and the guard once again stopped the peasant to check him up and down. Still nothing.

So this went on day after day, the guard always searching the peasant and never finding anything out of order, not even a crumb that couldn't be accounted for. Years passed, and the peasant slowly but surely became noticeably wealthier. He began to dress in more elegant clothes, silks and fine linens, and over time added assistants, so that eventually he would pass through the checkpoint in magnificent robes, with seven or eight boys in tow, each one leading his own donkey.

The guard would check, check, check. Nothing. But his suspicions never abated.

Ten years passed and then twenty and more, right up to the day that the guard retired. He left his station at the border and began living the life of the content pensioner, playing Pesë Katësh with his cronies and lazing in the bright cafés on the main street in town. One day, as the now former guard was sipping his morning coffee, he spots the peasant and his entourage parading up the street, making their daily journey to the border. So the guard runs up to the peasant and says, "I know you are up to something, friend, so please satisfy my curiosity and tell me, after all this years, what were you smuggling?"

The peasant smiled and put his arm on the guard's shoulder and, realizing that his old nemesis was now retired and could no longer arrest him, answered with one simple word:

"Donkeys."

See, my dear Counsellor, that is why I like the Buddha. He has a sense of humour! And not the so-called humour of the Christ — he calls Peter a "rock"; how the hell is that funny? — but a real jokester. Donkeys? That's funny!

It's also an apt description of our present conundrum, isn't it? For we Balkanoids are always looking at one thing — History is a particular favourite — and seeing something else entirely. (My word — I am pedantic! What is ever to become of me, Nexhmije Gjinushi? Will I become one of those dull old men, with soup stains on the front of his shirt, boring the world to death? I certainly hope not, my little Kosovo Maid. Perhaps it is just the earliness of the hour, and I've yet to have my morning coffee.)

More so, consider that this story provides some insight into that subject which I believe is of great interest to you: my father. You see, Father is like the donkey; the more you look at him the more you'll try to see. But no matter how hard you look, no matter what crevice you peer into, you'll never find anything.

Let the record show that my family left Crnilo under cover of night and made our way directly to The White City, that refuge for a millennium of the Balkans' lost and unwanted people. Beograd's the oldest city in Europe, older (or as old at least) as venerable Athens itself. For seven thousand years men and women have lived and died here, fornicated and prayed, slaughtered one another, expelled their brothers, stolen from their mothers and fathers. For seven thousand years they have danced within these pale limestone walls. The Huns came and levelled it; the Sarmatians came and built it back up. For a century, the Goths and Avars sparred with one another and the Byzantine Empire for the control of this city, and for a thousand years the Bulgars, Hungarians, and Serbs scurried under the great shadow of Constantine's kingdom, taking turns dancing with the White Lady until the Holy Romans took her back.

Nandor Alba. Alba Graeca. Castelbianco.

The names slip off the tongue like my father's Sanskrit incantations, sweet nothings for the soul.

Griechisch Weissenburg. Nandor Fejervar.

So we offered our own little invasion, Brati, Djordje, Jovo. My mother and father and I. It was a difficult adjustment. Mother and Father had become quite adept in navigating the nuances of life in Serbia's small towns and villages, but Beograd was almost too much for them to comprehend. We moved from flat to flat before settling into a small apartment building owned by Veselin Čajkanović, one of my father's distinguished relatives. It was a drab, Stalinist-era building, modern in the classic sense, concrete, functional — as close to being autistic as a building could come. Located in Vidikovac, a neighbourhood some ten kilometres south of Beograd proper, our building was carbuncled to a hilltop, affording us a startling view of the city's skyline framed by the conflux of the Sava and Danube rivers.

Even by our modest standards, the apartment complex left much to be desired. Filled with pensioners mostly, rotting like teeth in their damp rooms, or displaced families, as anonymous and ignoble as my own, bivouacked in their cramped quarters. The family directly across the hall, for example: nine in all, including a grandmother and a maiden aunt, living in a single-bedroom flat. The father, Fisnic Nikolić, had been a schoolteacher in Herzegovina. But the declining political climate and crumbling economy had led him to seek his fortune elsewhere. Now, he and his three oldest sons were *gajtos* in Potsdam, building roads to connect Germany's former East with its former West. When Nikolić and his sons came home to visit, the family swelled to thirteen members, so many, in fact, that they had to sleep in shifts, with five or more bodies sardined into the lone bedroom.

We were not so badly off. Soon after we arrived in Beograd, Jovo left to study — to my Father's surprise — at the Univerzitet U Novum Sadu Medincinski Fakultet, while Brati and Djordje had fallen in with those Arkan gangsters and were hardly ever around. With Beba Dobra sleeping with the wild dogs, there were really only the three of us. The flat was crowded enough, though.

Living in such cramped quarters my parents' relationship declined. Their arguments grew to be as constant and as natural as breathing. Father spent his time circling the flat in his housecoat, orbiting Mother while offering domestic advice and advancing his opinions on the state of the world. At first Mother was stoic in her acceptance of Father's intrusions, a real Kosovo Maiden. In time, though, she began a campaign of passive resistance, humming loudly to herself as he spoke or turning up the volume on *Senka'zi Deca*, her favourite television soap opera. Eventually, almost casually, she began to disagree with him — something I'd rarely seen before — and the trickle soon gave way to a flood. They came to argue constantly, about everything and anything, to the point where it became not a string of unique disagreements, but one single ceaseless antiphonal squabble, almost spiritual in its complexity and form.

Nothing was beyond dispute: the correct way to scrub a pot; the optimum heat setting for frying an egg; the most efficient bus route to Beograd Centrum; the operating hours of Muzej grada Beograda, the civic museum. In time, the net was cast further and further, as their life devolved into one endless philosophical/sociological/scientific/historical/cultural debate: the annual mean rainfall in central Kosovo; the relative health merits of pomegranates versus wild Serbian raspberries; asexual reproduction in seahorses; Plato's allegory of the cave; the literary merits of Ayn Rand; oil production in *fin de siècle* Nantucket — no topic was too obscure or lacking in inherent controversy. Granted, Father's arguments tended to be littered with questionable facts, dubiously notated, while Mother leaned toward contrary discourse (often simply disagreeing with her husband, no matter how mundane the topic) and blanket ad hominem attacks that sought to undermine Father's arguments by casting aspersions on his intelligence, mental stability, or manhood (and often, all three at once).

Instinctively, I understood. We all had our way of coping. It was not the loss of his position at the mine — that wasn't it at all. Father always lost his job. It was merely expected of him, and I suspect that we would have been secretly disappointed — Father more than any of us — with any other outcome. No. The real issue, the unspoken part, was the loss of Beba Dobra. It stung us, all of us, more than we could say.

We all blamed ourselves and everyone else, with mother assigning blame more than any of us. She blamed herself for not keeping a better eye on her youngest and most precious; how many times had she thought that the mines were no place for a boy, no place for anyone, really? She blamed me as well. Not overtly, perhaps not even consciously, but it was there, revealed in the way she held the knife when she sliced bread for my supper, the way she averted her eyes, just slightly, as she kissed my forehead. But most of all, she blamed Father. It was his mine, after all; how he could let it blow up and kill his own son? This was beyond my mother's limited comprehension. And so, she wrapped herself in a cocoon of facts or, more accurately, disputed facts. She could not bring Beba Dobra back to life, but she could question this life and, specifically, the man who had brought her here.

Alone with my parents in the flat, I had little opportunity for escape. The option of hiding in my room, favoured by young men and women around the world, I suspect, was not open to me. My room was the living room: I slept on an ancient divan, once property of the niece of Dragutin Dimitrijević (her uncle, under the codename Apis, was mastermind behind the Black

Hand's assassination of Franz Ferdinand and Princess Sophie). The divan itself played no major part in world history. It was dusty and hard, its horsehair mattresses compressed by five generations of Serbian asses, its velveteen cushions, once a rich crimson like St. Sava's blood, were by now faded and as brown as the river that bore the great martyr's name. My parents spent their days in the living room and adjacent kitchen; the divan became the dull sun at the centre of their universe.

I did find some solace in the tiny lavatory and holed away in that room, growing more bored. To pass the time, I tried reading the labels on bottles of medicine and hair products, first silently to myself, then out loud, pretending to endorse various products, like the announcers on the commercials that had only recently begun to flood our TV screens.

Months went by and almost a year in Beograd and the world rumbled on, past the Bosnian Troubles and the Siege of Sarajevo (where my brother Brati, the Stammerer, spent seven months on the front line, impatiently — and vainly — waiting for the Bosnians to tire of NATO drippings and mercifully surrender), past the months of hyper-inflation, with prices doubling every sixteen hours and an inflation rate that at its peak reached a breathtaking *five quadrillion* — 5,000,000,000,000,000! — per cent per annum (people used 100-dinar bills, not to buy things, but to wipe their arses), past the heroic invasion of Kosovo, which saw my other brother, the ever-silent Djordje, lose the tip of his thumb in a cooking accident deep behind enemy lines, before inadvertently capturing (then quickly surrendering to) a klatch of confused Italian cadets — all this as Father, Mother, and I orbited the flat, driving one another nuts.

We eked out an existence on my parents' dwindling savings and handouts from the farthest reaches of the Zanković clan, whose members, already humiliated by Father's role in the Crnilo disaster, could not bear the disgrace of one of them living in destitution. Father, in the wake of his public dismantling, went from door to door seeking employment. He had nearly exhausted every familial and social contact when he finally, thanks to the intercessions of our landlord Veselin Čajkanović — who was keen to have his rent paid — landed a job with Nezavisne Banke od Ljudi Srbija. It was one of the numerous mercurial financial institutions that rose and fell in those days, offering the people, unfamiliar with the emerging market economy, an alternative to the poorly run state banks.

Father's job was simple and well beneath his experience and education. He was a teller who stood behind a metal grate for up to ten hours at a time in the foyer of an impressive sandstone building, which had served, until the recent collapse of the Serbian infrastructure, as the offices of Pošta Srbije, the national postal service. Here, he collected hard currency — German deutschmarks, British pounds, U.S. dollars — from cautious depositors. As unreliable as father could be, he did have a way with people and a knack for getting them to part with their cash.

…I don't blame you being wary, Gospođa Ninčić; I was wary too until I invested in it myself. You heard me right, Gospođa Ninčić, *invested*. Don't think of it as a bank account, Little Dove; it's more a savings club, an investment in your future…Twenty per cent interest, per month. That's guaranteed, Gospođa Ninčić, and of course your entire investment is protected by the Narodna banka Srbije…

Alas, Father's banking career did not last long. No, it wasn't the result of that little incident on the Knez — perhaps you saw the pictures in the news? Father, dressed in nothing but a grimed T-shirt and piss-stained underwear, standing on the top balcony of the Srpska Kruna Hotel, pulling American dollar bills, purloined from the Nezavisne Banke od Ljudi Srbij's vaults, from a burlap sack and tossing them to the crowd below like some great God sowing the Earth at the dawn of time. Instead of the golden boot that little piece of manic theatre earned father a raise — it was the best publicity Nezavisne Banke od Ljudi Srbij could have hoped for. They were literally giving money away! Investments immediately went up four hundred per cent.

No. Father lost his job when the bank itself collapsed. You see, dear Counsellor, there was a reason why the enormous interest rates seemed to be too good to be true. I'll give you a clue: think donkeys! Had anyone looked at the bank's dealings with an open mind, they would have noticed that beyond the usual Serbian holdings — an aggressive position in the heroin trade, some strategic holdings in arms-running futures — the Nezavisne Banke od Ljudi Srbij's was essentially a pyramid scheme, with new depositors providing the capital to pay the interest to the old ones. As long as the bank was expanding exponentially, the whole thing worked swimmingly. But once Beograd's ready supply of hard currency began to dry up — well, the lie has short legs, as we Serbs like to say. It cannot run very far.

The bank president, a former baker and pimp with close ties to organized crime and Slobo's Radical Party, took a midnight flight to Paris with several suitcases full of hard currency. The bank's most loyal customers burned him in effigy. And Father was once again out of work.

For my part, I wasn't about to wait for the economy to catch up to my needs. I had by now started making forays into the black market. I had begun with the basics, moving jeans and sneakers, but those lines of products had already flooded the market and very much targeted a luxury demographic. I quickly realized that the bare necessities of life — food, drugs, sex, and other diversions — were where the money was. Given that the underground grocery trade was completely controlled by the government, I had to find more flexible products to move. I dealt in drugs, it's true, soft ones mostly: weed, coke, a little "e." Heroin, crack, PCP, meth — these were much harder to get your hands on and brought me in contact with more unsavoury clientele. I tended to avoid them if I could.

Looking back, I won't say I feel remorse. I did what I had to do, and at the time, I genuinely felt I was providing an important service. I was giving people the chance to escape this living hell, even if it was just for a few hours in the day. Escape was a much-needed commodity at the time and, in many ways, was perhaps the only thing holding the country together.

Lazar Internet Café was a necessary evil (although, to be fair, this could probably be said about almost any aspect of my life). This rundown little room was grafted onto the back of a wretched bar with the strange name that would translate, with difficulty, as The Peasants' Table or, perhaps more accurately (although, more obscurely), The Table from the Cabin in the Forest. It was an odd building, a former chapel, co-opted by Communists years ago.

The bar and café were owned by a father and son. Kosta Ilić, a squat bear of a man, ran the bar, while Bracha, that repulsive cricket, made a go of the café. You couldn't find a father and son more opposite. Ilić was like a comic uncle from one of those Russian films that never seem to get made anymore, a man as wide as he was deep, as loud as he was harmless, hirsute and kinetic, always slapping you on the back and given to imposing vast hugs on anyone who got in his way. Bracha was an argument for euthanasia. Tall and gaunt, with an adolescent dusting of a moustache (despite being almost in his thirties), the bulging, empty eyes of a serial masturbator, and front teeth that protruded at almost unimaginable angles, leaving him with a perpetual, idiotic grin. All this could be forgiven, Nexhmije Gjinushi, if it weren't for that troublesome personality of his. The general consensus was that kind as old Ilić was, he had been far too lenient on his son, while the mother (who had left the family years ago and moved in with Ilić's own brother, if the rumours are to be believed) had pampered and indulged the boy. The result: Bracha was a selfish prick, plain and simple.

He called it the Lazar Internet Café, although the irony was lost on Bracha. He saw it as a sincere attempt to reflect the greatness of a nation, and he'd adorned the room with patriotic images — Serbian flags, cheap prints of *Seoba Srbalja* and *The Kosovo Maiden*, a hand-painted image of Lazar floating over a green field surrounded by blackbirds, the hero of the people keeping a watchful eye over the low-level drug deals and young men subtly whacking off to internet porn.

But as I say, the café served its purpose and had the added benefit of allowing me to keep an eye on my father — who'd worn out his welcome under mother's wing — while I pursued my various business interests. I would drop him in the bar with his cronies and run around the back to work the deals.

Lazar's also had a significant role to play in my story, Counsellor, for it was here that I most improbably rediscovered My Sweet Angel of the Salivating Dogs. But I am most certainly getting ahead of myself. Let me take a step back and tell you how it all began. How I first met Tristina and how I first fell in love. Admittedly, it may not be entirely relevant to my defence. But I believe the story has a weight of its own, no matter how light, and that each pebble (and this is likely the lapsed Buddhist in me speaking) contributes to the whole.

14

NO DOUBT YOU'VE HEARD of the Great Dr. Pavlov, Counsellor? He and his drooling mutts? Good old Ivan Petrovich; it was he who brought Tristina and I together.

The occasion was a field trip, not long after we arrived in Beograd, an excursion that every Serbian school kid took to the Mother Bear. It was designed to give us students the opportunity to experience the greatness of Soviet culture first-hand. The Russians would bus us into Moscow, show us Red Square and the tomb that held the waxen head of Vladimir Ilyich Ulyanov, stitched to a bloated suit, preserved and displayed like a saint's relics, take us to the Circus and the Kremlin to see the dancing beasts, and, inexplicably, tour us around the hyperboloid Shukhov Radio Tower, of which Muscovites are inordinately proud.

Equally inexplicably, the coaches always stopped at the Pavlov Museum in Ryazan, some 120 kilometres northeast of Moscow, leading me to believe that the bus driver himself either had a secret girlfriend folded away in some musty corner of the museum's basement or found, as I did, its heated and richly decorated lavatory a highly desirable place to have a bowel movement.

In either case, there in the former Pavlov family home, where the future scientist was born and raised, you could find among the antediluvian beakers and Bunsen burners a pair of stuffed dogs: *Druzhok*, or Little Friend, and *Tygan*, Gypsy, a happy couple. Druzhok, it turns out, was the first of Pavlov's canine subjects to survive past the initial surgical phase of the experiments. You see, the animals weren't just passive passengers in Pavlov's investigations, anxiously sitting and drooling as the avuncular physiologist dangled a doggie treat in one hand — inches from their snouts — while scribbling notes on a clipboard with the other. No, these dogs were committed subjects or more, part of the equipment. Strapped in place, attached to inquisitional instruments of measurement, they did their duty.

Druzhok and Tygan were the lucky ones; they merely had cannula surgically implanted in their muzzles, bulky copper tubes that caught their drool and must have made the everyday necessities of a dog's life — eating, licking one's ass, even resting one's head — painful and troublesome. Later volunteers were not so fortunate. They had their insides outed and small metal boxes, designed to collect intestinal and pancreatic fluids, fused to their partially exposed digestive tracts. Induced sleep was too sweet for these dogs; Pavlov was a firm believer that in order to get effective data his subjects must be awake, alert, and alive. The torments of my life — of which there have been many — pale in comparison to what this loving couple must have experienced. Those poor dogs!

Pavlov's purpose was concrete, Nexhmije Gjinushi; he hoped that by understanding the digestive process, he could begin to unravel the mysteries of peptic ulcers, colitis, gastroparesis, and lay the groundwork that might someday lead to a cure. However, with his keen eye, Dr. Pavlov noticed that his canine volunteers would salivate, not only at the presence of food, but at the sight of the attendant who brought them their food. Pavlov hypothesized that the dogs had learned to associate the attendants with food, and this learning triggered an induced automatic response: salivation. By mistake, the professor discovered classical conditioning.

For his efforts, Nexhmije Gjinushi, Pavlov earned the first ever Nobel Prize for Medicine. For their efforts, Druzhok and Tygan got stuffed.

Druzhok was the bigger dog, a true mutt, part German shepherd, part Border collie, by appearances, with narrowed, Slavic eyes and a curious expression on his frozen face, as if it had just dawned on him that Dr. Pavlov was not at all the good master he seemed. Tygan was smaller and rougher, a black mongrel with white patches, and one ear cocked — a brilliant taxidermicological stroke that animates the whole face. And so the dogs stood in this glacial half-life, perpetually waiting for their master to bring dinner, forever on the cusp of drool.

I wondered at the time, how long will they last like this? They would undoubtedly survive World War III and the Nuclear Winter (for remember, this was back in the time when every Soviet schoolchild believed in the coming nuclear war as firmly as children in the West clung to their visions of Santa Claus) and on into the next millennium. It touched me strangely at the time, the fate of these dogs. Once vibrating with life, as was I, now rendered separate, inanimate: furniture for the ages. At least they had each other.

And so, there I stood, along with these shells, when I realized that someone else was spying on us from a distance. A girl, tall and slender, with a frizz of red hair and pale white skin — beautiful skin — so clean, so luminous, so very different from the ruddy, swarthy, fuzz-faced coal maids of Crnilo.

She silently watched us for several minutes, her fingers mindlessly ruffling the edge of her schoolgirl pleats. I tried not to look at her, focusing all my attention on Druzhok, leaning forward as if I were examining some particularly stimulating point of scientific interest.

"Are you going to do it?" she finally said, in a conspiratorial whisper.

"Huh?"

She came a few steps closer.

"Are you going to do it? Are you going to set them free?"

I must have looked quite baffled, Nexhmije Gjinushi, for she immediately glanced at me apologetically and turned to go away.

"No," I said, sharply. "I mean, yes. How did you know?"

My question was sincere, because I realized just as she asked it that it was, in fact, exactly what I was about to think. The words hadn't formed in my head yet, but somewhere inside me I had already decided to help the dogs escape.

The girl shrugged.

"It's terrible, that's all. Someone should help them."

I looked at the name tag, pinned to the lapel of her jacket: Tristina. What a strange name — and beautiful.

"I'm wondering how one would do it?"

"You just reach out and grab them, I suppose."

I looked directly at her face for the first time, my eyes meeting hers — brownish, wide, ancient, and familiar. We quickly diverted our glances.

"What's wrong with your nose?"

My stupid martyr's beak! All askew from its encounter with the lavatory wall. I quickly moved my hand up to cover my face, but Tristina stopped me. She stared intently for a moment, then nodded, appearing quite pleased. Perhaps the damage made me seem more dangerous? Did that appeal to her? Do girls like dangerous boys?

"There could be an alarm or something?" I finally said, breaking the silence.

"Hmmm?"

"The dogs. There might be an alarm."

"That is a possibility."

"I suppose one could get in a lot of trouble."

I'd heard of one boy who had been caned and expelled simply for taking a box of pencil crayons from the school; what would they do to a child who had pilfered significant relics of the Soviet Empire? I could not even begin to think.

"For every action, there is an equal and opposite reaction," she offered, then frowned at my obvious ignorance. "Isaac Newton."

I nodded, as if the name had just been on the tip of my tongue.

"I could say that I found it, I suppose, that I was just returning it."

"If you're afraid, I understand."

"It's not that I am afraid, far from it —"

I was going to recount a litany of my bravest acts, but before I could think of any, even before I had a chance to make one up, Tristina reached over the corded partition and grabbed little Tygan. She thrust the dog into my arms (it was surprisingly light but, of course, all empty inside), glanced to the left, then ran off.

And so there I stood, holding Pavlov's dog, suddenly overcome with the urge to run, and wondering obliquely if this would be considered a genuine example of classical conditioning. I turned and fled down the staircase, into the dark basement of the Pavlov Museum, ever thinking that I should just toss the mutt to one side, but never quite able to bring myself to do it.

"Atta-boy!" Miloš Obilić was now beside me, urging me on. "Run, run like a Turk! The treasure is yours, the glory..."

I slammed through a metal door, and found myself outside in the cold air. I could see my breath and Tygan's breath, too, almost; it was that cold. In the air was the sharp smell of the lavatory. I could see the back of my coach, the engine running to prevent it from freezing. Miloš Obilić now appeared crouched beside the bus tire.

He waved me on.

"Quickly! The coast is clear..."

I made a dash for it and reached the bus without being seen. I tried the nearest luggage compartment on the bottom of the coach. Locked.

I shuffled over and tried the next one.

It was locked as well.

By now, I heard the voices of two men, bus drivers no doubt, approaching. I grabbed the handle on the third compartment, turned it as quietly as I could. The door fell open and I quickly slid Tygan inside. She looked at me for a moment, her ear half-cocked.

"It's all right, girl," I whispered as calmly as I could. "We are going to escape."

But she looked at me again sadly with her sharp glass eyes. If she could have whimpered, she would have.

"I can't..." I tried to explain, but it was no use. In my little heart, I knew that Tygan would never be happy without her Druzhok. I gasped in exasperation, then quickly set off back in the direction of the museum.

By now the teachers and their charges were starting to make their way to the doors. I had to wait just beyond the dog exhibit for several minutes, pretending to tie and retie my shoe as a stream of students marched past me.

Finally, it was clear. I reached into the exhibit and grabbed Druzhok. I pulled sharply, but he did not move. I pulled again, with no success, then realized the copper tube coming from his mouth was attached directly to a complex array of scientific equipment.

I grabbed the tube at the point where it connected to a canister that had once collected Druzhok's drool. I gave a good tug.

Nothing.

I tugged again, this time with my foot against the cur's haunch, but again, the dog would not yield.

This time I grabbed Druzhok's snout just above the copper tube and placing both feet now on the collection canister, really put my narrow back into it. I pulled and pulled and pulled, until the entire operation suddenly succeeded. I went tumbling backward, Druzhok in hand, and was almost to the stairs when I realized that the force of my exertion had caused the dog's lower jaw to break off completely. I glanced back and saw the jaw grinning at me, still attached to the collection canister. I persevered.

Druzhok was vastly heavier that Tygan, and it took all the effort of my small muscles to get him down the stairs and down into the basement corridor.

Miloš Obilić was by the exit.

"It's going to be tight, Little Prince, but with God's grace, we can make it."

By now my body pounded with adrenaline. I charged through the door, the dog half hidden by my coat. Making my way directly to the back of the coach, I weaved past a couple of teachers. They almost took no notice of me, assuming, I guess, I was just another tardy student running to catch his bus.

Finally, I reached the side of the bus. I grabbed the handle to the baggage compartment and turned it.

At that moment, the bus revved up and started to move forward.

"Pray with me."

Miloš Obilić was on his knees in the mud.

"O Heavenly Father."

"We really haven't time for this."

"*O Heavenly Father*."

"O Heavenly Father."

"Who flayed the Turks and smote the Egyptians…"

"Who smote the Turks."

"Flayed."

"*Flayed* the Turks and smote the Egyptians…"

Obilić sighed. Even being a holy figment can be exasperating at times, I suppose.

"Deliver this boy, Thy humble servant, and his charge."

"Deliver me, Thy reluctant servant, and my charge."

"For the Power and the Glory of Serbia."

"For the Power and the Glory of Serbia."

"Everlasting."

"Is that really a word?"

"Everlasting."

"Everlasting."

"Amen."

"Amen."

And then, the most wondrous thing happened, Nexhmije Gjinushi. The coach stopped!

I will not speculate by what power: divine intercession or simple coincidence, it mattered not. The fact is, a line of students passed in front of our bus, forcing the driver to yield. That was all the time I needed. In full sight of a row of waiting buses, I unhatched the luggage compartment and slid Druzhok in beside the little gypsy girl. They lapsed into each other, Tygan's snout nestled into Druzhok's muzzle, just below his jawless smile. I made my way quickly to the door and banged on it. And just as I stepped up, the driver's curses harrowing my ears, I happened to turn; at that moment my eyes locked with the deep brown eyes of my Red-Haired Angel. Her bus had started to move too, taking her off in her own direction, pulling us apart.

I took my seat and tried, silently, to remember the exact wording of Miloš Obilić's incantation.

I returned from my excursion late that night and slithered into my bed. I did not fall asleep right away, the rough divan made sure of that, as my head still tumbling with thoughts of Druzhok and Tygan, still tucked away in the coach's luggage compartment, Tristina, and our great adventure. When I finally did fall asleep, it was one of those strange affairs where I seemed to skate across the surface of slumber without ever completely sliding into it. I had fierce dreams involving police and scientific instruments and Turks and holy relics of the martyred St. Andrej. I had richly erotic visions of dog-headed girls and the Holy Virgin that aroused and roused me several times.

15

SUCH IS YOUNG LOVE, my unpronounceable muse; it comes and goes. Did I ever expect to see her again? Of course not! I no doubt mooned over her for days or perhaps weeks, and then moved on to my next untouchable obsession. But when I saw her the second time, some ten months later, sitting at that dirty cubby in the café, it seemed an inevitability; in fact, it felt as if we had never been apart. We were connected by these chance encounters like a line between two arbitrary points on a map.

I remember the incident vividly. There was an odd electricity in the air of the Lazar Internet Café that evening, a tempered excitement that came with the knowledge that somehow our backwater country had managed to find itself on the international stage. War was already raging in your Kosovo (it must have been awful for you, yes? The night raids? Perhaps you lost someone near to you, a brother or uncle? I am sorry I have never inquired) — and the NATO guys had had their little tryst in Rambouillet and sent Slobo his ultimatum: withdraw or face the consequences. Little did they know he'd already heard that a thousand times from his lovely Mira and knew exactly what to do: ignore the warning and keep on fucking!

It was a time of great economic uncertainty, not only because the Communist ideal was crumbling around us — and along with it, all the infrastructure and investment the Russians had maintained — but also because people suddenly found themselves with a strange new freedom: the ability to voice their strongest opinions publicly.

The SANU Memorandum, Nexhmije Gjinushi — perhaps you've heard of it? This to my mind was the beginning of those *Miloševćian* social experiments that turned the angry eyes of the world toward Serbia. The uncivil wars, the "ethnic cleansing," Operation Allied Farce, even my present circumstance — this did not begin on the Field of Blackbirds 650 years ago; its genesis was in the dusty boardrooms of Srpska Akademija Nauka I Umetnosti, where, barely a decade ago, a handful of very smart men with glorious Balkanoid hairdos figured out what was wrong with the world.

I will spare you the details, Nexhmije Gjinushi. Suffice to say it was the usual lamentations of great men just past their prime: that the world was no longer good enough, that somehow, someone had treated them unfairly, and that the only way to fix the hitherto unrealized problem would be through radical political transformation, led by those wise men and all their magnificent follicles. In this particular case, it was the Serbs who had been hard done by in their own country, as — the wise eggs at Srpska Akademija Nauka i Umetnosti decided — a grinning Tito sat back and watched you Albanian Turks commit a cultural and literal genocide.

So we let the members of the Serbian Academy of Sciences and Arts have their voice. Our leaders dismissed it — even Slobo, then only President of the Yugoslavian state of Serbia, called it "nationalistic claptrap" — and the whole memorandum might have been forgotten if it hadn't struck a chord in the West.

The Americans were drawn to its thinly veiled attack on the Socialist International; support and money began flowing in, giving new life to the Serbian nationalist movement.

And so we find ourselves where we are today, my Kosovo Muse, with the Americans striving to destroy a movement they helped create, and me, in the midst of it all, pecking away on my iBook.

But still, you're confused? True, it's difficult to keep track without a program. Even I, as intimately familiar with the conflict as I am, have trouble keeping track. Who are the good guys again?

I suppose you could point to the breakup of Yugoslavia as the catalyst, and no doubt the border fracas with Slovenia was a sign of things to come. That was ages ago, Counsellor, when you and I were still children of a kind. And besides, it was hardly a tiff and over almost before it began. Bosnia was more serious stuff. Four years of Republika Srpska and Herzeg-Bosnia trying to get your kinsmen, the Bosniak Muslims, to change their mind over independence. How many people died in that one, Counsellor? I believe conservative estimates put the figure at around twenty thousand. Pocket change, really.

Then we come to your turf, my dear. It's been — what? — two years since the festivities broke out? Your liberators versus ours — out there liberating everyone to death; trying to outdo the other in terms of pure evil. No wonder NATO sat with their thumbs up their asses for so long.

For the record, though, we knew the bombs were coming — of course we did! There had been rumours for months. Most people disregarded them. The Americans would never attack. Their President, after all, liked jazz music and fornication. He was practically a Serb.

In any case, it was a day like any other. I had left Father with his cronies and headed round back to Lazar's Internet Café. My usual routine.

I remember Bracha's greeting as if it were yesterday, and I recall that I pretended to smile. I looked around the café. Ten grey screens glowed in the grey light of the grey room. It hadn't been painted since Tito was fornicating.

"Hey, Turk!"

Bracha had started calling me that — Turk! Hey, Turk! — all in good sport, he supposed. What a prick.

"I told you Brach; I am a pretend Buddhist, not a Muslim."

Bracha snorted.

"You have the Muslim nose, friend."

"The Muslim nose?"

"You know, the opposite of the Jew nose."

Bracha laughed and looked around the room, to see who was witnessing his brilliance.

Bracha and I had a parasitical relationship. I needed a home base and his Polish PCs to run my business, but he needed my services as well. Bracha's girlfriend was a bitch and a whore — what was her name? She would fuck anyone, but not Bracha — unless she was coked up. And who could blame her? She was not too bad to look at, straddling the lines between too skinny and too ugly, but never quite crossing them. But Bracha, he was hard to take. That pockmarked soccer ball face: you felt like kicking it.

The girlfriend needed all the Dutch courage she could find to sleep with that monster.

"You know, my grandfather was in Jasenovac."

It's true; Ilić's father had been in a guest in Ustaša concentration camp during the European war.

"Bracha, I know. You've told me a hundred times."

"You know what they called the clinging ones, the nearly dead?"

"Yes, you've told me. And I'm not really interested anyways, Brach. It's ancient history. Can I buy some time? I've got some pot, and I'm telling you, it's good."

"Muslims."

"Bracha, the pot."

"They called them Muslims because they were so thin and sick and so crazy that they'd talk to themselves. They'd sit on the dirt like Muslim beggars, begging to die, praying to Allah to make their bed in the sky."

"If you're not interested—"

"Okay, okay. Two hours, two ounces."

"You're crazy, Brach."

"I tell you, Turk, you're crazy; two hours, two ounces."

"I can buy a computer for two ounces, Bracha."

The monster snorted. "*Turk*—" this Turk thing was getting tired, way past tired, bone tired, dead "—go buy one, then."

"I'll give you one ounce of pot and one line of coke for six hours."

"Coke?"

"It's the real thing."

Bracha paused briefly. "One ounce, two lines."

Two lines. He must have been very horny.

"Okay. One ounce, two lines, seven hours."

The monster grunted and nodded. He turned his head, not wanting to let on that his prick had defeated him once again.

My transaction a success, I set off to find a free workstation. And that's when I saw her. In fact, even before I laid eyes on her, I had that curious sensation that I was about to see someone familiar. Have you ever had that sense, Nexhmije Gjinushi? Personally, I don't ascribe it to ESP or any other supernatural process. Perhaps it's the result of a smell too subtle to register on our consciousness or a transfer of electrons taking place at a subatomic level. Let the record show, though, that as I searched the café for an empty workstation, my eyes were immediately drawn to the cracked stained glass window at the far end of the room, a replica of the miraculous Theotokos — the Virgin Mother and Her Child — as revealed to St. Sava on his pilgrimage to Jerusalem.

A shaft of light was piercing through the window and drawing a halo, as sure as the one above the Holy Manikin, around my Red-Haired Angel's face.

I cannot tell you the date or time, Nexhmije Gjinushi. But I can tell you exactly what Tristina was wearing (a light pink hoodie, ostensibly from the GAP, but no doubt some Asiatic knock-off), the colour of her lips (a bright fuchsia, contrasting nicely with her eburnean skin, and just striking enough to distract the eye away from the pimples), and the exact position of her glasses, which had slid halfway down her nose, giving her an odd, professorial air — every detail of that second first encounter burned into my mind's hard drive. And that hair, that joyous, strange, wild, and hungry hair, the colour of which no word can do justice. Any effort to describe it (red is almost an insult, tepid and usual and completely unbecoming of a colour that seemed to belong to its own spectrum), would send the strongest among us scrambling for the thesaurus: incarnadine, latericeous, phenicious, conflagrant, igneous, rubedinous, rubescent, rubiginous, rutilant, vinaceous — all mere insults that only underscore my main theme, which is that, when you get right down to it, words are but tiny sparks and, while a useful shorthand when it comes to organizing the world, almost useless when it comes to describing anything beyond the most mundane.

"No one can love unless he is impelled by the persuasion of love."

I closed my eyes again and rubbed them. Miloš Obilić was there, standing above me, grinning like a lunatic.

"She's a beauty, yes?"

I did not respond, conscious of the fact that if Tristina were to notice me carrying on a conversation with an invisible phantom, my chances of getting her to go out with me would be severely compromised.

"Love, my son. Love."

"Hmmm?"

"Did your heart palpitate?"

"What are you talking about?" I answered out of the corner of my mouth, trying to be discreet. I quickly moved to an empty desk; Obilić galloped behind me to keep pace.

"When a lover catches sight of his beloved his heart palpitates. It is the way of love. And you turned pale, yes?"

I sat down and buried my head behind the computer monitor.

"I felt nauseous, yes, as if my head was spinning, but you tend to have that effect on me, Miloš Obilić."

"Every lover regularly turns pale in the presence of his beloved. She is the one."

"What 'one'?"

"Your beloved; the one whom God intends for you. God has chosen well, my son. She looks to be a good woman: strong legs, wide hips, and a firm countenance. Her people are suitable, I assume?"

"I know nothing about her or her people."

"Nothing and everything: a secret lover, then?"

"You could say that."

"Perfect. Public love is a sham; the most private of love is the truest."

I slowly peered over the monitor, and this time Counsellor, my heart most certainly did palpitate. Tristina was no longer at her station, her place having been taken by a spotty-faced monkey in a Sajkaca, now methodically cleaning the computer screen with a dirty handkerchief! After all this time, had I lost her again? I stumbled back to the café wall and, peering through the side window, looked for my red-haired angel.

"She's gone, my son."

"Where did she go? How will I ever find her again?"

"The easy attainment of love makes it of little value; difficulty of attainment makes it prized." He spoke with authority, then, sensing my mood, suddenly changed his tone. "Do not lower your head, Little Prince. This woman is a treasure from God, and He will lead you to her. Come, let us pray together."

Miloš Obilić dropped to his knees.

"O Heavenly Father."

"Shit, Miloš, not here —"

"O Heavenly Father."

My trusty hallucination looked at me sternly.

"*O Heavenly Father.*"

"O Heavenly Father."

"Who smote the Ethiopians before Asa, and before Judah; Who smote the men of Bethshemesh —"

"Is this necessary?"

"— because they had looked into the ark of the Lord; Who ordered the Israelites to go forth and smote the people of Amalek, and utterly destroyed all that they had, and spared them not, but slew both man and woman, infant and suckling, ox and sheep, camel and ass; Who called his people to smote the men of Babylon —"

"Enough with the smoting."

"— and commanded that every man that was found should be thrust through and every one that is joined unto them should fall by the sword, and Who ordered too that their children also should be dashed to pieces before their eyes, their houses spoiled, and their wives ravished. Take this boy, Thy humble servant, and set him forth on the path of righteousness…"

"Yes. Set me forth on the path of the righteous."

"And deliver him into the arms of that maiden that You, in Your wisdom, have selected for him…"

"And deliver me, oh my God, into those loving arms."

"So that he may experience, through her, the Glory that is Your eternal love…"

"Just deliver me, that will be enough."

"For the power and the glory of the children of Lazar…"

"For the power and the glory of…them."

"…everlasting."

"There's that word again."

"Amen."

"Amen."

16

OBILIC WAS RIGHT, NEXHMIJE GJINUSHI: love does not come cheaply. Bracha, that stick, demanded three joints and some German pornography in exchange for Tristina's phone number.

I played it safe and sent her a text — "Druzhok says hi."

I was surprised when she responded, but when I suggested we get together, she played it coy; the trail went dead. *No one can love unless he is impelled by the persuasion of love.*

A few days later she sent word through her sister Lena, wondering why I hadn't texted her again. The truth is, I was terrified — terrified that she would say no, terrified because I knew that this was a "no" that I could not accept, terrified that in the face of this feared rejection I would become one of the obsessed nuisances, tracking a woman like a dog, reduced by love, and the fear of its loss, into an emasculated imbecile. Terrified that I could never make her love me.

"I thought she wasn't interested," I told her sister.

"I think Tristina is very interested," Lena said.

"What did she tell you?"

"Nothing."

"Then how can you say she's interested?"

"It's not what she didn't say, it's how she didn't say it."

That's how it all began, the kind-of love story that permeates this testimony. I know what you are thinking. How can love be relevant to our case? Of course, how is love ever relevant, Counsellor? But, in this case there is a purpose. As I've told you before, my march was as much about finding my way back to love as anything else. In any case, as you can see my love story is all very modern. Sometimes I think that you imagine we are a backwards people, we Serbs. But we have running water, Nexhmije Gjinushi, and television and veejays and Serbian rap music, and our love affairs can ravel and unravel like an episode of *Friends*.

"So tell me about yourself?"

Fast forward a little, my dear. Tristina and I now sitting in one of the almost fashionable cafés on the Knez. Our first date.

"What do you need to know?" She shifted in her seat, Nexhmije Gjinushi. She did not believe that I was really interested.

"Just the usual: name, rank, and serial number."

"My name is Tatijana-Jasminka Crepajac — that is something you don't know. But I prefer Tristina —"

"Just Tristina?"

"Yes."

"Like Madonna."

"Yes. Exactly."

"And?"

"And?"

"Your rank?"

"My rank is Wary Girl, First Class. My serial number is zero."

"That's very low."

"I know. I've been working on it."

She wore a lot of rouge, trying to hide the pimples on her face. It was something that had happened here, the pimples, my Counsellor. Was it like that in your town too? Everyone in Beograd had them, from dew-skinned babes-in-arms to chalked and wrinkled *babas*. Ever since the sanctions started. We blamed Clinton; the President and his NATO cronies must have been putting something in the water.

"And what else?"

"Like?"

"For instance: where do you work, Tatijana-Jasminka Crepajac?"

"I work at a day spa. The name is not important because I am sure you have never heard of it."

"And?"

"What is this? An interrogation?"

"Perhaps. For all I know, you could be a Muslim spy."

"I see. Well, what else can I tell you? You know, I like music —"

"I like music too. House, techno…"

"But who doesn't like music?"

"Yes. You'd have to be deaf."

"Or dead."

We paused to sip our coffee.

"And what about you? Tell me about you?"

I shrugged and pretended not to be interested in the question.

"Nothing, really. You know, I'm a businessman, a computer genius. I like girls. I like to fuck."

She turned her head and stirred her drink. Perhaps I'd gone too far. She looked to the corner, where the lights of Knez Mihailova glittered a welcome. In light of the UN threats, they'd argued long and hard over those lights. The city fathers, old men in old suits and military moustaches, wanted the lights off. With so much uncertainty, why make yourself a target? But the shopkeepers and hoodlums — now, in Beograd, almost every influential man was either shopkeeper or hoodlum — wanted the lights to stay on. They believed it would be good for morale: let the bombs come if they must, let them rain down like biblical brimstone, but the people needed their restaurants, their coffee houses, their jazz clubs. Besides, the Americans would never bomb the Knez. This was strictly between Uncle Sam and the ex-Communists; the good people of Beograd were safe as long as they played it smart.

"I like books and other stuff, too." Religion I was back-pedalling, afraid my forced machismo had gone too far. "Buddha, but not God. But mostly I like beautiful girls. It's how I make it through the week. I think about beautiful girls, I think about beautiful girls to trick myself through each day."

She caught me staring at her wondrous red hair, tightly curled — kinky, the Americans would say, almost crimson — like a woman in a magazine. One did not see many red-haired girls in Beograd, Nexhmije Gjinushi — not real red anyways. Sure at the discos and raves, there were always those chicks with their hair dyed as red as elderberry wine. But Tristina was different; it was natural.

"And your pubic hair: is it red?"

She blushed and turned her head.

You must excuse my candour. I was not schooled in Capellanus. *De regulis amoris* — the Rules of Love — were beyond me. And I was young. And stupid. And brash. And just charming and desperate enough to be able to pull these things off on occasion. Besides, I took a very commercial view of these things, and favoured the direct route to a woman's underwear. *Show interest*: that was the key to any negotiation. Show interest and imply an offer.

As I understood it at that time, every negotiation was a two-way street. One who covets must have something that is coveted. In the sexual marketplace, that was easy enough to ascertain. Even by this point I'd figured out that girls were as easily attracted — distracted — as boys; the key to any successful sexual swap lay in convincing the other person of your desire for them. What was really being traded, then, was not orgasm or arousal but the confirmation of sexual allure. Orgasms were the product or the by-product — the value-added, the loss leader — and not the goal of the transaction. But negotiations were rarely about the actual goods or services being discussed.

"I have never kissed a girl with red pubic hair. I would very much like to do that."

"You talk too much."

"Perhaps you don't listen enough."

"Maybe I'm tired of listening to you?"

"Maybe I'm tired of talking to you." I think that, at the time, in my mind this was very much like sexy banter. If this was a hot movie or one of those books with the tits on the cover, I would have said something funny at this point, something nonchalant that would make her want me even more.

As it turns out, it wasn't necessary. She lit another cigarette, then folded her arms across her chest, smoking the way I imagined she imagined a beautiful movie star would smoke, smoking the way she'd seen the American women smoking in an old film. She lifted her chin up and blew the smoke harshly into the cool patio air. Neither one of us spoke. We were weighing our options. I stirred the muddy beverage the waiter had assured us was indeed coffee.

"What are you thinking about?"

She shrugged and took another life-affirming drag.

"Do you ever think about politics?" she asked.

I shrugged. "No. I am a lover, not a politician."

By now, my hands had moved to her knee. "Do you?"

She didn't answer right away. She was looking at the lights on the Knez. An old woman had now appeared down the street, pushing a makeshift, wooden wheelbarrow, and stopped to scrounge through a pile of garbage on the street. The old woman was embarrassing to look at: a serf, really, from another century.

"I think that everyone is a politician, in one way or another." The girl made a brief show of keeping her legs together as my fingers, hidden by gypsy tablecloth, skated along the crease of her nylons. Finally, she let his fingers gently part her legs. Her lips, I found, were already moist.

Were it not thus! *My blessing, my beatitude*, sullied by dirty nails and greasy fingers under the Knez's artificial stars. But we were young, and these are crumbs already dropped. And to my defence, who cannot but help, when confronted by Love in its purest form, to lean back on the rituals and rhythms of our smallest lives? Alighieri, when Beatrice first spoke to him (after a decade of imposed, almost sadistic silence) collapsed onto a heap of mere words — *"ciascun´alma presa e gentil core"* — attempting to turn his basest feelings into gold but, in the process, diminished through mere art the power of the moment. It's our default position: we are human.

"I try not to think about politics. It's enough just to get through the day. It's enough just to get through the night." Tristina was trying to remain nonchalant, as my fingers worked their sorry magic.

"The Buddhists say, *Imagine no direction — no east nor west nor south*."

"That's not Buddha. That's the Beatles."

"Same thing, I think."

She laughed, the first time that night. She covered her mouth with her hand. Like most people in Beograd, her teeth were awful and, only in the most intimate of situations, do they show them.

"You know what I miss more than anything?" she asked, my fingers now making her all warm inside.

"Hmmm?"

"Since the sanctions and all — what I miss the most?"

"Yes: chocolate."

"And real coffee."

She smiled for a second time and nodded. He could tell what she was thinking: perhaps he is a poet after all.

I slid my fingers down her leg and rested them on her knee. "You know what I don't miss?"

She took a long drag and blew the smoke out softly so that it hung around her head. She believed this would make her more alluring.

"The stars?"

Now it was my turn to look surprised. These days, the night skies were lit by flares, distant fires, searchlights. We had not seen a star in nearly three weeks.

I squeezed her knee and smiled.

"I was going to say deodorant. But, of course, the stars. You're right. No one misses them."

17

SO I SENT ANOTHER TEXT, and we had our second date. Coffee at my parents' place. I'd even bought real beans, Nexhmije Gjinushi, imported from Austria, at the cost of several premium joints and a small electrical motor. I never got to use the beans, though, since coffee that night consisted of several minutes of small talk that lead us inextricably to Dragutin Dimitrijević's ancient divan. With my parents snoring in their bedroom, Tristina slipped her skirt off.

From that point on, we were almost inseparable, bound together by a strong sense of mutual purpose and a sexual intensity that only the young and well-conditioned can maintain. In a matter of days, I came to understand Tristina, or at least, had absorbed a long list of facts about her life, which created a perfect illusion of intimacy. For example, have I told you, Nexhmije Gjinushi, that Tristina had a passion for tennis? Or that she did not eat red meat because, as she said, she would not eat an animal that she could not imagine herself being able to kill? Did you know that she was born in Kikinda, an ancient town in the very northeast tip of Serbia. She has a tattoo on her left shoulder, you see. The image? The Kikinda coat of arms, which features — and this is the God's truth, Nexhmije Gjinushi — the severed head of an Ottoman Turk, impaled on a sabre. An armoured hand holds the sword and beneath it is a small pink heart, like one a little girl might draw on the back of her hand with a felt marker. Tristina told me she got the tattoo on the eve of her sixteenth birthday, on a dare from her boyfriend at the time, a Hungarian.

I could tell you more, Counsellor. That her father was second cousin to the poet Miloš Crnjanski and held a management position at Naftna Industrija Srbije, the national petroleum corporation. That she'd once won a gold ribbon at Dani Ludaje, Kinkinda's annual pumpkin festival, for growing a seventy-four-inch gourd, the longest ever produced by any student in the district. That she was self-conscious in the washroom, and whenever she used the toilet, ran the tap to mask her activities. That she believed notionally in the Father, the Son, and the Holy Ghost but could never decide if they were completely spiritual figures, manifestations of the human psyche, or supernatural beings who had a material effect on the world.

Within weeks, we had found a small flat and moved in together. At night, we would make love, then lie in the darkness, peering out our small window, watching and waiting for the bombs to descend.

18

WHERE WAS I WHEN the first bombs finally fell, Nexhmije Gjinushi? Not, alas, with my Beloved Angel. Let the record show that I was sitting in that wretched bar with my father, Sinisa, the ancient orthodox cleric, and Kosta Ilić.

We were into our cups and paid little attention to the planes passing low overhead. There had been sorties before, insectual buzzings aimed to show the people that the Americans had both the ability and will to strike their city. But this time, the hatches opened and the vicious eggs descended.

Father had already drunk four boilermakers and was going on about the politics and how they did not interest him. He was dressed in a rumpled grey suit, an Armani knock-off, remnant of his banker days, and, underneath it, a stained white T-shirt.

"You could chop the country up into a thousand pieces if you like," he was saying, "dice it and toss it in oil and cook it in a stew, for all I give a fuck. You could take all the Muslims and Serbs and Albanians and fuck them sideways and bake them in a pie…"

Sinisa was leaning on his thin arms, trying to lift himself from an ancient wing chair slowly decaying by the fire. He tried to speak, but his words were interrupted by his own grunts of exertion. Finally, the old priest gave up and collapsed back in the chair.

"What's that, Father; more brandy?" Ilić asked.

Sinisa grunted again and cleared his throat.

"I said: O Lord, touch the mountains, so that they smoke."

The cleric smiled, quite happy with himself, and took a sip from a plastic tumbler emblazoned with the face of Winnie the Pooh.

Ilić smiled and commented to the old cleric that his words were very fitting, given the circumstances (an allusion to the bar's former life as a chapel, I suspect, Counsellor), while Father took a long draw from his glass and then began to mumble himself. I believe he was reciting a passage from the Bhagvad Gita, the sacred Hindu Song of God. In the wash of his bank's collapse, father had taken great pains to memorize vast swatches of the work and came to believe, for a time, that he was in fact the reincarnation of the God Krishna himself, the avatar of Vishnu, who had come to preside over the battles of the warring clans of Serbia, just as He had done five thousand years earlier when the Kauravas and Pandavas battled for control of the throne of Hastinapura.

The first bomb broke a window at the front of the bar, and a large chunk of the window landed in the pot of watery soup ruminating on an electric hotplate. The men continued drinking and spooning their lunches without raising an eye. Indifference was Serbian machismo. Besides, there were almost two million people in the city; the chances of being hit and killed by a bomb were very slim.

"On the radio today, they said that Clinton's testicles have not descended." Kosta Ilić instinctively buttoned up his coat. "The promiscuity, the military aggression, the masculinized wife — these are all classic compensatory mechanisms associated with latent testicular development."

"How on Earth would Radio Beograd know about the state of Clinton's nuts?" Father seemed quite incensed. "Do they have spies in the President's underpants? Have they bugged Hillary's vagina?"

"No need to get angry with me, boss. I'm only reporting what I hear."

The second bomb was actually part of a longer cluster. Twenty, maybe twenty-five rapid blasts, although blast is not the right word. They sounded more like loud, dull thuds, like a rain of lizards or toads on a corrugated metal roof — almost comical. Ilić, who'd made a show of plucking the glass from the pot and dipping his bowl in, sipped his soup and shrugged his shoulders. He made a little face and said, "That was a weird one," before thumping on the thin wall and calling to his son.

"Bracha! Bracha! Did you hear that one? Almost right up our assholes!"

His accent was surprisingly cultivated. Perhaps he was from Niš? There was a university there. At the start of the war, a lot of professors had abandoned their posts and gone underground. It was never smart to be too smart in times like these.

"He's a bastard, you know…" Ilić removed a small crystal of glass from his spoon.

"Who? Bracha?"

"No, God willing. Clinton. He's a bastard; no father."

"A son of a whore!" Sinisa piped up, suddenly and so aggressively that no one was sure if he was actually contributing to the conversation or just venting a lifetime of frustration.

"Yes, well, we can't hold that against him, can we, Father? Was not our Lord Himself conceived out of wedlock?"

The final bomb thundered like an ancient God, the hammer

of Perun, and kicked open the tin door of the establishment with a heavy boot of dust and debris and stones and shrapnel. Still, we protected our stools and boilermakers, a last line of defence against NATO's might.

Slowly, Ilić shook himself free from the dust and debris that had accumulated on his clothes, leaving only a few pieces of bright glass and wood clinging to his brown frock, like candy sprinkles on a fat doughnut.

"What could the Americans conceivably — Bracha! Bracha! — want from us, in this shitty little bar? I have no culture for them to expropriate and sanitize, I have no workers for them to exploit, I have no market for them to usurp, I am not in need of a lesson in democracy. Bracha!"

The son thumped the thin wall and growled like a fairy-tale ogre. "Quiet, Father, you're disturbing the clientele."

Ilić raised his hands in disbelief. "Half the building is crushed like a walnut, and *I* am disturbing the clientele?"

"Personally, I blame Slobo," Father said returning now to his bowl of soup. "Or better yet, Lazar and his field of blackbirds."

"Indeed!" Ilić roared his approval.

"This is how fucked up your stupid fucking country is, son." Father was pointing at me, as if I had some personal involvement in any of this. "The defining moment, the seed of Serbian culture — *the semen of its history* — hinged on a catastrophic failure. The entire course of Serbian history, the hinge that levers the national psyche, six hundred years of mournful celebration of an ignoble defeat."

"An ass-kicking of the highest order."

"Correct, Kosta. Lazar roundly, soundly gets his ass kicked and, since then, the politicians pull it out, this Battle of Kosovo, anytime they need to rally the people and the troops for another round of ass-kickings — just ask Milošević. In truth, there are no historic records of the event, just patriotic poems, written centuries later, designed for propaganda and nostalgia."

"Is there any difference?"

"Words written to make old women wistfully remember the beauty they never had and old men sink into their horse-piss vodka and dream of some girl, now toothless or worm-eaten, who's remained forever seventeen in their memories. This tells you everything you need to know about the Serbian nation."

Father set down his drink and pulled an antique silver cigarette case — once property of Trifko Grabež, one of the conspirators in the assassination of Ferdinand, if Father's stories were to be believed — out of his jacket pocket.

"Let me put it in the simplest terms." He lit a hand-rolled cigarette as he addressed Ilić directly, a wise schoolmaster addressing his prized student. "The truth is that the Battle of Kosovo is just a crock of shit. The truth is, we are a nation of Abrahams."

"I'm not disagreeing."

"And the very notion that the war in Kosovo is the natural outcome of a religious, cultural conflict that stems back six hundred years or more is a load of bullshit!"

"Pure undiluted bull crap! Forgive my language."

"Your average Albanian Kosovar is about as Muslim as a duck, while you'd be hard-pressed to find a Serb anywhere willing to die for something as impractical as his God."

"We are nothing if not a practical people."

"In the eyes of the world, the people of the Balkans have always been fighting and always will be, but — and here's where the whole thing falls apart — try as one might, it is impossible to separate the good guys from the bad guys —"

"The black cowboy hats from the white —"

"Exactly. You see, we are all wearing grey, morally and genetically speaking; anyone could change sides instantly, my friends, simply by changing the colour of their shirt. That's why no one in the West can follow this story. That both sides are both good and evil is almost too unsettling to consider."

Father took another long drag from his cigarette, then smiled. "But what do I know? I am a madman."

He looked at me sternly for a moment, then turned to the bartender and laughed.

"Ziveli!" Ilić called, raising a small tumbler of vodka. "To the madness that is Serbia!" he called and downed his glass in one long gulp.

It was only then it dawned on us that Sinisa, the old priest, was being uncommonly quiet. We turned as one and looked toward him. He still sat in the chair by the fire, his elbow on the mantle, his fingers clinging to a tumbler of watery brandy; but now the top half of his head was sheared clear off, neatly just above the eye line. A shard of shrapnel must have struck him with such force and surgical precision that there was hardly any blood; the priest's mouth was open slightly, and he wore a half grin as if he'd just gotten the point of a joke told long ago.

We finished our boilermakers and enjoyed another. Ilić signalled us with a slight shrug, and following his lead, we lifted Sinisa from the hard chair and carried him out to the street. We laid him on the carpet of soft rubble and left him to the dogs and medics.

19

FROM THAT POINT ON, Nexhmije Gjinushi, the planes flew low almost without cease, or with such planned intermittence that we instinctively understood NATO's game. It was a Chinese water torture, with pain inflicted not so much by the bombs that fell — true to Clinton's word, most of the air strikes seemed to be targeting military installations: radar towers, airfields, army bases — but through the spaces between bombs, the moments of anticipation.

At night, Tristina and I would huddle on the ancient divan I had liberated from my parents' flat, a single candle, despite the blackout, burning on the empty milk crate that served as our bedside table, and watch the bombs exploding in the distance. It was very much like an electrical storm: a brilliant flash of light followed by a thunderous crash. We would count the seconds between the sight and the sound — one, two, three, four — to determine how far away the bombs were falling. One night, we had barely reached three when the thunder struck; that was the closest so far.

I was proud of the regal history behind the divan and was explaining to Tristina the story of the archduke and his dear wife, Sophie, star-crossed lovers of a type that only royalty could assume. The archduke's father, the redoubtable Emperor Franz

Joseph of Austria, was against the marriage from the start; although of noble birth, Sophie, Duchess of Hohenberg, was not directly descended from one of the reigning European dynasties, one of the prerequisites to marrying into the Hapsburg family.

"Emperor Franz Joseph refused his consent, and even direct appeals by Pope Leo and Tsar Nicholas failed to move him."

Tristina was not paying attention: the bombs had got her spooked.

"Listen please, my mouse, it's a very romantic tale. One of the great love stories of all time. You see, it appeared that Ferdinand would rather abdicate than abandon the love he knew to be true. Finally, afraid of losing his role in the line of descent, the emperor relented on the condition —"

"Why are we fighting again?"

"Hmmm?"

"Why are we fighting?"

"We are not fighting, Angel, we are resting."

Her arm was wrapped across my chest, her naked body tight against mine, warming me in the cold room.

"I'm serious: why are we fighting?"

"For real or pretend?"

"For real."

"Because the Albanian Muslims who occupy Kosovo are madmen. Because these Albanians are backward *seljobers*, the enemies of progress and usurpers of the Serbian people who originally settled the region. Because the usurpers threaten the Serbian people and the Holy Christian Church, seated within their borders. Because the Albanians are locked in their ancient blood feuds and are murderous criminals who will take us all down to hell with them unless those of us from a more civilized race take decisive action."

"Now, for pretend."

"Because Milošević is a madman. Because Kosovo is rich in minerals and ore and exploiting those resources could make Milošević a very wealthy man. Because the Americans hate the word "no" and take an obsessive delight in revenge, a word that seems to be etched into their collective psyche with acid. Because the Americans and Russians, despite appearances to the contrary, are still in a pissing match, and Kosovo is their urinal. Because history says we should fight, and no one can argue with history."

Silence.

Tristina pushed me onto my stomach and started squeezing the pimples on my back.

"Can you imagine: what if it never ends?"

"The war?"

"Yes. No. I was thinking more the bombs. What if they continue to fall? Perhaps not all the time, like this. But just occasionally, like a spring storm."

"You mean like five seasons: winter, spring, summer, fall, bomb."

"Exactly. Like it became something just ordinary. Something you would dress for. Something you'd avoid, like a hail storm or dinner with your aunt."

"The weatherman could provide daily updates: cloudy, with temperatures above the seasonal norms, and slight chance of death in outlying regions."

"Yes, five seasons. You'd expect it. It would become part of the fabric of life. And, I suspect, you'd look forward to it, and when the first bombs of the season fell, there'd be a sense of excitement in the air, like the first snowfall. No one likes the last three months of winter, but we all look forward to the first days. There is something comforting in the certainty of the cycles."

We were silent, watched a couple of small explosions in the distant hills.

"It's the uncertainty I hate."

Tristina leaned forward and blew out the candle. And before we made love, always a prelude to sleep in those days, I was suddenly overcome with a strange elation and sense of connectedness, not only to Tristina but to...everything. The walls, the darkness, the darkened street light, the cars dozing in the black streets, the silent revellers along the Knez, Milošević and the Red Dragon, enjoying perhaps a late snack in the presidential palace, the Kosovo refugees, Hillary Clinton and the Allied Supreme Command, the blackbirds and the blueberries and the bluebirds and the raspberries and blackberries...

"You know," I said, moving one hand, stroking the small of her back, "I think everything is going to be all right."

"Of course it will be, my darling," she spoke quite softly now, then let out a deep sigh. "Everything will be all right and more."

We lay in silence for a few more minutes. Then, Tristina suddenly pushed me over and became very serious.

"What do you want from me?" she asked suddenly, in a tone that bordered on aggressive.

I was taken aback, and did not quite know what answer to give.

"I don't want anything, Pumpkin. I am in love with you."

This seemed to calm her somewhat. She put her head back on the pillow and stared at a cockroach scuttling across the no man's land of our ceiling.

"Promise me one thing, Zavida."

"Anything, Love. You name it."

"Promise me you'll get rid of this useless relic and buy me a proper bed."

20

ON THE THIRD DAY, Nexhmije Gjinushi, the bombing abruptly stopped. There was a curious, unsettling silence. No one believed that NATO would give up this easily. Then, shortly after lunch, a U.S. Air Force B-52 Stratofortress flew unusually low over Beograd, perhaps in a show of confidence, to demonstrate to the people that Yugoslavia's paltry air defence system had been neutralized: our poorly rationed surface-to-air missiles — only one hundred in total — were gone within days of the first attack, while the much-vaunted anti-aircraft artillery, some eighteen hundred pieces, were well past their best-before date.

On the third pass, the B-52's payload bays emptied and a rain poured forth. People grudgingly sauntered to shelter, and covered their heads, waiting for the explosions.

But all they heard was a tiny, thudded *plop! plop!* like a shower of toads, starting off in a trickle, then building to a relentless percussive *ping*.

It appeared to be raining small packages. Whether it was an act of contrition or a simple change in tactics, the Americans had given up on bombs and were now attacking Beograd with trinkets! I'm sure you've heard the rumours, Nexhmije Gjinushi, and perhaps dismissed the stories as many had as urban legend. But I was there, my dear, showered in that strange rain.

I remember crouching forward and retrieving one of the packets from heaven. A small bag of condoms, brightly coloured, emblazoned with the word *demokrtija*: democracy. I handed the packet to Tristina. "Bill Clinton sends his regards."

Nearby a puddle was forming out of little bubble packs stuffed with American sweets: Life Savers, Mars Bars, Butterfingers. And now, a snow of leaflets was coming down, declaring MILOŠEVIĆ IS SON OF A WHORE and SURRENDER = PROSPERITY. One old comrade, an absurdly long row of medals stitched to the breast of his ragged jacket, read the leaflet carefully, pondering it for a moment before crumpling it up and tossing it on the ground. "This is old news," he declared.

Even the *babas* laughed at that.

Tristina and I collected our fill, stuffing our pockets with candy bars and French ticklers, before the jet waggled its wings and comically departed. Of course, the regulars at Lazar's Internet Café did not believe our good fortune at first.

"You're losing your mind, Turk. You've been partying too hard this Ramadan." Bracha had taken to calling the days since the bombing began Ramadan. He treated me, of course, as the resident expert.

"Do you know what day it is today, *Turk*?" He had a way of spitting the word that in time made the café's customers, many of whom knew me well, begin to regard me with some suspicion.

"I've told you, Bracha. Don't call me that."

"I'm just saying, Turk, do you know what day it is?" By now, some of the cronies at the coffee counter were smiling. "It's the third day of Ramadan. We will keep fasting till the bombs stop. Isn't that right, gentlemen?"

The cronies gulped down the last of their coffee-cupped-camouflaged boilermakers and cackled. No doubt, they too thought Bracha was an asshole. But what can you do when you are a crony? It is your lot in life to gulp and cackle. It is your manifest destiny, once you've made the decision to never be a target.

One day a Westerner, a journalist, entered the chapel when Bracha was in the middle of this routine. Perhaps sensing a splash of local insight he could relate on CNN or the BBC, he asked Bracha in his broken, German-tainted Serbo-Croatian what was meant by Ramadan. Was this what the local had taken to calling Operation Allied Force? Without a word, Bracha smashed a bottle over the man's head, and several flat-nosed teenagers kicked him until he vomited blood. Bracha dragged him out to the street, pulling him by the hair to make a greater mockery. The cronies had gulped and cackled and slouched ever more slightly into the comfort of their own necks.

"Look Bracha, we need to talk..."

Before the rain of trinkets, Tristina and I had spent the day shopping for a proper bed. She had grown tired of sleeping on history, and while the divan was firm enough to support our lovemaking, it was too hard to offer a good night's sleep.

We'd gone to Robna Kuca, where Tristina selected the kind of bed she wanted, a simple platform bed: elegant, contemporary. The rest of the morning was spent with me working my contacts, zeroing in on a couple of guys who moved furniture and small appliances (it never did to single-source; to maintain the upper hand in the black market, you always had to have competing bids). In any case, I'd tracked down the bed, a Bauhaus knock-off, and arranged the terms.

We had come now to the Lazar Internet Café to close the deal. I needed to weed a functioning motherboard out of Bracha's hands as part of the bargain.

"Your story pulls at my heart strings, Turk, it really does. But I have no incentive to part with a motherboard."

"Three ounces, Brach, and a box of brand new American porno videos. Ten titles in all, the entire *Dildo Lesbian* series."

"That's a good starting point, my friend. But, do you have any idea how hard it is to get your hands on good computer parts?"

Of course, I knew exactly how hard it was, as Bracha was well aware.

"What is it you really want, Brother?"

"There's nothing that really interests me, man. Some coke, perhaps."

"Coke?"

"Coke, Turk."

A light went off in my head. Perhaps the rumours were true, that Bracha could no longer get it up and his girlfriend was screwing around behind his back.

"I told you, man, the coke flow has all dried up. There's nothing but shit out there."

"I want an ounce of coke, plus the weed, plus the pornos."

"An ounce, man? There's nothing around. Zilch."

"That's my price, Friend."

I paused a moment and bit my tongue.

"What's a matter, Turk? Do you smell a rat? Oh, I forgot, you can't smell at all. He can stink, boys —" Bracha winked at his cronies — "but he can't smell."

I could feel Tristina slip her hand into mine.

"We should go," she whispered. But I was determined to not let her down.

"Okay. Look Bracha, I'll find you some coke, a few lines, whatever I can scrounge up. But I can't promise you top quality. There's some real bad shit floating around these days."

Bracha pretended to be nonchalant as he considered my offer. I went in for the kill.

"So, let's say, half an ounce, and I'll throw in some Rohypnol just for the hell of it, and any two pornos of your choice. I might even have some man-on-man action, if you're interested."

It was my turn to wink at the cronies.

Bracha scowled and waved me away.

"Bring me the pills, bring me the coke, bring me the weed, and bring me the box of pornos, *Dildo Lesbians* one through ten. Now, get the fuck out of my café."

21

FOR THE WANT OF a platform bed, and an insect's desire to fuck, it was agreed. The coke alone, it appears, was no longer enough to get the ruptured beauty to lie down with the beast. Of course, Nexhmije Gjinushi, I could have no way of knowing that I was about to initiate a series of events that would bring me closer to my inevitability.

Now, it was around this time that I first started to hear about Beograd Magus, that mysterious figure, whose rise and fall parallels my own. I discovered the Beograd Magus by pure happenstance. I was either going from or coming to — I cannot recall which, dear Counsellor — the Peasants' Table. It was in the days after the first bombs fell, and certainly after the wondrous monsoons had begun. They had become commonplace by now (NATO, the practised, abusive lover, keeping us on our toes with bombs one day and showers of gifts the next), and I recall distinctly that I reached the Peasants' Table after making my way through a sudden cloudburst of Schick Slim-Twin Razors and plastic spools of mint-flavoured dental floss emblazoned with the name of the American Dental Association. The surreal had become the ordinary, Counsellor, very much setting the stage for my father's next transformation.

The first indication that something curious was happening struck me as I approached the hastily rebuilt entranceway to the bar; people were waiting to get in, lots of them. For an establishment used to accommodating a handful of unwashed gentlemen, this was a minor miracle.

I took my place in line with the others, listening attentively to the solemn conversations in the line.

"Where is he from?" one toothless rube was asking another. They were probably in their late thirties, but looked much older.

"No one knows for certain. Some say America, others, northern Bulgaria, Trnova, or some such place."

"But he is a Serb?"

"Most assuredly. He speaks, they say, perfect *ijekavski*, which suggests I suppose, a Croatian background."

"He lives on a diet of mushrooms and wild raspberries." A fat, pimpled girl had butted in. "He's a mystic or some kind of health food fanatic, I think."

The two men nodded thoughtfully and offered the girl a drag of their joint.

I finally made it inside the Peasants' Table. It took a moment for my eyes to adjust to the dim light. They were standing three-deep at the bar, and there was Kosta Ilić pouring beer as fast as his fat hands would allow. There was a buzz of conversation, and those men who were not lining up for drinks had crowded into the far end of the establishment where something clearly had captured their attention.

I pushed my way through, thankful for once for my diminutive stature, which made it easier to slip through the cracks in the crowd, and finally came to the edge of the crumbling apse that now served as a storage space for empty kegs and other debris. The anteroom itself was cordoned off with a thick purple rope suspended between two ornate brass stanchions, undoubtedly liberated from one of the nearby theatre houses during the recent blackouts.

Just beyond the barrier, my father. There he sat, the yellowed T-shirt riding up his gut so that a wedge of his hairy belly was exposed, legs crossed, forearms laid atop his thighs, his palms upturned, his eyes closed as if he were asleep, hovering, it seemed, a few millimetres above a table strategically centred in the anteroom.

I closed my eyes and rubbed them. And when I reopened them, Nexhmije Gjinushi, my father was still there, floating in thin air. I had a sudden urge to leave the bar, certain that this latest mystery would only lead to more trouble for my poor mother and me, but as I stood contemplating the correct course of action, I felt a thick hand land on my shoulder.

"You look like a man who could use a drink." It was Kosta Ilić, whose talons were hooking into my shirt collar as he spoke. He pulled me quickly to the bar.

"Perhaps the death of Father Sinisa affected him more than he cared to say." Ilić spoke to me out of the corner of his mouth as he quickly drew another *piva* for one of the curious locals who had come to witness my father's floating first-hand. "Father Sinisa was a religious man in his way — doddering, dogmatic, bigoted, but spiritual. Your father is a spiritual man too. Impious to a degree, yes, and something of a dabbler in the heretical ways of Oriental mysticism, but isn't that just another side of the Byzantine Rite? Why, I've even heard it speculated by more sober men than I that perhaps the good priest's spirit has entered your father's soul, and it's a wholly Christian miracle we are witnessing. It is not without precedence: the Abbess Irene of Chrysovalantou, it is said, could levitate, and once crossed a flooded river to minister to the needy without ever getting her sandals wet, while the Catholic Carmelite Teresa of Ávila often lapsed into almost orgasmic rapture and was at these moments given to bouts of levitation, particularly if they occurred during the application of the Holy Sacraments."

"With all due respect, Kosta Ilić, I am not sure that Father Sinisa's spirit was in any condition to enter anyone, let alone my father. And I must say, I have an uneasy feeling about this."

"That's to be expected, boy. Who among us does not find himself humbled and at least a little bit uneasy in the presence of such a miracle? For was it not our Lord who said: a prophet is not without honour, except in his own country, and among his own relatives, and in his own house."

"Maybe that's the part that is bothering me. Father isn't given to miracles. Massive fuck-ups are more his line."

Ilić handed off one *piva*, then drew another.

"That only makes it all the more miraculous. In any case, it is the strangest thing I have ever seen. It started off with just a moment, a spark of time when one could easily think that it was nothing more than a trick of the light or the shadows. There was your father seemingly awake and alert, mumbling his Indic jumbo or perhaps, as some have speculated, reciting the Uskoks cycle or some other classic of the Serbian epic tradition, and then, his eyes went as blank as a goat's, and I was left with the sense that he had indeed hung suspended in the air for the splittest of seconds."

Ilić paused again to serve another thirsty customer. The line of eager yokels ran almost to the doorway, while another dozen or so people were crammed up to the window (old women and children, mostly, prohibited by law or propriety from entering the premises) trying to get a glimpse of the Beograd Magus.

Kosta Ilić continued.

"As the days passed, the seconds grew to minutes, and it became apparent that some kind of miracle was in the works.

There we'd be talking or playing tablac, then the next moment the varnish would return to his eyes and he'd begin to drift, both physically and mentally. Now it seems he spends most of his waking hours in this ecstatic state, taking neither food nor drink, finding it unnecessary to either pass water or move his bowels. It truly is a miracle for the ages."

"Hmmm. I'm surprised he never mentioned any of this. Slipped his mind, I suppose."

"He has, no doubt, a lot on his mind."

"It's done wonders for your business too, Kosta, I see."

The barkeep lowered his eyes, humbly I suppose.

"I don't pretend to understand the ways of the Lord, Zavida Zanković; but yes, His blessings are manifold, indeed."

Ilić handed me another *piva,* then held my hand steady as he drizzled *rakia* along the inside of the glass, leaving a piss-coloured layer suspended over the watery beer. He winked, to let me know it was on the house, and pushed the glass toward me.

"Bottoms up, my young friend. Here's to miracles. *U zdravlje!*"

"*U zdravlje!*" I responded, and quickly downed my shandy, glancing again toward the apse and trying to ignore the thin wire, barely visible, that descended from a hook in the ceiling until it disappeared down the back of my father's shirt collar.

Kosta Ilić caught my eye and shrugged. "Would you care for another drink?" he asked, already reaching for my empty glass.

And so, I spent the rest of the night, a guest of Kosta Ilić's largesse, drinking myself into a silent, conspiratorial stupor. And now I am saving a day's work, Nexhmije Gjinushi. Even the ten cups of your thin NATO coffee can't keep me awake all night. I am so very tired, my dear. I am off to bed to dream. I will keep an eye open for you!

22

I MISSED YOU THIS MORNING, Counsellor. I understand from Vasile Lupu that you were detained on some urgent matters, and must admit I felt a certain jealousy. 'She's seeing another prisoner behind my back,' I thought — I really did! It had never occurred to me that I have to share you with other clients, that there are other detainees in other cells worthy of your attention.

And so my heart raced a little at the thought that some-where, perhaps in a room across the hall, there was another insignificant man in borrowed clothes, writing his story for you. I must admit, my reaction surprised even me. Am I harbouring feelings for you, Nexhmije Gjinushi? I suppose it is inevitable. What is it called when the captive falls in love with his captor? The Stocking Syndrome?

But you have my pledge: I will keep things on as professional a level as possible. Korbi Artë would expect no less — from both of us!

I will say though, and this is off the record, that I was afraid my confessions of yesterday had put you off, that you come to see me as nothing more than another of the male swine — the animals — that call this region home. But I revealed those intimacies in good faith, my Kosovo Muse. Leave nothing to the imagination, you said, and it is my sincere intention to do just that.

Vasile Lupu brought me other news as well, declaring that, according to the men on the cable news channels, the war is almost at an end. The Russians have turned down Slobo's invitation to come and join the party. They have enough problems of their own, I suppose, and haven't any jam left to initiate World War III. The hills, Lupu tells me, are now crawling with UÇK and Albanian troops, along with Norwegian special forces — the Hærens Jegerkommandos and Forsvarets Spesialkommandos — waiting for the signal to liberate Kosovo.

For my part, I will not hold my breath, and am fully aware that, if history has taught us Serbs anything (and I am certain that it has not), the difference between liberation and invasion is often merely one of salesmanship.

In any case, you will be happy to know that I have not let my time go to waste (there is a finite number of games of Pesë Katësh one can endure with Imbrahim Kaceli, my dear); I have been diligently tapping, compiling a corpus of evidence on my trusty iBook, strengthening our most futile case.

I'd left off with the Beograd Magus, Nexhmije Gjinushi, and I am happy to report that, understandably, Father's fame spread quickly. In no time at all, stories of the Beograd Magus had been picked up by the government media, and images of him dangling under the watchful eye of St. Sava — along with stories of a two-headed lamb, a statue of St. Tatiana that bled from the eyes, and a hen that laid black eggs — were portrayed as a sure sign of NATO's impending failure.

On any given day, the curious stood ten deep around the run-down chapel, trying to get a glimpse of the famous Magus through the windows or one of the many cracks in the walls.

They would line up for three-quarters of an hour for a chance to get inside the bar, which by now accepted deutschmarks and American dollars only, with the US $10 cover charge that included a complimentary *piva* and free photo opportunity with the floating saint.

My father, so recently ostracized, was now feted, a frequent guest lecturer at the Univerzitet u Beogradu, invited to all the gallery openings and smart parties (where the hostesses would insist he appear in his ragged T-shirt and underwear), with politicians leaping over one another for a chance to be photographed with this symbol of Serbian piety and wisdom.

Marija Milošević herself, Slobo's only daughter, came calling and dragged him onto *Srbija Danas*, a news magazine show and flagship of TV Kosava, one of the two television networks she owned. The station featured blockbuster movies and American sitcoms dubbed into German and Serbian, old Serbian war movies, and several fluffy propaganda exercises thinly disguised as news shows. Back then, Beograd was a media hub, boasting no less than thirteen TV stations. If nothing else, Nexhmije Gjinushi, we Serbs understand the power of diversion.

My father's interview took place, in TV Kosava's main studio, on the tenth floor of that glorious Ušće Tower, and was preceded by a short documentary film featuring moody images of him filmed in half-light and shadows, while making much of the converted chapel where his miraculous levitations took place and the ancient and recently deceased Father Sinisa, whose soul, the newscaster implied, may very well have taken root in my father. The little documentary concluded with a montage of images: my father, looking half-demented and wizened, gaunt, with his long, grey hair matted and twisted, dissolving alternately into details of St. Sava staring down from the wall, Petar Radicevic's patriotic painting of the Battle of Kosovo, news footage of lines of Serbian refugees (victims, one supposed, of the Albanian cleansing of Kosovo), NATO jets over Beograd and hysterical *babas* standing in the ruins of their bombed-out homes — all mixed together in a fiery paprika served to the strains "U Prolecnje Jutro" performed by piano and solo voice.

The documentary faded into a live segment. My father in the studio, down to his skivvies, sitting cross-legged in a chair. He made quite a contrast to our elegant hostess, her long straight hair dyed jet black, her lips painted crimson to match the colour of her jacket — Prada no less. She a crass princess; he a reluctant saint.

Marija sat stiffly in a swivel chair, a stack of index cards in her hand. She welcomed her viewers in that stilted, professional way of hers (she has studied professional broadcasting, they say, at an institute in Omsk) and introduced my father.

At first, the alchemist did not seem to notice Marija. He ignored her opening salutation, sitting with his eyes closed, breathing deeply, and apparently, reciting a silent prayer.

"Dobroslav Zanković? G. Zanković, are you with us?"

Slowly Father opened his eyes.

"Are you meditating, sir?"

Father shrugged. "Of course."

"What is that like for you? Can you describe that experience for our viewers?"

"I...it is not 'an experience.' It is a non-experience. I merely meditate and, in the process of meditating, clear my mind of all thoughts, my body of all sensation."

"Well, I am told that many things happen when you enter a transcendent state."

"What happens in the physical realm is beyond my awareness."

"They say you levitate, as if by magic, and several miraculous cures have been attributed to your name. They say you speak directly to the saints."

"They say a lot of things. I only claim to seek understanding."

"Of?"

"Hmmm?"

"What are you trying to understand?"

"Nothing. Only understanding."

Marija Milošević was growing somewhat irritated by Father's lack of clarity. She was a journalist, after all, who lived in the world of questions and answers. She tried another tack.

"Dobroslav Zanković, if you have one message for the people of Serbia, what would that be?"

Father appeared genuinely surprised.

"*One* message? I have *no* message."

"But surely, you've come from the wilderness, in a manner of speaking, at a critical point in the history of the Serbian peoples —"

"History is a blanket we wrap ourselves in. It warms us at night but offers no real protection against bullets or fear."

"If you let me finish, sir, I think we can all agree that your emergence has come at a time when important events are unfolding, events which will have an impact on the Serbian people for the foreseeable future. And here you are, levitating, performing astounding miracles, espousing a system of beliefs…"

"I must stop you there, good lady. With all due respect, I am not espousing anything. I have no beliefs. In fact, the whole notion of belief is a contradiction, for once one believes, one has accepted certainty, and any certainty is an illusion. Can you believe in an illusion? The concept itself is incongruous."

"But is not a lack of belief in itself a belief?" Marija crinkled her eyes and turned her head, her posture suggesting that, perhaps, she was entering into territory not covered during her tenure at the Omsk School of Broadcast Technology.

She interpreted Father's silence as a small victory and returned to her index cards.

"Many Serbians have interpreted your miraculous levitation as a sign from St. Sava himself that the NATO aggressors will ultimately fail, that their attempt to bend the will of the people, to break the spirit of Serbia, is futile. What do you say to these good people?"

Father paused and thought for a long time.

"I cannot speak to the will of God or St. Sava, I do not pretend to understand the intentions of NATO, nor do I care to try and look into the future or predict what may be. I will leave such mysticism to politicians, gypsies, and the Blessed Church. What I am trying to understand, though, is the fear beneath it all. The fear that drives us to God and holy men; the fear that drives us to die on a field of blackbirds, in the name of second-rate sagas or third-rate saints; the fear that compels us to love and hate and lie and cling to those things dear to us. So, I am trying to watch fear, to observe it, not to suppress it and not to sublimate it and not to try to escape from it; but to understand it, to hold it in my hand like a toy, to neither control it nor be controlled by it. No doubt, you want to tell me that the history of Serbia is not a history of fear, but the story of great men, brave men, who have fought back, again and again and again. But I reply that the history of Serbia is fear, just as the history of America is fear, or the history of Russia or Ancient Greece, or the histories yet written — any history, by its very concept — is the story of fear, and the barbarian we keep trying to conquer — fear — is unconquerable. One cannot surmount fear, one cannot defeat it; one may only embrace it, observe it, and try to understand it."

Father abruptly stopped and began rocking back and forth slowly, humming to himself a single, droning note. Milošević sat tense in her chair, smiling obliquely, not certain, Nexhmije Gjinushi, if what she had was good television or simply a potential mental patient on the verge of a complete collapse. She cut to commercial.

After the break, we returned to the studio. Father's rocking had become more violent, and as he spoke his prayer, his voice slowly rose up. The words would have sounded as nonsense to most listeners, who perhaps assumed father was speaking in tongues, but I recognized the words immediately. A hymn from the Rig Veda. Excuse my Sanskrit, I'm a little rusty, but I believe the words, roughly translated, are as follows: *He who gives breath, he who gives strength, whose command all the bright Gods revere, whose shadow is immortality, whose shadow is death: Who is the God to whom we shall offer sacrifice?*

"G. Zanković, please: a question if I may…"

"He who through his might became the sole king of the breathing and twinkling world, who governs all this, man and beast: Who is the God to whom we shall offer sacrifice?"

Ms. Milošević was visibly irritated. She liked her holy men on message. But the cameras kept rolling, perhaps hoping that something sensational would happen.

"He through whose might these snowy mountains are, and the sea, they say, with the distant river, he of whom these regions are indeed the two arms: Who is the God to whom we shall offer sacrifice?"

At this point, Father began to shake violently, lapsing from the chair into convulsions on the floor. The fit became ever more violent, as Marija Milošević, now standing, called his name.

Father started up again.

"He through whom the awful heaven and the earth were made fast," he boomed. "He through whom the ether was established, and the firmament; he who measured the air in the sky: Who is the God to whom we shall offer sacrifice?"

As the cameras rolled, one of the more compassionate studio technicians, still wearing his headset, ran to my father's side, then another. The first one cradled his head, and the second one lay upon his legs, barely containing the spasms that rocked Father's body.

"Watch the tongue," someone cried. "He mustn't swallow his tongue!"

And amid the chaos, our good lady Milošević stood poised. The camera focused on her for a moment, then slowly pulled back and faded, as the sound of the disorder continued in the background. A moment later, the screen went black, then TV Kosava cut away to a music video, a group of schoolchildren singing "Računajte Na Nas," a patriotic pop song that never fails to bring a tear to the eye of even the most elderly *baba*.

23

AS FATHER'S ANTICS GALVANIZED the nation, Counsellor, my domestic bliss continued. I probably knew, somewhere deep in my animal brain, that it would not last. But not even I, at my most cynical, could have imagined that it was already starting to dissolve.

It had been raining glossy German and American magazines and counterfeit dinars all afternoon. The magazines were full of colourful pictures of famous American movie stars and offered tips on cooking for one and improving one's sex life. The dinars were very, very convincing and immediately sent black market currency exchange rates into the toilet.

"The Buddha told a story…" I was making conversation, Counsellor.

"Did he ever do anything else?" Tristina was only half-listening. She was trying to straighten her hair. She did not like the natural curls and was bent over the kitchen table with her hair splayed across a towel, flattening her curls with a hot iron.

"Quiet please. The Buddha told a story, or maybe it wasn't the Buddha. In any case, someone told a story. It concerned a priest or more likely a monk. The priest or monk lived in a temple high in the mountains. It was an isolated place, where devotees gathered to meditate, work, and study."

"Is this a long story?"

"We'll see. So, one day, a warlord arrived with a vast army. He wanted to take over the temple because its position, with impenetrable stone walls and distant vista, made it strategically important. The warlord assembled all the people who lived and studied in the temple and its surrounding grounds, hundreds of men, all of them, their heads shaved, dressed in saffron robes. The warlord berated the holy men, dismissed them for leading lives of inactivity and self-indulgence. He ordered them to surrender the temple at once or die. The holy men did not move. They all looked to their leader, the head monk or priest or whatever..."

"I could help you with that, you know."

That, she heard. "You'll only burn it. Then I'll have to cut it all off. Would you like that, making love to some bald and toothless *baba*?"

I tried, but could not imagine her bald and toothless or even old. I was convinced she would remain young forever.

"Anyways, the warlord summoned the head monk. They dragged the withered old man forward, scraping his knees on the rough stone floor and shredding the hem of his robe in the process. The warlord repeated his demand. Surrender or die."

"It's all very dramatic."

"Indeed. And so, there was silence. The old man seemed detached, unconcerned. Perhaps he was deaf? And so the warlord grabbed the old monk roughly by the beard, forcing their eyes to meet: 'Surrender or die.'"

"Shit!" Tristina quickly brought a finger to her mouth. She had burnt her little pinkie with the iron.

"You should be more careful. I don't want you to burn our beautiful table."

"Shhh. Finish the story."

"Okay. So faced again with the ultimatum, the old monk still did not respond. Angrily, the warlord drew his sword, pressing it to the old man's throat. 'Speak,' he demanded. 'Do you realize you are looking at a man who could kill you without a second thought?' The old monk smiled. 'And do you realize you are looking at a man who could die without a slightest hesitation?' "

There was a pause, as Tristina finished running the hot iron through her hair.

"The point?" she asked, finally.

"I suppose, the message is one of choice. One can choose to be a force that acts upon, and therefore, can be acted upon. A reaction, waiting to happen. Or one can choose to stand outside of action — which is, of course, a kind of action in itself. Ah, the Mongols and their love of contradictions."

Tristina sat up and checked out her hair in the cracked looking glass above the stove. She was happy, but not too.

"The Buddha seems very indecisive to me," she spoke casually, without really thinking about things. "He seems to have created a whole philosophy, a whole spiritual way of life, built around his inability to make up his own mind. That is the genius of the Buddha, if you ask me: he managed to convince everybody that his deepest character flaw was in fact the cornerstone of a profound system of intellectual practice. He must have been a wonderful politician."

She smiled at me and I inched even further in love.

"Shall I?" She nodded toward the stack of baggies on the counter, and I raised my eyebrows in agreement.

Tristina took the big baggie of coke and started divvying it up into small portions: three tablespoons per portion. She was very precise.

It was a pleasant domestic scene, me weighing and divvying

the merchandise as Tristina handled the packaging. A real mom-and-pop operation.

Outside, the flying fortress was making another run. The whole apartment shook as the leviathan breached and shuddered above them. Then a new noise, thinner than before, a very distinct clacking like a hard insect exploding under the weight of a heavy boot. I looked out the window.

"It's music now, I think. CDs and cassettes."

Tristina looked excited. "We should go out. Maybe we'll get something good. Some U2 or Backstreet Boys."

Typical Tristina. Her tastes were very pop.

I got up and grabbed my coat. Personally, I hoped for the new Chili Peppers.

We held hands as we walked to the door.

"You know," I said, offering Tristina a cigarette. "I'm really beginning to like this war."

To the Buddhist mind, Nexhmije Gjinushi, humanity exists in both heaven and hell. The torments and puzzles and cravings of this world are steps toward or away from enlightenment. One could be in heaven or hell right now depending on which path one has chosen.

The problem, my Kosovo Muse, is that this heaven, like every other heaven and hell, is an illusion. Eventually, the time will come for you to move on, to be reborn. While this sort of resurrection is the ultimate goal of the Christian faith, for Buddhists it is the biggest insult. They want to live beyond life and death, above hope and suffering, above truth and enlightenment, beyond existence: they want Nirvana. (The spiritual realm, my dear, not the band.)

Tristina was dubious. "Why wouldn't someone want to suffer?" she asked that morning, in between popping the pimples on my back. She was such a Serb.

I thought of bringing it up again, as we wandered the Knez. How much greater the Serbian people would be had they only been defeated by Chinese Monks and not Ottoman Turks. They would have learned the futility of desire, the illusion of history. Serbian history was a Buddhist exercise anyway, an exercise in misery, a pointless purgatory where there was no redemption in suffering.

Tristina had agreed to come with me for the score. It was going to be a simple transaction. My source, Rutgar, was not too paranoid and, for a German, fairly level-headed. We had agreed to the terms: I would trade some of my stash for half an ounce of coke. On the surface, it was a sweet deal, but I knew the coke would be shit, despite Rutgar's assurance that he had a direct line to some Dutch aid workers who smuggled the best stuff in with their medical supplies. It would be cut with flour or worse.

The arrangements had been made over the phone. No one worried about being caught back then. The country was virtually bankrupt. We could barely afford to line the politicians' pockets, there was certainly no money left over for any real police work. The ones we really had to look out for were the gangsters, real bad boys, who didn't like anyone making a deal without them getting a piece.

The drizzle of leaflets had slowed to a light shower. "Tomorrow's weather forecast: overcast with a slight chance of dildos."

Tristina laughed and hugged my arm. It was already dinnertime; the bombers were retreating in the distance, low in the sky, disappearing into the clouds like the sun.

My thoughts were stopped short. It wasn't the sound of the great flying fortresses, humming their mantra anew in the distance — we had come to welcome the sound that heralded gifts from the sky (there had been the occasional cloudburst since we'd set out: a sprinkling of toothpaste and a hemorrhoid cream; a sudden shower of antacid pills; a flurry of embroidered cushions, brand-new and still in their plastic IKEA wrapping) — but the almost imperceptible whisper of rubber tires on the littered street. Cars were an oddity in Beograd these days. Even the politicians preferred the anonymity of walking.

The score was made, and we had been strolling the Knez arm-in-arm for hours, like partners in a folk dance promenade. Even our steps were in rhythm. We had just passed the ruins of a bombed-out kiosk (vandals, not NATO, no doubt) as Tristina talked about the future, a refreshingly new topic of conversation around these parts. I had my plans, but she had her plans too. Commerce. She was saving her money from the spa job to go someplace safe, the university in Warszawa perhaps — her mother was an ethnic Pole — to study investment banking. I had been silent, half-listening, half-contemplating the cosmic everything.

I did not turn when I heard the car roll to a stop. I'd been particularly vigilant lately. There were rumours. Nothing substantial. But the word was that there'd been some kind of problem with Bracha's girlfriend. Something to do with the coke I had supplied, although I suspected that the creep's own pharmaceutical experiments had backfired, and he was blaming me to remain in his girlfriend's good graces. One version had her head exploding like a mortar shell. Another had her bleeding from the eyes and ears and lapsing into a coma as Bracha comforted her like the Kosovo Maiden in Predić's garish painting. In reality, anything was possible. The bitch had done so much coke, it was medically conceivable for her head to explode, Nexhmije Gjinushi. It was completely feasible, from a scientific point of view, that the nasal cartilage and sinus membranes had finally dissolved and she now wept blood like a miraculous virgin.

I did not turn at the sound of tires, but quickened my pace. I could hear four distinct clicks behind me as the doors were unlatched (a sedan: that was not good. Mostly gangsters and pimps drove sedans; they were the only ones who could afford all those doors). I allowed myself to turn when I heard the last of the four doors chunk shut. It was a good solid sound, a German car, no doubt.

From the corner of my eye, I did not recognize the car.

I tightened my grip on Tristina's arm and pulled forward. "Turk!"

It was Bracha, no doubt about that. I pretended not to hear and again quickened my pace.

"Turk. We need to talk."

I pushed Tristina forward and hissed to her: "Keep walking." I turned around and smiled.

"Brach — nice to see you, man."

Bracha didn't speak. He was either trembling with anger or crying or both. Three men stood with him. I did not know their names, although a couple looked familiar. They all wore expensive track suits and gold chains. They were not cronies. This was deep shit.

The next moments unfolded in silence, Bracha too angry to speak, I, too frightened. Only Tristina had the wherewithal to say anything, although this amounted to little more than repeatedly asking me *what the fuck was going on*.

Bracha hit me suddenly on the side of the head and then again on the shoulder with a metal object. At first, I imagined it was a ceremonial sword, like the ones the old veterans carried in the Kosovo parade. But soon I realized it was nothing so romantic: a tire iron, rusting at the ends, the white paint chipped and scuffed. It had seen service before.

I tried to protect my face with my arms.

"Bracha, slow down…"

Bracha responded with a torrent of bestial abuse, largely unintelligible gruntings.

The tire iron came down on my shoulder and back, then clonked my head again. It was a fairly narrow piece, taken, no doubt, from someone's old Yugo. I could taste blood in my mouth, and remember feeling surprise at how little the tire iron hurt. It was almost comical.

Finally, his energy seemingly spent, Bracha bent over me. He placed a foot on each arm and emptied the contents of a plastic bag onto my face. Bracha rubbed the smooth powder into my fresh cuts, forced open my eyes, and smeared powder on the unprotected surface with his thumb. That stung, and when I opened my mouth to address the pain, Bracha poured more powder in. He clenched my jaw and throat with his hands, until I almost passed out.

"This is good shit, eh? This is damn good shit." Bracha punched me now several times in the face: three, four, five… I soon stopped counting. I just waited for it to end.

Finally, Bracha sat on my chest, both hands clenching the front of my shirt. He seemed to be sobbing.

I opened my eyes and blinked several times to free them up and get rid of the stinging. I spat the bad coke out onto the pavement. I could taste it, mostly baby powder. Not good shit, but nothing that could kill you.

"I told you, Bracha. I couldn't vouch for the quality. Let me make it up to you —"

Out of the corner of my eye, I could see one of the hoodlums, looking bored enough. I recognized him from the clubs — Ratz we called him — a tall blond guy in Nike head to toe. He was shaking his head. Everyone knew Bracha was a pussy.

As my eyes cleared, I could see the other two *bitangas* holding Tristina. They had her arms and one guy had gagged her mouth with a wad of surgical gauze. It looked very professional.

Bracha got off my arms as the pain started to set in. The blond guy from gymnastics helped me to my feet, not gently but, again, very professional, like a surgeon might if his job was to roughly help people stand. Ratz put me in a kind of choke hold that was remarkably effective: I could barely breathe and felt completely under his control, but as long as I remained perfectly still and submitted, things were not too bad.

I watched as Bracha limped toward Tristina, almost dragging the tire iron. I could see Tristina's eyes but could not tell if she was frightened or bored: if there was a border between the two emotions, she had found it.

"Turk, you fucked up my girlfriend. Maybe I should fuck up yours?"

"She's not my girlfriend, Brach. We just met at chapel."

The hoodlums all laughed, and even Tristina seemed to smile through the gauze, but Bracha paid no attention. He was trying to say something — probably something diabolical or clever, like the bad guys in an American action movie might say just before pulling the switch, but it just came across as random mumblings. That was Bracha's biggest problem: he couldn't accept that he was an idiot, something humming, less than human.

He pulled Tristina's skirt up; I saw her brace herself without struggling. Every Serb girl knew there was a time to struggle and a time to submit and put your faith in the unreliable God.

"Maybe I should pry her open, Turk. How would that be?"

I instinctively moved forward, but Ratz adjusted his grip, in the process, turning my head so I could not see what was going on. I was pinned, crippled. And a strange thought came to me: Miloš Obilić? Where was he? Why did he not appear now, at this moment, when I needed him most?

I tried not to picture Bracha pulling Tristina's panties down, running his fingers, almost lovingly, through her pubic hair.

"I think she likes that, Turk. I think she wants a real man inside her?"

I tried not to listen. I concentrated instead on the sound of my own breath: in and out, in and out. The NATO planes were coming in again, their meditative hum growing louder.

Only to the extent that we subject ourselves over and over again to annihilation can we find that part within ourselves that is indestructible.

Nearby I heard a light thud. Bounty again was falling from the sky, but I could not turn my head to get a good look.

And I tried again not to think about what I could not see. Perhaps he was using the iron now: men like Bracha know no bounds. I could imagine her wincing in pain, yet finding that place too, inside her head, Nexhmije Gjinushi, joining the legions of Kosovo martyrs perhaps or the bands of brides and sisters and mothers of martyrs marching to the celestial plains.

Something landed not two feet from me. A book. NATO was sending us books now. I could see them scattered across the Knez. One fell by my feet and spilled open, a thick old book with yellowed pages and ornate lettering. The title, in English, ran across the top of the pages: *Leaves of Grass.*

Leaves...of grass? That made no sense.

I lifted my eyes and struggled to see Tristina and, in the effort, came to realize that this was what it meant to be a Serb. It meant being a poor Buddhist. Detachment was possible, but only detachment-as-mental-illness, a passionate indifference to the suffering of oneself masked as indifference to the suffering of others.

I watched the slobbering Bracha, the hoodlums disgusted and indifferent, then closed my eyes. You must understand, Nexhmije Gjinushi, history was taking its course, and there was not a damned thing I could do about it.

24

WAS I ANGRY, COUNSELLOR? You cannot begin to understand.

For weeks afterwards, months, thoughts of revenge grew like weeds in my mind. At night, as I lay in bed, my head was filled with thoughts of my hands around the fat insect's throat, his baby eyes bulging even further out of their sockets, his face turning red, then blue, then purple as I blocked the life from him. Even later, after being shanghaied into Milošević's army, these dreams of anger would sustain me, through the long marches across the Yellow Valley, through the nights of unwanted and unwilling guard duty. To this day I savour the thought of gouging his heart from his chest with my bare talons.

You will not be punished for your anger, you will be punished by your anger — the Buddha said that, Nexhmije Gjinushi, and while there may some wisdom in those words, I believe that indifference too can be its own punishment.

The Saviour was the one that did it. A gift from the Gods of NATO, the book struck Bracha at exactly the right velocity, in exactly the right spot, at exactly the right time. He folded over like a lamb with its throat slit and crumpled onto the ground. The gangsters, taking this as a sign their work was finished, relinquished their holds and hightailed it out of there (not before relieving Bracha of his wallet and cellphone, and the last of the bad coke).

Rather than running into each other's arms like people in a Hollywood movie, Tristina and I tentatively stepped forward and met at the fallen Bracha, exhausted adversaries or comrades. We weren't sure.

"You okay?"

Tristina nodded slowly. "Yes. Yes. I think I am." She was holding the waist of her skirt with one hand, the other was crossed over her chest.

I looked down on Bracha. Definitely out. Dead perhaps. Neither of us cared to check for signs of life. A little blood trickled from his ear, a result of either the book hitting him on the head or his head hitting the pavement as he fell. We didn't care. In truth, I kicked the fallen man's kidneys a couple times. Tristina bent over and picked up the book, the one we'd come to call the Saviour: *Seven Habits of Highly Effective People*.

"Habit number one: watch for falling books, Tygan."

We wandered off in relative silence. Tristina stooped every once in a while to collect another unconscious volume.

I tried to forget the whole thing. Tried to forget about the books. Tried to forget about Bracha, who unfortunately lived, but who was left by the accident submerged in an even grander idiocy. And now Bracha's girlfriend (who had not died, but whose nasal bones had crumbled, leaving her looking like some venereal leper of old) took care of him and found in his simplicity something she could hold on to.

I tried to forget about Ratz and the hoodlums, and I found another Internet café with another Bracha who was, mercifully, only half as loathsome and ten times hornier. And night and day I worked and worked, determined now to build a little nest egg so I could take Tristina away from all this. We were going to escape, you see. I had already decided. We were going to escape from this world, this once and future former country, to the Great Nothing: America. It's true, Nexhmije Gjinushi. I am almost embarrassed to say that my dreams were as simple-headed as all those of the other dull pencils. Of course, every boy and girl east of Dresden dreamed of the West, dreamed of running away to join the neon circus of blue jeans and Kentucky Fried Chicken and fluorescent condoms.

And as I wheeled and dealed, Tristina lay in bed and recovered and slowly started to talk of the future again and read the books she had collected.

"I'm finding myself indifferent to tennis..." Tristina was sitting up in bed. Propped on six or seven pillows like a countess in a Russian novel, a bowl of soup resting on the grade-school atlas: a makeshift tray. The Saviour lay open on her lap. "The sound of the balls. I'm very ambivalent to that. As they strike the racket, the court: two different sounds. I am very indifferent to both. I was quite a good player in high school, you know..." Her voice trailed off, absorbed by a spoonful of cream of mushroom soup.

The soup. That had been a complicated one. I'd parlayed a stash of German porn and a couple of very stale joints for a nearly new distributor cap and a caseload of American razors. The cap was for a friend who made a business of selling black market petrol (was there any other kind?). As payment, he took me along for a drop-off at a converted mansion on the Dedinje. The place was a warehouse of sorts, gateway for food and dry goods making their way to any of the government-front restaurants and cabarets that littered the Old Man's Hill. I left with whatever I could carry: soap, canned soups, and British meats, and a dozen Blue Crescent first aid kits.

The soup seemed to burn her lips and Tristina withdrew

and blew, her mouth making a perfect circle. For a moment, she seemed erotic again.

"Some compared me to Majoli, you know. I beat her once. Just a single set, but all the same..."

The self-indulgence — I know it sounds awful, Nexhmije Gjinushi — was beginning to bother me. Believe me, I understood: she'd been through a lot. But now she was becoming like one of those old women you see walking the streets, the professional widows who wrap themselves in their mourning shawls for years, staying buttoned up, not in loss, but grief itself. Like these *babas*, Tristina was allowing herself to become defined by misery.

"Nevertheless, tennis. It doesn't interest me anymore."

She sighed deeply, almost theatrically, and resumed her reading.

"Seek first to understand, then to be understood."

"Hmm?"

"Habit Number Five. Very Buddhist."

Tristina sighed deeply and shook her head. "This is not Buddhism, Zavida. Everything is not Buddhism."

"I know, my love. In fact, nothing is..."

After dinner, Tristina roused. We walked the Knev that night for the first time in God knows when. A thick mist had infected the street, diffusing the lights and almost dousing our cigarettes. Tristina walked beside me, just out of reach of my hand. Her steps seemed deliberate, purposeful. I tugged her thumb.

"Come, my little martyr. My ass is freezing."

Still, she dallied. She stopped at the Tri Sesira, closed since the Americans had upped the ante. We used to laugh at all those stodgy places, Tri Sesira, Dva Jelena, Zlatni Bokal. Now she seemed wistful.

We stood contemplating the boarded-up windows for several minutes, neither of us uttering a word.

I took a hip flask from my pocket and offered my Red-Haired Angel a swig. She reached for the bottle almost automatically: homemade vodka that burned when she swallowed.

"I'm thinking of taking a trip," she said finally. "My mother. My sister. Novi Pazar, we think. My father believes..."

Her voice trailed off, and she took the flask again.

"Tygan, we should marry — yes?"

More silence. I reached for her hand. She did not let me take it.

Then we turned and walked through the moist lights of the Knez.

"I wonder if they'll bomb tonight?" She sounded almost excited.

"Stranger things have happened."

Tristina laughed, but just a little, then reached for another cigarette.

25

THE FIRST ARGUMENT was over some trifle. The botanical nature of the tomato, I believe. She maintained it was a fruit; I was steadfast that it was in fact a vegetable.

"It has seeds, that makes it a fruit."

"Cucumbers have seeds. Are you telling me cucumbers are also fruits?"

One argument led to the next. The correct name of Mr. Spock's planet (answer, Nexhmije Gjinushi? The Vulcan Home World, and not simply "Vulcan" as you might expect). And then the race was on. Nothing we could do would please the other. Toilet seat up, toilet seat down; toothpaste tube squeezed from the bottom or top — that sort of shit.

And while we still lay together at night, and still made love like Satan's own minions, Tristina never answered my question, and I never asked it again.

26

BY NOW, DEAR COUNSELLOR, the rains had ended. The trinkets no longer fell from the heavens. No more lubricated condoms in five fashion colours. No more Hanuta wafers or chocolate toffee bars from Sweden. No more ProPed High Cut Support Pantyhose. No more *TV Guide*, *Cinema*, or *Haus + Garten*; no more *Swank*, *Abgespristsk*, *Raisert*, *Schwanger*, or *XXXBrits*. No more books. The storm had abated. There was the odd cloudburst, a shower of magic realists here, a sprinkle of German noir there. Then nothing.

Gone too were the surgical strikes, those hypnotic, semi-precise high-tech wonders that had turned the nightly news into the most popular show around. Attacks straight from Hollywood, no doubt. The bombing had become impersonal, random, as if the Gods had grown weary of the game and no longer cared to hide their disdain.

A few weeks back, Counsellor, at a place called Grdelica Gorge, some three hundred kilometres south of Beograd, NATO planes hit the Beograd–Thessaloniki train as it crossed the Južna Morava. The missiles killed fourteen people; bumpkins, mostly, heading to the big city for Easter holidays.

Days later, twenty people, most of them children, were killed when bombers missed an army barracks and pumped eleven Block III Tomahawk land-attack cruise missiles into the residential part of Surdulica, a small industrial town known for making crappy auto parts. On the news that night, the Gods dismissed the action as a "mistake," and added that "technology is not perfect and never will be."

This came as a shock to many of us: if technology isn't perfect, what hope is there for humanity?

Even the posh assholes in Dedinje weren't safe from the Gods' misguided love. Two day's previous, NATO's humanitarian shells scored a direct hit on Dragiša Mišović. Three patients from the neurological ward were killed, while numerous others, including a woman in the midst of a caesarean section, were injured. Their crimes? Conspiracy to be Serbs. Consorting with History.

"Serbia's iron will cannot be broken!" Milošević declared from his bunker deep inside Mira's pussy. "We have stood up to the greatest military coalition in history…"

True. The Serbian Will could not be broken. It was malleable: it could be kneaded into any form the Gods desired; it could be twisted in shapes unrecognizable. But. It could not, would not, break.

That was the problem.

Yet, even as I write this testimony, Counsellor, Beograd is fading in my imagination. The end would come quickly, and oddly, it was Crnilo that proved to be the catalyst.

I can date with some certainty the moment the end began. Tuesday, April 6, the thirteenth night of bombing, when according to the state news agency, NATO aircraft descended on poor little Crnilo.

Their target was supposedly a military barracks on the edge of town, set up (ironically, I suppose) to provide technical and manpower support in the wake of the infamous mining disaster.

Some of the missiles apparently fell short of the target, striking an apartment block and killing five civilians (including, it was rumoured, the beautiful Dušan Mićić).

NATO acknowledged their "blunder," and commenting on the error, Air Commodore David Wilby said to the press: "Despite our meticulous and careful pre-attack planning, the law of statistics will, at some stage, go against us and we will be exposed to technical defect."

NATO's technical defect roused the ghosts of Crnilo, as news agencies soon dove into their archives to uncover that other tragedy that had befallen this quiet mining town. It did not take long for some intrepid reporter to make the connection between Dobroslav Zanković the Beograd Magus and Dobroslav Zanković the Monster of Crnilo.

The backlash was sudden and complete. Editorials across the country denounced Father as a fraud and Marija Milošević herself led a camera crew into The Peasants' Table ("a scrofulous carbuncle on the ass of our fair city," she called it, in a moment, I dare say, Nexhmije Gjinushi, of genuine insight) to uncover the primitive system of wires and pulleys Father and his cronies had used to deceive the willing nation. Viewers were treated to the sight of one of Milošević's producers, sitting cross-legged and wearing a special harness they'd discovered in the back closet, levitating on cue as he hummed the American national anthem for effect.

That evening, a mob ransacked The Peasants' Table, smashing tables and chairs and carrying off every last beer keg and bottle of watered-down vodka. The Internet café was spared only because of Bracha's bold insistence that he had no connection to the owners of the bar and by the presence of armed goons at the entrance and in the parking lot.

Father had the good sense to disappear. At first, he bivouacked in his Vidikovac flat, waiting for the latest storm to pass. He remained philosophical and defended his latest deception in the simplest of terms.

"It was good for business and provided me steady work at a time when I dearly needed it. Besides, we really didn't deceive anyone. In my experience, people are hard to deceive. While they rarely see what they want to see simply because they want to see it, they often don't see what they don't want to see merely because they don't want to see it."

In time, though, the storm clouds did not lift. It was time for him to escape again. He left one evening wearing one of mother's old cloaks and a feather hat taken from the personal collection of Sofija Dimitrijević. And that was the last any of us would hear of him for ages, Nexhmije Gjinushi. There were rumours, of course, and unsubstantiated reports from friends of relatives and relatives of friends. He had taken up with Albanian bandits. He was working as a double agent for the Croatian secret service. He had become a raspberry farmer and herbalist in some tiny hamlet in the darkest reaches of southern Serbia. Who knows? Any testimony I could provide as to his whereabouts or activities in the ensuing months would be strictly hearsay and inadmissible, I suspect, in any court of law.

27

MY OWN DEPARTURE FROM BEOGRAD was equally inauspicious. One minute I was enjoying a shitty coffee with friends at the Kafe Agronom, when a group of uniformed men arrived. Middle-aged thugs, gaunt or tubby — take your pick because there were no in-betweens. Some dressed vaguely like police, in black uniforms and flak jackets, others dressed more like soldiers or paramilitaries in drab military costumes, a parody of green, and the Arkan crest on their homemade berets. They carried that sense of entitlement granted every disenfranchised man the day he is handed his automatic weapon.

Some of the guys started catcalling — it was stupid, yes. Instinct told us to slip away, but the hot mud, marinated in vodka to make it palatable, loosened our brains and tongues. When one of the tin soldiers asked Luka Nikolić for his papers, all hell broke loose. These were Stalinists, we had decided, forgetting about the guns until Luka's brother Dejan had his face split open by a rifle butt. Eight of us were conscripted on the spot, pressed into the service of the Provisional Armed Forces of the Federal Republic of Greater Serbia.

The next morning I was out of Beograd, making my way to the Yellow Valley, to Fuckhole or Shitsville or wherever the impersonal gods had in mind. At the time, as I have told you,

I convinced myself that it was only a momentary parting from Tristina, that this love existed outside of time, had always existed and always would, that every step I marched away from her would be one more step on my way back. Her silence at the end I understood. I left without any ceremony; I was shanghaied after all, and that doesn't leave one time for long goodbyes. My kingdom for a phone!

Let the record show that we marched for six days. Up the hills, down the hills, deeper into the region they called the Yellow Valley. It was still early in the spring, which made it even more difficult to traverse. The ground was damp and fallow, and the traction of our army issue boots was no match for the mud of the steep Drenica slopes. The grass was still curled and bruised from the harsh winter's snow, and the dogwoods that stubbled the valleys had yet to flower.

Still, it was amazing how much ground you could cover when you were driven by alcohol and indifference. At first every step had been a chore, each tick and tock a reminder of the stupid fortune that had swept me up.

In the meantime, letters would have to do. It was old-fashioned and oddly comforting to write these letters, the ultimate cyberspace, where you are in communication with a person who only exists in your imagination. I could only envision her face as I wrote, imagine and hope that this piece of paper, this inanimate It, would somehow (by magic, I suppose) find its way to her. And then, I could only imagine her reaction to it: happiness, horniness, anger, indifference, a myriad of responses limited only by my mind's eye and alcohol intake. Such an impersonal medium, Counsellor, these letters. No wonder no one writes them anymore.

28

DEAR TRISTINA:

Blessed Mary, I am going crazy without you. Just thinking about you right now, my cock is ready to explode. I am not sure how much longer I can hold off before seeing you again. I am tempted to pull my cock out right now, but I am trying to practise the Buddhist virtue of patience.

There's no privacy here, of course, it's just a bunch of guys in a wheat field trying to make do, but that doesn't stop me. Last night, just as I was falling asleep, I imagined that you were lying in the bedroll with me, and you had your tongue deep in my mouth and both hands on my cock and balls. Just the thought of you touching me, I almost came right then and there. It just took a few strokes (my hands are no substitute for yours) and I shot my wad right in my tighty-whiteys. That's the only way I can sleep, imagining you are there with me and that we have just fucked. Then the world seems okay and I can sleep.

What a strange picture we must make, me and all the other guys. If you came up on us at night time, you'd see a dozen bedrolls on the ground, and a dozen blankets popping up and down like they had rabbits in them, drunken rabbits dancing to some inaudible song: *The Song of Kosovo.*

The only sound you'd hear is a dozen guys trying not to moan too loud, and trying not to call out our absent lover's name. And once we're all done, and turned over to sleep for the night, you know what we do? We call out "Good night" to one another, very friendly, almost lovingly.

God, I miss you!!! Do you miss me too? Your silence is starting to worry me, but I understand. You have been through a lot, and who has time for letters these days?

I can't tell you what shit this is. We have new orders, and on the move to God-Knows-Where, Kosovo, in search of the elusive and crafty Turk. The point of the whole exercise escapes me. We are in a country full of Muslims. Why we have to go off looking for particular Muslims is anybody's guess. I would think one Muslim would do just as well as another; in fact the randomness of our approach has a lot going for it. Much more representative of Slobo's strategy, which I figure is I-Don't-Know-What-the-Fuck-I'm-Doing-But-if-I-Keep-Doing-Stuff-Maybe-People–Will-Think-I-Have-a-Plan. But I understand the approach. Given that we are looking for particular Muslims (although we know nothing about them, specifically, except a few anthropomorphic nicknames — the Leopard, the Badger, Korbi Artë, aka the Golden Falcon — and the fact they are "terrorists"), and not just Muslims in general, then we can maintain the illusion that this is a just, or at least justifiable, fight between known combatants. It's all about protecting your ass, as near

as I can figure. War crimes are on everyone's mind.
With the outcome already decided (you have to
understand, my love, everyone — absolutely everyone
— is certain we are going to lose this one). A bunch of
sloppy Serbs taking on the might of the most powerful
nation on earth — plus NATO! This is the Field of
Blackbirds all over again. This is defeat waiting to
happen. (Serbia can hardly wait!!!) An international
tribunal can't be far behind. The brass — all of them —
are already working on their alibis.

But yes: the New Orders. Vojnovic himself briefed
us. He came down to the fire last night and talked for
what seemed like hours. Most of us pretended to listen,
trying to get our chores done before darkness took over.
(Kovač, the brownnoser, sat in rapt attention, jotting
feverishly in his little black notebook. Our sergeant,
always on the ready in case Vojnovic should need a
handy dog to spit on). The mission was vital for the
survival of the Serbian Nation, he told us, and "the fate
of the entire war effort rests on your shoulders" (those
were his exact words). Our mission was simple and
complex all at once: we were going north (he was never
more specific than that) deep into the Yellow Valley
to root out Albanian warlords trying to pry Kosovo
from its rightful place in the Serbian Federation. The
warlords, Vojnovic told us, were in league with a cadre
of international terrorists — Afghans, Palestinians,
Neo-Nazis, and other NATO puppets. They were
forcing Serbs from their homes, uprooting them from
where they had lived peaceably with their Albanian
neighbours for centuries (Kovač, of course, nodded
violently, and looked and sat even more rigidly, as if

he felt Vojnovic was signalling him out personally for special attention). There were documented reports, Vojnovic told us, of Serbian maidens as young as nine — little girls — raped by gangs of Albanian paramilitaries, of the wholesale slaughter of Serbian men and boys, anyone with a hair on his balls, their vital organs harvested and sold to Asian medical clinics, with the wholesaling of human body parts, along with a significant hand in the heroin trade that flowed through Kosovo, which financed the Albanian's illegal and immoral insurgency. It was all Ethnic Cleansing this and Ethnic Cleansing that (Ethnic Cleanser: what a perfect name for laundry soap. My friend Boz and I might market it after the Defeat!).

The speech was meant to be rousing, I supposed. But I for one couldn't wait for the man to shut up. I wanted to get to bed. I wanted to get back to thoughts of you.

But enough of politics. I want to tell you about my sex fantasy. It's a good one, and it involves you (of course!). For some reason, we are on a beach somewhere on the Adriatic. I don't care where (you pick). Anyways, we've gone on vacation somewhere and we've just come in from a swim in the cold sea, and our bathing suits are clinging to us, and I can see that your nipples are very hard. Whether from the cold or just because I am turning you on, I'm not sure. We quickly lie on our towels and snuggle to warm up, and start kissing. We kiss very softly at first, but then your tongue slips out and fights its way past my lips, and soon my fingers are very, very softly tickling your shoulders and the back of your neck. You stop my hand suddenly and push me back onto the blanket, and take out a tube of suntan lotion and pour some into your hands. You turn me onto my stomach and rub the lotion onto my back. I can feel the water drying as you massage my shoulders and back muscles, and feel the hot sun warming my skin. The smell of suntan lotion is everywhere, and it makes me hot (remember that night on the Knez, when the smell of coconut oil was everywhere?).

Shit.

Nikolić just farted. A big loud wet one. It sounded like a duck with its head under water, sighing. He broke the spell, the fat pig!

Good timing, perhaps. I think I should leave the fantasy be for now. Otherwise, I might have to take matters into my own hands right here and now. Patience, dear boy. Patience.

Anyways, the time is coming for lights out. We are on the long march, my mouse, and there might be terrorists under every pillow. If I never see you again (and I know I will, if only you'll have me) remember, I died with a hard on, dreaming of your warm pussy.

xxxxxxxoooooooooo
Vida

P.S. What's with you, sweetheart? I haven't heard a word. Please, please write soon!

29

THE MARCH WAS THE WORST PART. We could have taken the lorries the whole way, Nexhmije Gjinushi, there was no godly reason not to. It was Kovač. He wanted to toughen us up. Make men out of us, he said, which was absurd from the start. We were Serbs, after all, born men, sons of sons of men.

"We'll walk from here," he told the bewildered driver at the checkpoint just south of Prizen. "We'll march, like soldiers."

He was a countryman of yours, Counsellor, although an ethnic Serb, who now fancied himself a drill sergeant. He quacked orders and pecked at his men's souls. Once, he'd run a pharmacy in a chi-chi Priština suburb. At war he remained inconsequential, seething with resentment toward his mostly Muslim neighbours (we both know, my dear, that you Albanians are notorious for your lack of religious commitment; it's one of your most endearing features) who, if they hadn't exactly handed him over to the UÇK, had certainly stood by as the militia's thugs pushed him out of his home. He'd had a good life, he'd tell us. He tried to sound angry, but I suspected that, in fact, his heart was broken.

He was an odd man, Jadranko Kovač. Given to bouts of tears, forever popping mild prescription narcotics, speaking obsessively about his wife, some fat, demi-dowager, no doubt, with minor political connections, and their seemingly imaginary son who supposedly fled to Canada some time ago (when their embassy was pouring out visas like walnut liquor to anyone with a professional degree), expounding on his pet theory that Martin Luther was less Catholic reformist than Orthodox Christologist. Yes, he was Serbian through and through: romantic, opinionated, perpetually on the verge of defeat.

"Kosovo is a living entity," he'd tell us boys. "Scientists have proved it. It actually expands and contracts; it breathes. You've heard them say how Romania is the asshole of the world? Well, Kosovo is the lung. Kosovo and the Amazon rain forest."

To be fair, he sweated it out with the rest of us. Quacking, pecking, waddling, dragging his own thirty-pound pack, he set the pace. Nice and slow, just how the farmboys liked it.

He always referred to us as farmboys, this hillbilly with the low Albanian drawl, despite the fact that all of us were students of one kind or another, and none of us had ever had dirt under his nails. Whether Kovač was suitably romanticizing the cause — a radical Christian peasant workers' collective crusade — or simply an utter dimwit, I couldn't tell. Probably a little of both.

Already, I'd recognized that the Company Men were different. You'd see them lurking in the background, aspiring to something greater (and therefore less) than human, like priests or turbofolk pop stars. Us farmboys kept our distance from these serious army guys, but not Kovač. He was in there like a fly. They found him a nuisance; anyone could see that, even in the dim light of the distant barn. But they were no doubt used to nuisances like this. Petty officials like Kovač, uncleverly hiding their self-interest, eager for approval, eager to be empowered enough to unleash their tiny vendettas. But the Company Men — they wore serious uniforms, tailored by the poshest Beograd haberdasheries, with bright sashes, waist-length capes, and sharp caps. They spoke only in low, serious voices, intently looking into each other's eyes, ever vigilant, perhaps, for signs of betrayal. In real life, I could imagine, they were all bank presidents, captains of industry, or culled from the very highest levels of organized crime.

Kovač slunk outside the circle of Company Men, like a hungry dog waiting to be cursed by strangers.

"Does he want a glass of Kool Aid?" Božić had taken a seat beside me on an upturned manger. "Is he ready for his drink?"

I shrugged and scraped some stew onto a heel of stone-hard bread.

"They tell me there's chicken in the soup: beak, feathers, assholes..." Radmilo Božić slurred his words a little. Barely dinner time and already half-cut. He was Beograd too, and while I had hardly known him, it was nice to have a familiar face to share my apathy.

"They say Zekavica himself is in there."

"Which one's he, then?"

"Wait and see. If Kovač starts sucking one off, then we know it's Zekavica." Božić poured some liquor into a glass and offered it to me. "Drink up, we need our wits about us."

What was happening? Who knew? The plan was lost on us mere mortals, so I'm afraid I will not be much good as an informant. But there were definitely some heavy hitters, like Zekavica, the celebrated field commander, and Ristić, who was rumoured to be General Ojdanić's right-hand man, and therefore firmly in Milošević's pocket. And the troops: there were at least five full companies, not to mention a tank corps six-vehicles strong, and several lorries hauling heavy artillery.

Overkill. So far, they had done no more than arrest a family of gypsies and commandeer a deserted barn.

"What the fuck are we doing here, Boz? I should be with Tristina now, we could be making our way to America or anywhere west of here."

Božić shrugged and topped up his own glass. "Cry me a river, friend. But this is certainly as good a place as any to get drunk."

I watched Božić toss back his vodka, then I grabbed the bottle and poured myself a shot. The liquid electrified me, warming my fingers and filling my head with cotton.

"Have you ever fucked an Albanian girl, Boz?"

Božić frowned and thought. "Many times; six maybe seven different girls. I used to come here, you see, with my uncle to hunt for mushrooms. Biggest fucking *vrganj* you've ever seen. Sixteen, seventeen inches across, I shit you not."

"No shit?"

"For real."

"And..."

"Hmmm?"

"The girls! What are they like?"

"Like girls anywhere, I suppose."

"I've heard they all die virgins."

"No, they like to fuck, I can tell you that. And I can tell you too, of the six or seven Albanian girls I had my way with, three of them took it in the ass. That's almost fifty per cent. How many Serbian girls let you fuck them in the ass? Hmmm. One, maybe two in all of Beograd."

Božić laughed and I started laughing too. Not that either of us had said anything particularly funny, but we were just at that perfect part of the buzz when everyone and everything seemed connected and wondrous. It was the laughter of mitigated joy.

"I tell you what they do have, though, and it's not a myth. These old women who cut their hair and wear pants. They spit and curse and carry guns. You'd swear they are men."

"Lesbians, then?"

"No: *virgjëresha*. Something in between. It's some strange custom. They vow to never fuck a living thing, and in return, they are allowed to live like men."

"Hmmm. I think lesbians would be cooler."

"Way cooler."

I leaned back on my makeshift seat. In the distance, I could hear the mosquito hum of a NATO bomber, somewhere just south of the moon. Even out here, in the middle of Dogfuck, Nowhere. The Gods were omnipotent. I sighed and thought of Tristina. At least, I thought that this was the time I should think of her. But I giggled instead; Boz was giggling too.

"I was just thinking, kid, one on each side..."

"And we're the meat in the sandwich, brother..."

We laughed again and, with our free hands, clinked glasses before downing another shot. It wouldn't be long now. A couple more drinks and we'd be too drunk to think of anything, too drunk to think, too drunk to love or hate or hope or care. Just a couple more drinks and I could pass out in my bedroll and fall into a blackness that dreams could not disturb.

30

MID-MORNING WE RECEIVED THE ORDER to push out. We marched at a moderate pace along the dirt road that ran through the forest; spruce, pine, the occasional beech here and there, a grove of ancient walnut trees (the region is famous for these, as you may know, Nexhmije Gjinushi). We marched in silence mostly, everyone enjoying a cigarette (two fresh packs each, with Vojnovic's personal compliments) and exorcising the demons of the previous night's vodka. The only sound was the occasional song of a bluebird, rising joyously over the low rev of the tanks.

For a while, ten minutes maybe, we went up a gradual incline. It grew noticeably cooler, as the hills to the east blocked the rising sun and the shadow of the trees engulfed us. In time the forest grew thinner and the trees gave way to browning pastures and small agricultural plots. Some goats wandered freely, lifting their heads to glance at us invaders, before turning their attention to more pressing matters.

Božić arched an eyebrow and glanced at me. Where was everyone? I shrugged. The region was famous for two things, Vojnovic had told us: walnut liquor and terrorists. We could only assume that the bad guys had already headed for the hills. I checked my watch.

"Hey, Boz, check it out: high noon. Time to run those var-mints out of town."

We called the village Flori, I don't know why. I saw no sign identifying it; there was no marking on any map that I had seen. Still, that's what we called it, although even the word village seemed an exaggeration. Clusters of modest houses, hanging in terraces, gradually descending to a village square, dominated by a rough but elegant mosque. Surrounded from all sides by muddy hills, the village seemed designed for attack.

The tanks descended first. Two of them plodding like oxen, their gears screaming under the strain of deceleration. They were followed closely by the police units, the party men with serious caps, guns and faces drawn. Half of those men split off and began what seemed to be a systematic investigation of the houses. We watched as six heavily armed SUP men kicked down the door of the first house and stormed inside, guns aloft. It looked very precise, professional. These guys knew what they were doing.

Of the group that remained on the descent into the village square, my troop brought up the rear, a courtesy, I assume, acknowledging our utter lack of experience (our combat training had consisted of putting on a uniform). In fact, as I would come to understand, the formation was simply standard operating procedure. Rookies were put at the back. In case of ambush, they provide a useful buffer between the terrorists and the real army.

The tanks came to a halt in front of the crumbling mosque, and soon the assault force — police and paramilitaries, three-hundred-strong — had surrounded the grounds of the building. There was a curious moment, as Boss Hogg (I never figured out his name, but he was definitely Vojnovic's right-hand guy, always walking in his shadow, always nodding and jotting little notes on his wrist) conferred with his lieutenants — and the rest of the world came to a stop. I caught myself trying to listen in on their conversation, as no doubt all the other men were trying to do, trying to get a hint of what was to come.

Then came the comic bit. In the midst of all this strength and firepower, one of the green berets, on the nod from Vojnovic Jr., stepped forward and politely knocked on the door.

Nothing.

He knocked again.

From inside the mosque came an old man's voice.

"Go away," he shouted in wheezing Albanian.

Even the Green Beret had to smile.

"I'm not going anywhere, grandfather. Make it easier on yourself. Come open the door. Don't make me break it down."

There was another long silence.

"Go away!"

The voice was as ancient and dry as a sound of a horsehair bow rasping across the single string of a *guslar*.

Everyone — even Boss Hogg — laughed.

"Don't try my patience, grandfather. I haven't had my morning coffee yet."

Another long pause, and finally I heard the sound of the old man sliding the buttress to one side. An ancient mullah stepped into the light. Thin as a cricket, slurring a rain of invectives on the silent commando.

"Do you realize you are looking at a man who could kill you without a second thought?"

"And do you realize you are looking at a man who could die without a single hesitation?"

Which was older, the mullah or his mosque? It was impossible to date either of them. The mosque, for example, seemed ancient indeed, but did not appear to be made of stone at all.

Whitewashed concrete perhaps or even plaster. How many hundreds, thousands of years had the mosque, or at least a mosque, stood on this spot, how many times had the armies come and knocked on the door? And how many times had this old mullah answered it?

At that moment, there was a short burst of gunfire, unmistakably an AK (the water-splash explosion and the start of the burst gave it away), and we turned as one to look uphill. There was a small commotion as a couple of the commandos marched half a dozen Albanian men up toward the woods. And that's when it hit me. This was real. These were real people, and this was a real village, and these were real guns. There would be no good or evil here; that would be decided later. There was only one simple rule: do not, under any circumstances, take a bullet in the head.

The sound of the Kalashnikov inspired the SUP and a team pushed past the old mullah. There was a rush of angry voices from inside, but another burst of gunfire soon silenced that. I strained to see inside the mosque, but a cadre of Serb police crowded the entrance, waiting to receive anyone who came out, and effectively blocked my view.

A few more moments passed and I could hear the calm tone of a man speaking within the mosque. I couldn't make out the words, but the calm man was clearly explaining something. The rules, no doubt. The sound itself was rather soothing. After the harsh cough of the AK, to hear the man's rich tone, like a radio DJ, was a welcome relief. For a moment, I suspected that order and sense had been restored and what would unfold now would be a carefully plotted inspection of the village. Vojnovic's instructions had been clear: they had come to weed out the last of the terrorists, end of story.

Later, with the clarity of hindsight, and the wind at my back, I would come to understand things differently. End of story, for example. There was no "end of story," because it is not the nature of Story to end. True, the literate world had tried to corral Story, lasso it, and tie it up with Beginning, Middle, End, and keep it in a civilized and civilizing pen (the libraries of the world were full of such "stories"), but that did not contain the nature of Story or its corporeal, primordial power. The Rig Veda. The Avesta. The Diamond Sutra. The Arul Nool. The Emerald Tablets. The Pyrig Tablets. Liber Linteus. The Apocrypha. The Talmud. All tried, and failed, to contain the serpent.

The Story writes itself, Nexhmije Gjinushi. The Story stands outside story just as sure as the Song of Kosovo is beyond mere song. And so, in a nation unwritten, beyond definition (because wasn't that what they were really fighting for, the final, finite, and unattainable grammatical rules to define the Serbian nation?), and for a people without history (in that they made no distinction between past, present, and future, and therefore could not understand history in any material way), in a world where everything was fluid, no distinctions could be made. In other words, in the midst of pure Story to end was not just impossible, it was inconceivable.

But that realization would come later. At this moment, Counsellor, I was drowning in story. The orderly sweep of the village had quickly deconstructed. A sudden explosion at the hilltop (an incendiary bomb, probably, launched by the support troops across the mountain) sent the mosque crowd pushing to the exit. People — old women and children mostly, with no man under fifty in sight — stumbled out of the large wooden doors, only to meet a rain of fists and rifle butts. I tried to grant the commandos the benefit of the doubt: they were trying to restore order. But seeing some old Albanian *baba* on her hands and knees, her face bloodied by a policeman's fist, shook what limited faith in the cause I might have had.

Across the village, people began emerging from houses and buildings that only moments before had seemed deserted. Some carried small packs and sacks or just held cans of food and water in their arms. The commandos tried to contain them with short bursts of gunfire, but the shooters had to be wary of their own men, and the villagers seemed well-versed in the art of evasion. They ran through the twists of the old streets in a dozen different directions at once, yet all seemed to converge, almost magically, in a field thick with wheat at the north end of the village.

Not all of them got away, of course. The old people, men and women both, had neither the ability nor inclination to run. They waddled to no place in particular, shielding their heads with weakened hands as they cursed and scolded the invaders. Children too, the youngest, were boiling in fear, some of them unable to muster any defence beyond falling to their knees and closing their eyes as tightly as humanly possible.

And then there were the stragglers, the thoughtful ones or the most frightened, who'd waited in their warrens until the last possible moment. Most of these were quickly contained by the troops who now vastly outnumbered the remaining villagers. But a few managed to dodge the police and paramilitary and make a break for the fields. Two such stragglers made their way to the narrow corner where Božić and I had ducked to wait out the storm. The girls, sisters no doubt, practically ran into our arms. I held the one girl, a modest little cow, maybe twelve or thirteen, by the shoulders for a moment. My first impulse was to try and soothe her. But this was impractical and likely in neither of our best interests. "Run," I said, releasing her. "Run like shit. Go! Go!" I tried to boot her ass, to underscore the urgency of the request, but she was already gone. Just in time too. As the girls emerged from the maze several metres up the hill, an ellipsis of automatic gunfire tracked them. A moment later, they were lost in the fields.

Rattled, Božić and I sat down on the stone curb. He held up his hands; they were shaking.

"Look," he said, laughing. "Frightened by a little girl."

I held up one hand too and laughed. "They make them scary here, Boz."

He slapped his pockets and dug out a pack of Vojnovic's ciggies, taking out a single smoke. Carefully, he milked the tobacco from the end, capturing it in the open cigarette pack. Then he took an empty casing from another pocket and unscrewed the top. With his hands still unsteady it was no easy task stuffing the end of the cigarette cylinder with the premium pot. Still, he was well-practised and, a moment later was lighting up.

He took a deep toke and politely offered me a hit.

There was a long pause as we closed our eyes and waited for the pot to kick in.

"Did they make it? The girls?"

Boz shrugged. "I think so. I think they were just trying to give them a little scare."

"Us too."

"Ya."

"No one would shoot a harmless little girl."

Boz nodded, unsure, though, as if it was an optimistic opinion or a declaration of philosophical uncertainty.

We sat in silence, each one wondering how much shit we'd

be in if someone found out we'd let Cinderella's ugly stepsisters go.

"That was our good deed for the day," Božić finally concluded, flicking the spent joint to the ground. "Now" — he added, reaching for his pocket flask — "God owes us, big time."

31

DESPITE MY BEST EFFORTS, Nexhmije Gjinushi, our forces managed to capture several hundred villagers. The paramilitaries, who seemed well versed in the etiquette for these sorts of things, had lined the villagers up in rows and quadrants, ten people to each row, five rows to each quadrant. Instinctively, the hillbillies stood at rough attention, silent, many of them holding passports or other identification papers at the ready in case one of us, like a conscientious conductor, cared to check them out.

The SUP quickly separated the men from the other villagers and assigned them, as if following a prescribed formula, into six or seven groups, a dozen plus to a group. The word "men" is used very opportunistically here, being applied to any male over the age of, say, thirteen. Case in point, one mother clung to her son's arm and then, as her son was being led away, to my leg. She was protesting — "He's only a boy! He's only a boy!" she cried — as another woman, a fading yellow nurse's uniform under her overcoat, tried to simultaneously calm the mother and reason with the Serbian police.

"It's true, he's just a boy. He's not even thirteen."

The police officer, a gruff sergeant with a droopy eye and a giant Romanov moustache, was unfazed.

"Too bad for him he's not a shrimp."

And that was that. He was taken off with the rest.

Once the men were assigned to their groups, the SUP brass made themselves scarce and a strange something took hold of the Albanians. A collective silence descended. The men and women seemed to be communicating with simple looks and sideways glances. None of them spoke.

The men were led off in their groups, as the women and children stood, confused, in a herd at the edge of the wheat field. Already, half a dozen policemen were circulating amongst them, roughly searching the detainees, taking whatever they could. The police were brisk and efficient, sticking their hands into undergarments, ears, mouths — anything. When one fat old farm woman, her arm in a sling (from some previous police encounter, no doubt), was found to have a stash of leks and deutschmarks rolled up in her ample bra, the cops pushed her to the ground, hiked her skirt up, and pulled her panties down past her knees. I averted my eyes, the sight of the woman's singular indignity in itself left me feeling undignified. But that didn't deter the cops. One of them dug in her box and ass with his fingers, while another one held her by the neck with a billy club. After that, they moved on and found a crowbar. They cracked her cast open: bingo; another wad of bills rolled up inside. And so, the process (minus the cast, of course) was repeated with her three children, two girls and a boy; the oldest could not have been more than eleven.

Thus the police made their way through the crowd. When they were more or less finished, the sergeant climbed on the front of the tank to make an announcement.

"Attention please," he shouted, although he needn't have bothered: he had their attention. "Once we're finished processing you, you are free to leave." The sergeant hung on the word "processing" to ensure no bit of irony was lost on his charges.

"Does that mean we can return to our homes?" several of the women asked at once.

The old sergeant smiled.

"I'm sorry, ladies, but this village has been declared a disaster zone. For your own comfort and safety I must insist that you evacuate the area. Immediately."

The women flooded him with questions, but the sergeant calmly unholstered his service revolver and shot it in the air. The questions stopped.

"There really is no time for questions, ladies. Every moment you are here compromises your safety. You need to leave, and you are to leave now. Go find yourself a safe haven. I suggest Albania," he said, pointing due east. "It's one hundred kilometres that way."

Some of the older JNA and Arkan Volunteers were pulling young women from the crowd, one or two at a time. It was all done rather matter-of-factly, with the men merely tapping the women on the shoulder — as if this were a ball and they were inviting the women to dance — and pointing them off in the direction of a plumbing service store that had been turned into a temporary command post. The women didn't say a word, although many of their mothers protested, mildly. Not that they were happy about it, but they comprehended: this was part of the ritual.

Kovač, to his credit, wanted no part of it.

"Is this absolutely necessary?" he asked, to no one in particular.

Finding himself completely ignored, he tried a more direct approach. He walked over to a couple of the boys from his own troop, who had selected some homely and frightened Albanian hen and were leading her to a quiet corner behind the mosque. Kovač pulled the woman aside, said a few soothing words to her in her native tongue, and sent her on her way. He turned to his charges and admonished them, finally concluding: "Let's keep our heads, gentlemen; this is for Greater Serbia."

One of the boys stepped back, and grabbed his balls. "This is Greater Serbia," he said.

But Kovač was already on the move. He was confronting a couple of SUPs, regular men who weren't inclined to give a dilettante like Kovač the time of day. The old pharmacist had gotten between the cops and two young girls, sisters, from the alley earlier that day.

"Please, gentlemen, they're only children," Kovač implored.

"Would you rather we fuck you?"

The men didn't wait for Kovač's reply. They pushed him aside and carried on with their business.

I tried to gently detach. Whether this was a sign of enlightenment or mental pathology, I can't say for sure.

Even I (who not so long ago had felt himself worldly, but now felt, at best, naive, at worst, not of this world at all) understood the dance; the guys were taking the women away to screw them. Four, maybe five guys on one girl, and then the same four or five guys on another, and so on and so on . . .

The intent was purely bestial and Darwinian; beyond the fucking, which was an end in and of itself, the act was an insult to the village men — the terrorists — who had run and hidden in the mountains and a larger insult to the Albanian race, your race, Nexhmije Gjinushi, which would now be diluted and defiled with Serbian seed.

32

SERBIA'S ANCIENT SONG CYCLES. Nexhmije Gjinushi, tell of a curious visitation Prince Lazar received on the eve of the Battle of Kosovo. As he prepared to sleep, a falcon landed in a tree nearby. Unlike you or I might have been, Lazar was not impressed. It was a time, we can assume, when falcons were commonplace and royalty such as Lazar used to be attended to by all manner of man and creature.

The falcon eyed the prince sternly for a moment, pausing once to strike an aphid that wandered too close to his perch.

"I am an Angel of the Lord," the falcon declared. Lazar, who did not appear to be surprised by either a talking bird or the presence of a hypernatural being, merely nodded and turned to give the messenger his full attention.

"There comes a point in the life of every Serbian man when he must make a choice, Holy Lazar, and that time has come for you."

Lazar drew a block of firewood closer and sat upon it.

"I am listening, Sacred Prince. Continue."

The falcon pulled a downy feather from his belly and set it at Lazar's feet. Then he drew a small ruby from under his wing and laid it beside the feather.

"This stone," he said, nodding his head toward the ruby, "represents the earthly kingdom; from the Sava River to the north to the Dinara Mountains to the west, from the convergence of the Carpathian and Balkan mountains to the edge of the Balkan Peninsula, Kingdom of the Macedonians — this, my Honoured Son, the Holy Spirit offers up to you."

The falcon then leaned his beak in the other direction. "This feather," he said, "represents the heavenly kingdom, which is bounded by no river or valley, by no mountain or plain, that owes no vassalage or political allegiance, which cannot be divided or corrupted, and shall exist for all time as constant as the light that shines from Thy Father's Holy Visage. This, my Honoured Son, the Holy Spirit also offers up to you. But I must tell you, Sacred Prince, that there are consequences to your choice. If the former, you will sweep the Turks on the field of Kosovo, you will smite them and their children and their children's children, you shall found a kingdom that will shine on this earth for a thousand years, and the bards will sing of your glory from one corner of the kingdom to the other. If you choose the latter, your troops will be decimated and you yourself shall feel the edge of the blade and the cold embrace of death; your earthly kingdom shall grow fallow and eventually rot to nothing, your children and all the Sons of Serbia will become vassals to indifference, and your name will be swallowed by the wind. But you will have chosen the righteous path, Blessed Friend, and your people will be a righteous people, and you will sit forever reflecting on the visage of the Lord."

The Holy Bird had finished and grew silent, and Lazar himself grew silent. It was a riskier decision than one might suppose, given that the devil himself was wont to appear in animal form and tempt mortal men with all sorts of wondrous bargains. Could this be a black trick? After several moments,

Lazar slowly reached forward and carefully picked the small ruby from the dirt. He drew it to his eye, holding it between his thumb and forefinger, and inspected it closely. Never had he seen a stone of such purity and richness of colour. He smiled at the Angel Bird, then, as if he was dispensing with a dry burr and not a solid gem, he crushed the ruby between his fingers.

"The Lord is my shepherd, I shall not want —" Lazar dropped to his knees, continuing the psalm. "He maketh me lie down in green pastures, He leadeth me beside still waters…"

It came to pass that the falcon's promise was fulfilled. The Serbs were routed on the Field of Blackbirds, the soil wet and red with the blood of a thousand Serbian warriors and almost as many of their Muslim adversaries, and Lazar was taken prisoner. He was beheaded at dawn, following the prescripts of medieval warfare, the executioner using Murad's sword (the sultan himself having been felled on the battlefield by a single arrow to the eye). No Serbs were present to witness Lazar's martyrdom, a disrespectful precaution aimed to avoid any political repercussions and to ensure the finality of the act — for without any such witnesses Lazar's spirit could not hope to enter the Eternal City.

But Murad's troops erred, for they did not realize that a young Muslim boy who witnessed the execution was in fact the son of a Serbian woman and, thus, a Serb himself. The boy begged the executioner to allow him to keep Lazar's head.

"Though he was an enemy," the boy argued, "he was a man of highest character, who sat in God's favour. To leave his head in such a place, carrion to be picked at by vultures and wild dogs, would surely be an insult to the Prophet Himself."

The executioner accepted the logic and allowed the boy to carry Lazar's head away in a sack.

And so the boy wandered through the corpses and scavengers

that littered the battlefield, pushed forward by some unseen force, searching yet uncertain of what he was searching for. After many hours, the lad stumbled on a log and took a seat, exhausted. He laid his sack upon the ground, and at that moment a beautiful maiden appeared. She was ministering to the dead and dying, ensuring that the last moments of those who still clung to life were as comfortable as possible and that the dead were washed and anointed as custom and decorum dictated.

As the maiden moved toward the boy, something curious began to occur. The sack at his feet began to vibrate and a great warmth and light came from within it. The boy spread the top of the sack open and was immediately awash in vibrant golden light. He turned his head to protect his eyes, but the maiden called to him, saying, "Do not be afraid, young child of Kosovo, for it is the light of God and will not do you any harm."

And as she said this, the head itself began to rise, and then floated gently as if carried by invisible hands till it found Lazar's corpse lying by a small mound of stones. Miraculously, the body was intact, untouched by the dogs or vultures or treasure hunters that scoured the field.

And there, before the maiden and the boy, the first miracle occurred, as the martyr's head reattached itself to the body, ensuring that proper sacraments could be applied to his worldly remains and signalling that the covenant between God and the Serbian people had been fulfilled. The earthly kingdom had slipped from their grasp, and from that moment forth they would be the chosen people of God.

The truth behind the mythology is irrelevant, Nexhmije Gjinushi. That the Serbian kingdom lasted more or less intact for another century after the Battle of Kosovo, that the battle itself was far from decisive, that the ancient themes of conquest, liberation, reunification were in fact liberal arts inventions of the nineteenth century — just as all modern history was a fiction invented to soothe the pangs of nationalism — these facts are irrelevant. The people needed Lazar, the Church, the governments, the Turks, and Albanians as much as the Serbs needed a dead saint to organize and give meaning to an otherwise disorganized and unforgiving world.

And so, we counted men as surely as Serbian soldiers have counted men for 700 years, culling the called from the chosen, and ensuring, through our baseness and brutality, that we are truly God's Chosen People. Let the record show, I did my bit. After the prisoners were assigned their groups, I was part of the contingency assigned to escort the largest group of men to a undisclosed spot deep in the woods. There were perhaps twenty-three or twenty-four of them, mostly very old and very young. The prisoners kept asking us what was going to happen. We did not — could not — answer.

"No talking," Božić barked, motioning with his gun (just as he'd seen the guys do in war movies) to get his prisoners to keep moving.

Kovač was less discreet, chattering away to whomever would listen (and they all did eagerly, recognizing his Ghegish accent, and hoping against hope that they would find in this, their countryman, an ally).

It was hard to keep track of their conversations, though. Words came in torrents from Kovač's lips, and he seemed to be offering nothing more than a laundry list of gripes he had with his own former neighbours.

"And none of them came to help me. I lived with them for decades, ate with them, drank with them, laughed with them, but none of them would lift a finger..."

The instructions were clear, although the point was uncertain. We were to march the prisoners up to the top of the same hill the troops had descended earlier that morning. There, we were to lead the captives off the main road and through the spruce and beech, past a large stand of walnuts, to a small clearing beside a natural spring. That was the designated drop-off area, at which point we would hand our charges over to another crew.

The job was simple enough, and it took us less than ten minutes to reach the rendezvous. There we hooked up with a small team of black-shirted police, who immediately assigned shovels to a number of the prisoners. One of the old men refused his spade. A cop, a young guy, built like a pit bull, took out his service revolver and held it to the old man's temple.

"Do as you're told, Gjysh. Don't make me shoot you."

Still the man refused. And so the cop pulled the trigger.

That was that. The old man fell on the spot, and one of the younger cops immediately began to rifle through the dead man's pockets. As the others looked on in terror — many of them the old man's brothers, nephews, cousins, no doubt — the Pitbull raised both hands in frustration.

"What are you waiting for? Dig! Dig!"

33

"I'LL MAKE THIS VERY EASY ON YOU, GENTLEMEN." This Pitbull was one cool customer, Nexhmije Gjinushi; he did not miss a beat. "They say you can't put a price on life. But I can. If you want to live, it will cost you twenty thousand deutschmarks."

The prisoners were standing in front of the shallow trench they'd only just finished digging.

Several of the Kosovars began talking at once. The Pitbull silenced them.

"One at a time please, brothers. I can't talk to ten of you at once."

A distinguished man in shirtsleeves stepped forward.

"Twenty thousand deutschmarks is crazy, sir, with all due respect. None of us has that kind of money."

"So you're saying you don't have the money?"

The man suddenly closed his mouth and dropped his head. He took a few steps back, and stumbled slightly on the small pile of dirt left by one of the diggers. With his head bowed, one could see that the man had begun to go bald on the top. He had grown his hair, which was otherwise short and conservative — very Western — long on top and artlessly combed it in effort to hide the bare patch.

I glanced at Boz. Neither of us knew what we were supposed to do. Božić stood with his rifle at the ready, as if at any moment he would be happy to shoot someone. I smiled and tried to catch my friend's eye. I made a face like an American action hero and shook my rifle as I swept it back and forth. Boz smiled too and did the same: just a couple Rambos massacring an army of gooks.

The prisoners ignored us. They understood: the Pitbull was the one you had to worry about. Those with shovels dug deeply, intently, perhaps figuring that if they dug down far enough, they could hide themselves. Those without shovels dug too, deep into their pockets and shoes and the hidden corners of their thin coats and pants, collecting and counting their money. A small group of older men gathered together, wordlessly gesturing to one another. They had a frantic, family resemblance, all of them with small eyes, too close together, and high flat foreheads that left them looking slightly imbecilic. One of them, the youngest of the group, a man in his mid-forties perhaps, my father's age, was the most urgent. He was accepting money from the other three and silently pushing them to find more.

"Don't skimp, you assholes. Give it up."

Not far from the group a boy worked with a shovel. He was awkward, plunging the spade into the earth softly, where it bounced off roots and stones. Then he'd lift it, having barely collected any dirt, and tilt it almost immediately, pouring most of the dry ground back in his hole. The boy was still a teenager, very thin, with an oversized smudge of a moustache and pale hands. Sixteen . . . fifteen — who knows? But very delicate. He had no coat, just an old Black Sabbath T-shirt, and you could see the arms, void of muscle and hair, strain with each load of dirt. Take away the moustache (in fact, even with the moustache in this hillbilly village, Counsellor) and the boy could have passed for a girl.

I formed the story in my head. The frantic peasant was the boy's father or maybe eldest uncle — clearly he was the one in charge — the other imbecilic, imperfect copies, assorted uncles all. They looked to the boy with love and fear in their eyes, before scraping their pockets one more time. Collectively, they were trying to solve a problem; together, they were trying to buy back the boy's life.

This father counted and recounted the money. Apparently, they were still several thousand deutschmarks short. He began to move outside his little circle, quietly asking other men for money. By turns, he begged, pleaded, bullied. Still he came up short. The son, the silly, pretty, unhappy boy continued to struggle with the shovel. You could tell by the way he held it, he was used to being pampered. Perhaps he was the youngest of the family, the baby, and had been taken care of all his life. Whatever the case, he dug and dug without the tiniest inkling that the hole he was digging was his own.

34

I MUST APOLOGIZE, my Kosovo Muse, for falling asleep mid-thought. I had a terrible sleep — the damned music! It was snaking into my dreams all night long. The melody descends from the hills surrounding us, gets upturned and dispersed with the soil every time a shell lands, and just hangs in the air.

I awoke this morning to a symphony of *guzals*, shrieking like burning children, which slowly dissolved into the sound of Homer Simpson mowing the lawn. I opened my eyes, and there he was, wearing Marge's flowery dress and a floppy hat, looking very much the way I imagined my father looked when he fled Beograd. I was admiring this Homer fellow, when it struck me — I was watching my screen saver! I'd fallen asleep with the iBook on. I rushed to the computer to make sure that I had not lost all my good work.

But not to worry, my dear. The iBook did not let us down. My testimony was safe and sound, just as we left it.

The day is not all good news, though, is it, Nexhmije Gjinushi? Vasile Lupu served me some disappointment with my morning coffee. You have been detained again, my dear. As you may well imagine, I am started to get concerned. There are, I believe, not two days left before I must face the music, and we have barely had a chance to discuss my case.

I asked Vasile Lupu point blank: is something the matter? Had I somehow offended my lovely Counsellor? But he's a cagey old owl, and just shook his head.

"I'm sure she is doing the best she can...under the circumstances."

Hoot! Hoot!

I know your ways, Vasile Lupu!

So let me say at the outset, Nexhmije Gjinushi, that if my behaviour has offended you or in any way put you off — please accept my sincerest apologies. I am trying to change, my dear Counsellor, I am trying to become a better person (this is no excuse, Nexhmije Gjinushi, but you must admit, history is against me). Perhaps we can put the events of two days ago behind us and start afresh?

You have to understand, I have been through a lot, and as we sat together sipping our tea and coffee, my mind filled only with the scent of your sweet perfume, my eyes fell in sync with the slow rise and fall of your military blazer, and my thoughts were not at all on the words you were speaking — legal terms, matters of fact, reams of details about my life, all questions answered dutifully and with the illusion of attention — but on the whiteness of your skin and a curiosity as to the taste of your lip gloss.

Why am I telling you this? Because it's true, Nexhmije Gjinushi, and at the end of the day that is what we are after, isn't it? The kind of liberation that can only come from honesty, the justice that will not be found in Korbi Artë's Albanian courtroom or any place of judgment on this earth.

And so, as we sat sipping our hot drinks, I could not help but notice that, as the conversation continued more lazily than had been our custom, your eyes seemed to linger on mine slightly longer than usual, and when you leaned forward to jot down something on your yellow notepad, I could see that you'd left the top buttons of your blazer and blouse undone, affording me a view of the very edge of the cleft between your breasts and of the rim of red lace that ran across the top of your brassiere. Forgive me for reading more into this than perhaps I should have.

"In the strictest legal sense, the prosecution will have to make a distinction between your intentions and your actions; legal precedence is very clear on this point, I am told..."

What happened next I cannot excuse beyond saying that I am, at the end of the day, just a man, and a young one at that. And it was nothing, really, but enough of something to make me wish that I still believed in God and the Holy See so I could say a thousand Hail Marys and atone myself in your eyes and the eyes of My Sweet Angel of the Salivating Dogs.

We both set our cups down at the same moment, our hands almost touching. You glanced up at me at that moment, and almost without hesitation, I leaned forward and kissed you.

True, your lips were pressed tightly together — that was my first sign, duly ignored — and I am afraid I mistook your hands reaching up to push against my shoulders as an invitation to advance. And that's when you stood up, disturbing your tea.

"I have a —"

A what? boyfriend? cold sore?

You never finished the thought, but turned abruptly and walked out of the room. I suspect now you are angry, Nexhmije Gjinushi, and somewhat afraid, having been nurtured, no doubt, on stories of the animal passions that drive Serbian men. But I am different, my dear, or at least I am trying to be.

Of course, I cannot know your mind.

So let me leave it at that, and hope that we can move on.

For my part, I am diligently plunking away at the keyboard and have picked up the thread where I left it. I was back in the woods, a little later, and no doubt already quite stoned, contemplating the nature of heaven. The Orthodox view had been well hammered in, but the logic of it, like a nail sticking out from a floorboard, always caught me up. If heaven, by its very definition, was perfect, and therefore eternal, and therefore immutable, and therefore outside of time, Counsellor, did logic therefore not dictate that the entire course of History itself was predetermined? Since there was no Ever, the people in heaven would have always been there and would always be; and by extension, would not hell itself be eternal and the inhabitants of hell, the damned, remain the same for the infinite past, present, and future? And did not therefore this implied permanence itself imply a kind of perfection? Could hell be perfect? And more to the point, if heaven was without beginning or end, where did Salvation fit in?

The Buddhists, you see, had thrown the whole notion of Eternity out the window. Heaven and Hell became active processes ("A wise man makes his own heaven; a fool his own hell." Hadn't the Buddha, or someone like him, said that?). It was the culmination of decisions and measured responses — not reactions — to circumstance.

At that point in time, for instance, I was choosing to move beyond passion and desire. I lit another joint and inhaled this heaven.

"What day is it, Boz?"

"I don't know. Monday. Friday."

I took another toke.

"Why do we need to watch them? It's not like they're going anywhere."

"The dead need to be watched. Check your rule book."

"Yes, but technically, they aren't dead. Merely escaping. *Na nevidišu nema krivice.*"

I nodded and drank in the sophistication of Božić's ironic argument. The shootings, as the Pitbull had gone to great pains to explain, had never happened. There were no executions. No mass gravesites scattered through the forest. As far as we knew, the villagers had all hightailed it to Albania. Yet, here we sat, on an upturned log, as far away from the pile of escapees as we could get and still reasonably be considered "guarding."

Already we had covered the bodies in lime and a thick layer of dirt. Buddha or not, that was gruesome work. We drew straws to see who would spread the lime, since this was the more distasteful of the two jobs. Božić lost. He tried to spread the harsh powder without looking, shaking the plastic scoop as he turned his head. The escapees were freshly dead, and therefore did not look dead at all. That was the hardest part.

"Just pretend they are sleeping, Boz."

We smoked three whole joints: one to get our nerve up; another while Božić limed the dead; the last one helped me finish the job. Although we were completely stoned by then, neither of us laughed as we usually did after a few joints. I felt sick and could only hold my lunch down by looking at the trees and the mountains beyond. Božić made a makeshift scarf out of a linen napkin he'd found on the road and covered his face and nose.

"This can't be right," he'd say every once in a while. Each time he repeated it, it seemed as if the thought had just come to him.

When my turn came, I stood with my back to the trench and flung the dirt over my shoulder, without turning my head. How would the Buddha have handled this situation? Would he have laid down the shovel? Would he have cried? Would he have laughed? The Buddha was fond of laughter, as I understood it, and maybe he would have found humour in the whole situation.

Fuck it. Fuck the Buddha. Fuck Kosovo and the undead Albanians. Fuck Kosta Ilić's skeletal son, my inadvertent patron saint. Fuck it all! Excuse the coarseness, Nexhmije Gjinushi, but this is how I felt at the time. Everything layered upon everything else.

I lost my footing for a moment and had to brace myself with the shovel. My eyes fell to the gravesite and I caught one of the escapees wordlessly watching me. It was an impossibly old man with a neatly trimmed beard. His mouth was slightly agape, as if he had been stopped mid-sentence, and his grey eyes were still fleshy and lacked the glass of death.

I quickly turned my head and thought back to years ago, when my family had taken a rare holiday at the beach. I remembered the smell of frying potato pancakes and the feel of the hot sand on my bare feet. The sun was scorching, and Dobra Beba and I ran around looking for a speck of shade to rest our burning toes. And later, after the blankets had been laid out and the heat forgotten, we buried Father. We dug a deep hole, Beba and I, and Father, who was usually never one for games, was only too happy to lie down in the cool, wet sand. His huge belly rose out of his swim trunks like fermenting bread, and it had taken ages to bury him with our tiny plastic shovels. And every time my father moved, even the slightest, the sand would tumble off him. These men, even in their haste to escape, did not move. The dirt stayed exactly where it was put.

In the end, money hadn't helped them. The Pitbull had them all line up with their backs to the shallow trench. He went to each man, personally collecting the cash himself, counting it out carefully, feigning disappointment when the sum fell short of the negotiated price.

Few of the men had the requisite funds. All of them had something, anticipating before they fled that a bribe might be in the offing; that was the way things worked here. But twenty thousand deutschmarks! That was more than most of these men saw in two years of hard labour. Still, there were a couple. The distinguished gentleman wasn't just trying to hide his bald patch. Turns out he had all the money he needed and more to save his life. The Pitbull set him to one side with a couple of other geezers, both old and fat, with the stench of political connections about them.

The imbecilic father was keen to hand over his money, as well. He stood in front of his son, trying to shield the boy from the Pitbull's gaze, and offered up his bribe. The Pitbull counted carefully, made a sour face, then recounted.

"You're six thousand short, my friend."

The father started to make his case, his Serb hesitant. But the Pitbull held up his hands.

"I'm sorry, sir. No discounts today. Every life is priced to sell as it is."

The father, and now the boy's uncles, began to argue and plead, but the Serbian officer raised his side arm in the air to restore order.

"Listen ... Listen! You will all get your freedom. So calm down. We'll start with these guys here." He casually pointed his gun towards the distinguished man and the two apparatchiks.

With a deliberate grace that could only have been achieved through careful practice and calculation, the Pitbull squeezed off a quick shot, hitting the fatter of the apparatchiks square in the heart. He did not fall like a man shot in a Hollywood movie — no dramatic stagger or gentle folding to the ground. He dropped directly to the earth, as if gravity had suddenly accelerated. The Pitbull immediately fired a second shot that hit the distinguished gentleman on the side of his head: I averted my eyes and thought only of the man's bald spot.

As the second shot slipped out, the prisoners began to scramble. Some of them turned to run, stumbling over the piled earth. A couple dropped to their knees, hands folded in prayer or supplication, begging the guards not to shoot. A few, the wiliest no doubt, bolted directly to the trees. No matter. The soldiers had already begun shooting before the first man reached the closest bush. In thirty, maybe forty, seconds, it was all over.

Thirty-seven men. That was the final tally. I counted them myself. It made the job easier, somehow, as if reducing the men to an ordered and orderly piece of work, an inventory or accounting, moved them slightly to the right of humanity.

That they were freshly dead, too, proved helpful. As Božić and I lifted the men and carefully placed them in this cool bed, I could almost imagine they were sleeping. Of course, it did not help them one bit. But it helped me immensely. It allowed me to feel respectful and something less than monstrous. At times like this, that was a victory for everyone.

Božić by now was chain-smoking Vojnovic's free ciggies. Me too, although I'd never been much of a smoker. And with every puff I felt a trace of a chemical calm.

"We must remember to thank Comrade Vojnovic next time we see him."

"Indeed." Božić paused just long enough to light up another. "We're selling our souls remarkably cheap these days."

"What can you do?" I drew in, the cherry at the end of the stick glowing enough to lighten my face. "It's supply and demand, and this is definitely a buyer's market."

Božić nodded. He looked pensive now and turned as if he were going to say something. Then he closed his mouth, tightly.

I didn't know which way to turn. I had a joint going in one hand and cig in the other. I was tired of making decisions and took a drag from each, simultaneously. I would write Tristina, tell her everything, and maybe she would sleep tonight with me in her dreams?

35

TO BE CLEAR, NEXHMIJE GJINUSHI, I had no plan at the start. This is a trifling detail, perhaps, but I want the Court to understand that I merely reacted to circumstances as they presented themselves. In fact, my immediate reaction (and Boz, I was sure, would say the same thing) was to completely disconnect. For a moment or two, my brain simply could not process what was happening.

The first tingling of movement in the dirt I assumed to be either an optical illusion, my half-asleep eyes playing tricks in the dimming twilight, or simply the result of bodies shifting as the gases and juices realigned. But then when a corpse sat bolt upright, I truly almost shit myself.

I scrambled to find my gun, but even as I grabbed it, my hands were shaking so badly I could barely hold it. When I finally got a grip on the rifle, I almost pulled the trigger by mistake. It would have been a rude awakening for Božić too, with the muzzle about six inches from Sleeping Beauty's nuts.

By now the zombie — this demi Obilić — had rolled to one side and struggled to its feet amidst the rubble of the unofficially dead. Sprinkled with dirt and deathly white lime, the undead boy struggled to find his footing, took a few cautious steps, then staggered forward, a sloppy parody of running.

I considered firing off a shot, but there were so many good reasons not to. First, I had yet to stop shaking madly, so the chance of hitting this target, any target, was remote. Second, the last thing I wanted was to alert the mad apes of the SUP that something was amiss. Pitbull, who already treated us like cattle, would probably tear us apart with his teeth if he found out that one of his escapees was actually trying to run away.

Only then, as I started to give chase, did a plan begin to form. Escape: now here was an idea whose time had come.

As poor a soldier as I was, the boy — who, I would come to learn, had the hayseed Albanian name of Veton Dardani — was a worse adversary. I found him not twelve hundred metres from the camp, curled on the ground, sobbing like a baby girl.

I gave him a boot, not hard enough to hurt him: just enough to get his attention.

"What the fuck are you doing?"

The boy continued sobbing.

"Princess: get up! Fuck! You can't run away lying on the ground crying."

I reached down and pulled the boy to his feet.

"Save your tears for heaven. Can you run?"

The boy nodded, meekly.

"Then run."

The boy stood mute. Was he really an imbecile?

I waved my hands frantically, as if swiping a mosquito, until finally the dull boy took the hint. He began loping off, rather without direction.

"This way, Shithead." I lunged forward and grabbed the boy's arm, pushing him off in the opposite direction from the camp.

I followed at a discreet distance. Every so often the young dolt would turn to see if I was still there. A few times he smiled at me, a dim-witted grin you'd expect from a child used to being mistreated. I simply waved him on further and was beginning to think that perhaps the lad was truly mentally deficient.

How clearer could the situation be? He'd just watched half the men in his village murdered, and yet, instead of running to freedom, he loped along his edge of mortality. You could make the case: he was just a boy and didn't know any better. But youth didn't keep him from the executioner's gun, why should it be an excuse now?

Perhaps it was the shock, the loss of blood — that could have been clouding Veton Dardani's judgment. The right side of his body was painted in blood, emanating from the shoulder; his arm hung limply at his side. How he'd survived, only God could say. I do not remember carrying the boy to the pit, so it's possible he had been one of the first hit, and fell into the grave before he even had a chance to move. This would have left him in a fortuitous but unenviable position, at the bottom of the pile of corpses. Or maybe, slight as he was, he had been shielded by one of the older men and was shot just before or immediately after the man collapsed on top of him. It's even possible that, given his schoolgirl temper, the boy had simply fainted dead at the first sign of trouble. Nevertheless. He had done it. He had been licked by Death's cat tongue but not devoured. It was true what the old soldiers said: cowards die a thousand times.

And so we plodded forward, me shushing the boy and waving him on with my free hand. The dim-witted boy, the happy prisoner, turning around every ten yards, smiling like a stupid love-struck child, making sure his jailer was still in sight.

36

THAT NIGHT WE LAY TOGETHER, as familiar as man and wife, me, Zavida Zanković, spooning the shivering Veton Dardani, my arm around the boy's waist. Along the distant ridge, shells were dropping, and the ground purred like a happy cat. The boy, the merry dolt, was asleep. He could sleep through Death itself.

I removed my coat and placed it over his shoulders.

"Sleep, you horse's cock. Sleep..." I whispered.

The boy smiled, and snuggled closer.

I adjusted his head — the ground makes a poor pillow — and tried not to think of Tristina. Nostalgia was no one's friend at times like these. Even to think of her now, asleep in her warm bed, her hand on my belly...

In this place, even the present was nostalgic! Then again, the future was no less wistful. I tried to take stock of my situation, but realized that, at this point, my plan consisted of not getting killed and somehow making my way back to Tristina. Beyond that, the details were fuzzy.

I fixed my coat, which had slipped from Veton Dardani's shoulder, and patted the boy, feeling the sudden urge to kiss his cheek, as a father might do to a child. Just a small reassurance or reaffirmation of connectedness. The Buddhists, no doubt, had a word for this, but they could frankly go fuck themselves.

Buddha and his whole bag of simpletons, in their saffron skirts and designer assholes, they could go fuck themselves sideways with a spoon.

I moved even closer to the stupid child. *Stupidity is a gift from God* ... Where did that come from? TV? The Gospels of Mary Magdalene? Or had it been in one of the leaflets dropped from heaven?

"Good plan, Little Prince."

I turned and instinctively reached for my gun. Miloš Obilić stood not three metres away, smiling vastly, his last rotted teeth clinging to his gums, and holding a small curved knife, properly called, I think, a *bichaq*. Obilić winked and pushed the knife toward me.

"You have lulled the Turk into your confidence," Obilić whispered. "Now, you can slit his throat as he sleeps."

I pushed his hand away.

"Not now, Miloš Obilić. I am too tired for your hallucinations."

Miloš Obilić dropped his hands to the side and sat down on his haunches. "Sleep weighs heavy on all us Serbs, my son. Ivan Kosanchich, that bold knight, once went seven hundred days and nights without sleep, pondering the sad fate of these holy people."

"Miloš Obilić, please, quiet. I am not Ivan Kosanchich. I need my rest. Perhaps you can stand guard? Is a ghost capable of that?"

I closed my eyes, and was drifting off to the rhythm of Miloš Obilić's laboured breathing, when he spoke again.

"Ah — I get it, young master."

"Miloš Obilić, please —"

"You have a greater good in mind. Perhaps you're planning to ransom the young prince, or — yes! Have him lead you directly to the enemy. Like a falcon, returning to his master's gauntlet."

"You overestimate both of us, Miloš Obilić."

"It is a brave plan, my son. Bold. We will take them by surprise, like Boshko Yugovich, and slay a thousand Turks as they sleep."

"It is a bold plan, I'll admit."

"And cunning, my son. The bards will sing of this a thousand years from now."

"I'm not so sure of that, Miloš Obilić. But please, sleep."

"Of course, you need your rest before you prove yourself in the field of battle."

"I've already done a good job at cocking that up, Miloš Obilić. I think I will have to find some other way to distinguish myself."

"I'll not hear you speak —"

"You are my hallucination, Miloš Obilić, and I order you to shut up! The dogs of sleep are pursuing me, good father, and I am ready to surrender."

37

IT WAS STILL DARK, Nexhmije Gjinushi, when the drunken singing hammered me back to consciousness.

"*Hi, hi, my American Pie…*"

The accent was unmistakable.

I put my hand firmly over Veton Dardani's mouth, and the boy allowed his lips to come to rest on my fingers. He barely stirred.

The voices were coming closer, the drunken singing having given way to boisterous conversation. I shook the boy harshly and, dragging him to his feet, urgently signalled him to keep quiet. Miraculously, the nincompoop complied.

We'd barely tumbled into a thicket when the Albanian soldiers passed by. Nine of them, close enough that, as one of them stepped, a clod of dirt popped up and struck me in the eye. I blinked firmly and struggled not to move.

Two stragglers stopped to light their cigarettes. "Panajot Pano — I'd stack him up against Džajić any time —"

Both were my age perhaps, and looked as out of place in their battle fatigues as I must have looked in mine. One of them — who, with a golden tooth and a shock of bleached blond hair, appeared more suited for the disco than the frontlines of the Battle of Kosovo — pulled his dick out and started to piss in the bushes not one metre away from where we were hiding.

"I'd give it to Džajić on size and speed, but Pano's touch was magic, soft as butter."

"Džajić is no slouch —"

"I'm not saying he is. In fact, I'd say he the most underrated player in the world today." The pisser turned as he spoke, the stream now landing inches from Veton Dardani's face. The spray shattered and sprang directly onto his lips. For a moment I feared he would give us up, but the boy did not move.

"If he was playing in the Bundesliga —"

"I hear you. I'm just saying, as much as Dragan Džajić is underrated, that goes double or triple for Panajot Pano. . ."

I could follow their conversation, clearly. Like any good Serb, I could understand Albanian well enough. And even though I was not force-fed it in school — like those poor Albanian louts in Kosovo, whose schoolmasters required them to master the Serbian tongue — I could carry on a passable conversation. It occurred to me at that moment that I, the captor, was now at the mercy of my little prisoner. All Dardani had to do was utter a single word and that would be it for me. These UÇK boys would probably shoot me on the spot. And as I loosened my grip on Dardani's shoulder, he tightened his grip on my arm. The machinations of war were beyond him. He was frightened and knew only that I had somehow offered him solace and protection.

We lay in the thicket for almost an hour after the final strains of "Kokomo" had faded. I can only assume Veton Dardani was too tired and frightened to speak. I know I was.

Finally, as the first sun of day leached through the thick canopy of coniferous trees, Veton Dardani spoke.

"What is happening?"

It was the longest sentence he had strung together since I first encountered him. His voice was soft — which didn't surprise me at all — and he had a squeaky lispiness that made him seem younger still. But his Serb was flawless, and his accent more cultivated than I would have imagined. I was surprised. This was no country bumpkin.

"What is happening? That is the million-dollar question, friend. We are apparently the last two people on Earth, the last hope for humankind."

Dardani looked at me.

"My Serbian is not perfect. I do not understand."

"That makes sense. My Serbian is perfect and I do not understand."

Dardani smiled briefly, then looked hurt. He could not tell if I was playing or simply mocking him.

"I am *teasing*, bro. You are asking me to tell you what's going on, and I really don't have a good answer. You and I have somehow wound up in the middle of a drama hatched by madmen and performed by beings somewhat less than human. Pigs and goats with credit cards and nice pants. Beyond that, and the fact that I don't know if you will kill me or I will kill you, there seems to be nothing else to say."

The boy nodded and snuggled closer to me.

He was silent for a long time, trying to adjust his position to find some comfort. He still wore my coat for warmth, which suited me fine. It was as rough as sackcloth and scratched my skin whenever I moved in the slightest. He adjusted the sling that braced his injured arm — which had now swollen like Popeye's after a can of spinach. I'd made the sling the night before from a couple of plastic garbage bags I found tangled in a juniper bush. Dardani had been unspeakably grateful for this makeshift medical intervention, bowing deeply several times after I offered it to him.

Eventually, he seemed to find a comfortable position. He put his hand in mine, without any trace of self-consciousness.

"Why did you not kill me, sir?"

"I — Zavida please, or Vida. I did not kill you because I have no interest in killing anyone, least of all a boy. In any case, had I tried to kill you, I would have probably shot my friend Bož in the nuts by mistake."

"But my uncle and the others..."

"I had no part in that sorry mess, and further —" I was suddenly struck by the full impact of what the boy had been through. I softened my tone. "And further — I needed you, bro. You are my ticket out of here."

I expected the boy to be taken aback by that statement, but he merely nodded as if what I had said was self-evident.

"I understand, Zavida. I will do what I can to help you. But you must promise me one thing."

"And that is?"

Veton Dardani thought for a long time, struggling to find the right words, I supposed. Serb can be a difficult language, nuanced, with an array of odd tenses and moods.

"Promise me, Zavida," he was almost whispering now. "Promise me that you will never leave me alone in the woods."

38

WE ATE WHAT WE COULD. Unripened walnuts, almost inedible. Over-ripe mulberries, the few that the blackbirds had left, which putrefied the moment you put them in your mouth. Clumps of dirt — a good source of potassium, according to the fifteen-minute survival video that Kovač had shown us — and a nest of termite grubs we stumbled upon. Veton Dardani had contemplated dining on the bark of a wild plum tree, its fruit having withered to tiny turds. I knocked the bark out of the boy's hand. I did not know the Albanian word for poison, so I merely snarled and cuffed him in the back of the head.

Our days were spent mostly in forage, filling the gaps with conversation where I learned something of my little prisoner.

His story, it turned out, was even sadder than mine. Veton Dardani had come from Suva Reka, an ancient industrial city some three hundred kilometres to the north. His father, Besnik, was a senior official with the ultranationalist political party the LDK — Lidhja Demokratike e Kosovës — and an executive at the OBI/Kosovavera, a worker-run subsidiary of Cadbury-Schweppes, which produced ginger ale and orange pop for Kosovars, along with a selection of regional table wines for the Czech and German markets. The company had continued to function throughout the political troubles (although the wine exports were hurt when the company refused to list Yugoslavia as the country of manufacture), and even as Serbian forces systematically destroyed the city's infrastructure, Veton Dardani's family remained well off. He still attended the finest Christian private school, studied oboe in Priština with Anđelko Karaferić, and had earned, he told me, his green belt in sambo, a kind of Russian judo. I could not imagine this Dardani, milky-skinned and as fragile as a sparrow, karate chopping his opponents into submission, but stranger things were commonplace in this world of mine.

Had he lived somewhere else — to the north or east perhaps — Veton Dardani might have made it through the war with little disruption. But as you know, Counsellor, Suva Reka was a hotbed of Albanian nationalism and swarmed with UÇK. The local Serbian paramilitary police decided to make an example of the city. Roads and railway lines were systematically destroyed, politicians arrested and put on trial for crimes against Greater Serbia, and as ancient rivalries played themselves out, ordinary citizens were evicted from their homes and chased into the hills — or worse. The final straw for Veton's father was an incident at the Kalabria restaurant. I say "incident" because I can think of no other word big or small enough to describe it, although the word itself does not even come close.

You are perhaps familiar with the details, Nexhmije Gjinushi. It occurred inside a modest pizzeria in a popular shopping mall in the heart of Suva Reka, days after the first NATO bombs fell on Beograd. Some fifty members of the Berisha family — women and children mostly — had taken refuge in the restaurant as a band of Serbian paramilitaries shot up the other stores. The spree of violence and murder had begun a few kilometres away

236

in a housing compound owned by the Berisha family patriarchs, Fajik and Vesel. In mid-morning, local Serb strongman Misko Nisavic and a pack of his Boss Commerce dogs (many of whom had direct connections to a revived Black Hand) descended on the Berisha compound, separated the family members into groups, and sent the women and children packing. They were told to make a dash for the Albanian border, but in the midst of the terror, they instead took refuge in the pizza place. Over the next couple of hours, as the slaughter of their husbands, fathers, brothers, and sons continued, more and more women and children looked to Kalabria for sanctuary.

Eventually, the paramilitary surrounded the front of the restaurant, smashing windows and firing rounds to further frighten the people inside. At what moment was the conscious decision made to elevate this everyday terror to the level of clinical monstrosity, it is impossible to tell; but at some point, as the women ducked behind tables, trying to shield babies and toddlers with their bodies, one of the policemen unpinned two grenades and threw them through the front door.

Anyone who wasn't killed by the initial blasts was shot moments later as the gunmen made their rounds of the rubble. A crying baby, executed with a single bullet to the head. A toddler, his gut slit open by shrapnel, begging his mother for a glass of water, executed. An elderly aunt, a hundred years old, they say, lifting her hand to offer comfort to a dying boy. Executed.

By the time the attack ended, the Serbian police had killed forty-six members of the Berisha family. This is how the Sons of Lazar found their glory on the ancient streets of Suva Reka.

Within days of the massacre, Veton Dardani's father sent him packing south to live with an uncle. A successful man, familiar with the ways of Kosovo, Besnik Dardani should have known that for his people, as for mine, no distance would suffice, no corner of the universe would be too remote, no plan would be too complex or sophisticated or insane enough to provide any protection against the dogs of history.

39

EVENTUALLY, VETON DARDANI and I came across an abandoned encampment. There was not much there really: some charred logs in a circle of stones, some spent shell cartridges and bits of litter. But we quickly set to work. We scrambled for crumbs on the ground and found in a pile of discarded paper several unfinished Chipsy bags. I had meant to portion the bounty out over the course of two or three days, but we gorged ourselves on potato crisps and ended up on our knees in the ashes and filth, licking the last grains of salt from the bags.

It wasn't just hunger that pursued us. We kept encountering well-trod paths and pieces of discarded garbage at almost every turn: here a wad of magazine pages someone had used to wipe his arse; there a discarded Lucky Strike package. I even came upon a discarded fatigue jacket, the crimson UÇK arm patch catching my eye from several metres away. The coat was worn almost to shreds along the bottom, and was coming apart at the elbows and seams, but it provided modest protection against the cool night air and that was good enough for me. Eventually, I surmised that we were either in the midst of a heavily manned Albanian sector or that a single troop of UÇK men had picked up our scent and were tracking us down (I also entertained a third hypothesis, that we were accidentally trailing a group of UÇK men who had become lost in their own forest, which would be much in keeping with the farce in which we found ourselves).

It was no surprise, then, when a few days later we came upon a second camp, empty but clearly not abandoned, with two cauldrons of stew bubbling on a propane stove. We were sorely tempted. It had appeared almost by magic, like a hidden kingdom in some fairy tale. In fact, we were several metres into the camp before we realized that we had left the woods and entered a kind of makeshift civilization.

We leapt back into the forest and scurried off, hunched over like nervous dogs as we ran. After a couple hundred metres, we crouched to the ground, turned toward the camp, and started to laugh. It was restrained, to be sure, but laughter all the same. We were like naughty schoolboys almost caught breaking into the girls' dormitory after hours.

"Let's try that again, Dardani, but this time we need to be less discreet. Perhaps you could play your oboe, and I will attach a flashing disco ball to my head…"

Veton Dardani was alternately laughing too hard to even speak and wincing from the pain in his arm, now pink with infection.

"Or better," I suggested, "you can paint a target on my ass and I will run through the camp naked with a cowbell around my neck…"

The mood was broken by a rustling in the bushes. Veton Dardani and I immediately dropped to the ground and covered our heads.

Silence again, as we remained perfectly still. Veton Dardani grabbed my hand and held on tightly. He did that a lot, huddled in the dark, hiding from death and hunger; he would hold my hand and explore my fingers with his own, as a young child might do. Sometimes, he simply hugged me and cried, oblivious to my relative indifference. "Crying will get us nowhere," I'd scold, without any genuine anger. I accepted my role: the apathetic nanny watching over my charge.

We lay on the ground for five minutes or more without moving, barely breathing, until I summoned the courage to lift my head. Slower than time itself, I tilted my neck upward, expecting to arrive nose-to-muzzle with a rifle. Instead: nothing.

I scoured the bushes for signs of life. Still nothing.

And then we heard it again, a heavy rustling in the bushes. If it wasn't human, it was a large-enough animal, a fox or lynx perhaps. I felt around and found a small branch near my side. I picked it up and tossed it in the general direction of the noise. Again nothing. I began to rise, and just as I indicated to Dardani that he could get up too, a long-eared owl swooped out of an ancient walnut tree and nearly clipped him in the head with its massive wing. Veton Dardani fell to the ground once more and I almost lost it again, literally having to cover my head with my shirt to avoid laughing out loud.

"It's a good omen," Dardani told me, earnestly, once I had sufficiently recovered.

"What is?"

"The owl; it passed on my left. That's a good omen. It means fortune will soon find us."

"Fortune? Well, I hope She comes alone."

We quietly moved through the woods until we happened upon a rocky outcrop in the trees. From our vantage point, we could see the entire encampment. It was set up in a small clearing, surrounded by thick brambles on three sides, with a rocky vista on one end that overlooked the steep valley. Beyond the camp, I could see some low-lying hills. It occurred to me that, since our escape five days prior, and despite our almost constant travel, Veton Dardani and I had probably traversed less than twenty kilometres from our starting point.

Tents sprouted in the camp like giant, camouflage-coloured mushrooms, while I could see the propane stoves humming away in an area that had been obviously designated as the galley. There wasn't a soul in sight.

I took a long look at the pots on the stoves, steam rising from them, and ran my hand across my belly. I looked at Veton Dardani, then back at the pots.

"Stay here," I ordered.

My little imbecile folded his arms and crouched, content to be invisible, as I set off down the hill.

It was a risk, to be sure. But hunger is an impatient master. I crept through the underbrush, as wary as a glacier, stopping at random moments to listen to the wind. Emerging from the brambles just a few metres behind the makeshift kitchen, I crawled on my belly and knees until I was well within the tarp walls.

I stood and lifted the lid on one of the huge pots. Cabbage stew with reams of elbow macaroni. A bounty almost beyond belief.

I searched the galley for something to carry the food in, but besides a row of dirty tin cups, there was nothing. I pulled my shirtsleeves down, and using them to muffle the heat from the pot handles, I picked up the heavy container and lugged it back into the woods.

That afternoon, we gorged ourselves. Using spoons fashioned from chunks of bark, we stuffed our mouths, happily burning our tongues in the process.

As we reposed in the aftermath of the feast — I with my pants unhitched, my boots and service revolver in a neat pile beside my head, and Veton Dardani half asleep beside me, still swaddled in my requisition coat, one arm curled as a pillow, the other, hot from infection, across my chest — it suddenly occurred to me: the pot! I'd have to return it or run the risk of alerting the UÇK troops to our presence. True, we'd barely made a dent in the stew, and I hated to give up my bounty. But there was no reason why we couldn't just stay right here, watching the watchers, dipping into their encampment whenever we fancied a bite to eat. It was certainly no more unsafe than wandering through the mountains, running the risk of stumbling into a UÇK unit. At least here, from our vantage point, we'd have a decent idea where the soldiers were.

As I contemplated the best way to approach the camp again, I realized that Dardani was staring at me through half-opened eyes.

"What? What are you staring at?"

The boy shrugged.

"I was looking at your nose."

"And?"

"And nothing. I like it. That's all."

We fell silent once again.

"You know, you don't have to stay with me. Those are your kinsmen down there. You could go to them, I'm sure. They would help you, get you medical attention —"

Even as I said the words I understood the inherent madness behind them. I was giving up my prisoner, the one, almost imperceptible bargaining chip I held in this Celestial game. Not to mention that the boy could not help but turn me in, either wittingly or not, at the earliest possible opportunity. But I kept talking and offering him his freedom. Perhaps I recognized that his injury could only slow me down. At some point, flight would become necessary again, and I could travel much more distance much faster on my own. Or perhaps the words came from somewhere baser, fundamental. Perhaps I felt compassion, or at least a sense that by giving Veton Dardani what I could not give myself — the illusion of escape — I was at least approaching something that resembled compassion.

But my dull bird did not respond to the offer.

"Well?"

He only shrugged again, and continued to stare.

We passed maybe three minutes in complete silence, when finally he asked: "Do you love me, Zavida Zanković?"

What a strange question, made even stranger by my realization as he asked it that, yes, in fact, I did love him. Now it was my turn to hesitate, and I managed to stammer back to him. "Who has time for such nonsense questions, Veton Dardani? I must return the pot before those guys get back to their camp, or we're fucked for sure."

I stood and picked up the pot. The handles were cooler now, although it felt no lighter than before.

"Go to sleep, Veton Dardani. Close your eyes and wrap yourself in sleep. I will be back soon."

40

I DON'T BLAME VETON DARDANI. I was the one, after all, who dallied, captivated by the sight of the field phone. He was merely responding to circumstance and more — trying to protect me.

The sound of warplanes purred in the afternoon sky, and over the din, another shot rang out. I saw a trail of leaves fly as the bullet skimmed through the bushes. These are strange things, bullets. I don't know if you've ever had the chance to watch them in flight, but they have an elegance all their own. They do not travel perfectly straight, as one might expect, but follow a slightly elliptic trajectory — all very precise, however, and determined. Bullets are by no means wishy-washy. The surprising thing is that you can see them at all. You'd think they'd move too fast for the human eye to process. But you see them; you just don't have a chance to react.

We'd moved off of any recognizable trail by now, and while it made the going more difficult — especially for Veton Dardani, whose injury was taking its toll — it seemed more prudent than sticking to the trails. Undoubtedly, at the sound of the first shot, any UÇK in hearing range would have come running. The trails were likely crawling with them by now.

Veton Dardani's exhaustion, meanwhile, was reaching

mythical proportions. My overcoat weighed upon him, as if made of stones, and as he ran he lifted his feet and legs in a most mechanical way, as if his thin shoes were actually concrete boots, moving himself forward with no muscle support at all, simply sheer force of will.

I'd made my offer to him again — several times. He could simply give himself up to the predators, who would welcome him as one of their own. But again and again he refused, offering, in lieu of any coherent explanation, a simple shrug.

The UÇK encampment had not been as deserted as it seemed. I had made it back in without a problem, set the pot back in its place without an issue, and had already turned to leave when I spotted an olive green box with a drab handset emerging from its top. I recognized it immediately as an old-school field phone and wondered: perhaps, here was my ticket to reach Tristina. The phone itself sat on a collection of metal boxes surrounded on three sides by camouflage netting. I quickly made my way to the makeshift desk and examined the piece of equipment. I had seen some of the Arkan guys using a phone like this before, and while it looked familiar enough, there was a point when familiar became unfamiliar, and I could only begin to guess how to use the thing. There was an old-fashioned handset and an analogue dialling pad — those I could figure out — and a small, black dial that I assumed was volume control. But how did one use the phone? How did I make it work? Did I simply pick it up and dial? Would I be automatically channelled to a UÇK operator? Would using the phone somehow give up my position and ruin my very basic plan, to not be killed?

I picked up the receiver and listened. There was no dial tone, so I clicked the hook switch several times. Still nothing.

There was a toggle switch on the top. I tried moving that, but still no dial tone.

It was then that I noticed another, smaller box beneath the phone, which seemed to house some electrical apparatus. I pressed a large red button, and the phone sprang to life.

By the bones of St. Sava, I was finally blessed with some good fortune. I decided to simply dial, and punched in Tristina's parents' number. I was surprised to hear the phone ringing on the other end. I imagined what I'd say when she finally picked up. I'd apologize, of course, for leaving (although it was hardly my fault) and for everything. I had not protected her, you see, in her time of greatest need, and wasn't this yet the most basic obligation of man? No wonder she did not respond to my letters. She was angry with me, no doubt, and justifiably so.

And so I let the phone ring and ring and would have been content to sit there for a day or a month, waiting for someone to pick up, when something caught my eye. I turned to the right perhaps at the exact second the UÇK recruit turned his head to the left. His face was old and oily, his hair long and unkempt, and his eyes held a look of reluctant sorrow that quickly intensified as they encountered mine. I would have expected surprise, but any element of wonder had been squeezed out of him years before. Now all he could manage were shades of sadness. He was lying on a cot, his shirt and pants open, his fat belly spilling to the sides, a Russian girly magazine in one hand, himself in the other. He stopped mid-stroke when he saw me and sprang up, knocking over pans and boxes as he scrambled to find something. He began to yell, too, some kind of incoherent signal to his comrades, before coming at me wielding a long bread knife.

He might have caught me too, if a moment later the sound

of a pistol shot hadn't rung through the air, and the bullet hadn't lodged in a sack of flour just above my adversary's head.

My attacker changed his course and ducked behind a row of metal containers, his now-limp cock still dripping from his pants. I thought of making a joke — "You better put that thing away, before someone gets hurt!" — but in truth I began to make my way out of the encampment as soon as the opportunity presented itself and continued running like the devil to only God knew where.

And so we ran. Not stealthily, like foxes, our noses to the ground, our eyes fixed and alert, sliding through the undergrowth but, like clumsy horses across a field of ice, slicing into branches and tripping over every stone and on every root.

We had only the vaguest of plans. I led the way and had merely decided to go up, continuously up, for as long as we could, for no other reason than I knew that up was more difficult, more physically exhausting, and would seem like such a foolhardy strategy that the UÇK boys would assume we would never do it.

The adrenaline helped. We were running on pure juice for the first ten minutes or so. But while I've heard stories of people who pull off fantastic physical feats in the face of extreme adversity — the mother who single-handedly lifts the tipped tractor off her child or the father who fights off a pack of wild dogs with his bare hands to protect his young son — we were having none of it ourselves. After the initial burst of adrenaline, we both began to tire. The incline was steep, and the further up we went, the less hospitable the terrain became, a world of craggy outcrops and sheer rock faces. Our pace slowed to a trot.

Soon, as desperate as we were, we had to stop and rest. We took refuge in the burnt-out hollow of a Bosnian pine, victim of some long-forgotten forest fire or statistically improbable lightning strike. We huddled together, catching our breath, safe at least for the moment.

"I have run..." I began, panting so hard I had to stop and recover my thoughts. "I have run...out of...ideas."

"We could...we could just surrender."

"You could, of course. You *should*. You're Albanian. Me...I'm as good as...dead, if I surrender."

"I will tell them...you saved me. I will tell them that...you are one of the good ones."

I looked at Veton Dardani. Could he really be so simple?

"Look, Little Brother, this is Kosovo. This is where the blackbirds feast on the eyes of dead heroes. It is a place...a place that exists nowhere but in political rhetoric and our collective delusions. It is a place where there are no good ones, only living ones and dead ones and the others in between. Like us."

"Sometimes I don't understand you, Zavida Zanković. You speak in riddles."

"It is the fake Buddhist in me, I suspect."

"You're at it again, Zavida Zanković."

Veton Dardani turned, leaned forward to look past the burnt-out husk that was our sanctuary. "We could survive for weeks here, I suppose. Months if we had to. You are a soldier, after all, trained in the art of survival. And I am not afraid of Mother Nature. My parents have sent me to summer camp in Greece every year since I was eight."

I laughed.

"What, Zavida Zanković? What?"

I shook my head but said nothing. It had occurred to me that, in the midst of this inhospitable Earth that conspired to maim and kill me at every turn, I was surrounded by innocence.

Beba Dobra, Veton Dardani, my father, in his way (malicious and unbalanced, yet innocent all the same), the lovely Tristina, my Red-Haired Angel of the Slobbering Dogs, even Miloš Obilić, that celebrated psychopath, even he was not without his blinkered charm.

"I will tell you a story, Little Brother." At the suggestion of a story, Veton Dardani huddled closer and leaned his head on my shoulder. "It concerns the Buddha, the Master himself, who one day found himself wandering in the woods, not unlike the ones we find ourselves in today."

Veton Dardani splayed his legs to one side. "I have heard of him, this Buddha. He must have been a very wise man."

"Let's just say he's had good handlers. In any case, the Buddha was wandering — not lost. The Buddha was very strategic when it came to direction. It would not do for a man who had built his reputation on wisdom to ever find himself lost. Instead, he had constructed for himself an imaginary journey, one that sought no physical destination, but a destination that existed only in his mind."

"I'd be lying if I said I understood you, Zavida Zanković. But go on."

"It's very simple, Little Brother. The Buddha claimed to be on a road to Enlightenment, a very specific road that he called the Eightfold Path —"

"You are losing me."

"Right view, right intention, right speech, right livelihood, right effort… and some others. It was the Buddha's way of saying that for all of us — Chinese, American, Serbian, Dog-fuckervillian, whatever — all of our lives are like a journey, an imaginary journey, and that our goal is really not to arrive anywhere in particular, no place real in other words, but to learn and practice the proper way of living —"

"Like the Christian Ten Commandments?

"Something like that, yes. To learn and practise the proper way of living, to follow this path, which exists only in our mind, to make our way to Enlightenment."

"Which is a sort of heaven?"

"Sort of. I think Nirvana is more a kind of heaven, but Enlightenment is the key that opens the gate that gets you into heaven."

Veton Dardani thought for a moment, digesting it all, then nodded. "Go on."

"So: you have the Buddha wandering in the woods, not lost, mind you, perhaps physically uncertain of where he is, but unwavering in his belief that he is on the right path, when he comes to a wide river, rushing and churning —"

"Like the Ibar or the Sitnica, when the winter runoff hits?"

"That's right, just like the Sitnica when the snows have begun to melt and the spring rains have arrived. And so here is the Buddha, contemplating the great river, when over on the far bank he spots a young man; let's call him Veton."

Veton Dardani smiled, pleased that he'd now joined the Buddha in the world of Story.

"And this boy, young Veton, who is a disciple of the Buddha, is anxious to cross the river and meet the great teacher. He calls across the water and says: 'Illustrious Master, I want to come and study at your feet. I want to cross the river. Can you tell me; how do I get to the other side?'

"The Buddha paused. 'I cannot hear you, Blessed Student. Speak louder please.' Veton spoke again, raising his voice to be heard above the rushing river. 'Wise Master, I want to come and hear the truth spoken from your very lips. But I must cross the river. Can you tell me; how do I get to the other side?'

"The Buddha shook his head. 'Young Prince,' he called back,

'speak louder. The water rushes by so quickly and drowns out the sound of your voice.'

"Veton clasped his hands by the side of his mouth and shouted as loud as he could. 'Glorious Teacher, I want to touch your robe and learn the way of the truth from you. But I must cross the river. How do I get to the other side?'

"The Buddha furrowed his brow and appeared confused. Finally he called back, 'I hear you, young pilgrim, but do not understand. Why do you need to cross the river? You are already on the other side.' And with that, the Buddha walked away to continue his wanderings."

Veton Dardani lifted his head.

"And that's it?"

I shrugged.

"Excuse me, Zavida Zanković, but your Buddha sounds like a bit of a nutsack. The boy obviously wanted to come and meet him. Why would he blow him off like that?"

"Well, I think the Buddha felt there were larger lessons at stake—"

"From his point of view, perhaps. But it was still a total asshole thing to do to that kid."

"Okay. I don't disagree with you. But it is instructive. You see, Kosovo is just like that river. It's an imaginary place, really, and a place where we are always on the other side. No matter where we are standing, there is always the other side. That is the one constant: the separation that is defined almost exclusively by your point of view."

Veton Dardani sighed.

"I was hoping for a much better story, Zavida Zanković. Do you know any with wizards and elves and noble-hearted warriors?"

Now it was my turn to sigh.

"Close your eyes, Little Brother, and I will tell you a fairy tale about princes and maidens and righteous knights, and the true story of how Miloš Obilić, with his vast and glorious moustache, slew Sultan Murad, son of Orhan I and the Valide Sultan Nilüfer Hatun, on the Field of Blackbirds…"

41

I HAVE NO WAY of knowing what time it was, Nexhmije Gjinushi, or whether it was the rain or the wind that woke me. At first, I was certain I heard voices; I convinced myself it was merely the wind whipping branches in the trees.

Another sound, and this time it was unmistakable. Voices rising above the elements.

I shook Veton Dardani, my hand covering his mouth so he would not give us away. He opened his eyes slowly, closed them, and then opened them again, quickly appreciating the gravity of our situation.

We had few choices. Running seemed foolhardy. The rain and darkness would make it impossible to gain any ground. But here, crouched in the hollow of a tree, we were sitting ducks.

Already, the voices were all around us. Who knew how many men there were: a dozen, probably more. They spoke in low voices, an almost constant babble from one hidden place or another: melodious Albanian spoken too softly, too quickly for me to catch anything more than a word here and there.

Veton Dardani looked at me for direction, but I could only shrug.

We sat like this for several moments. The boy's lips were moving, silently, and I at first thought he was praying. But no.

Rather, he seemed to be having a conversation with himself, weighing the imaginary pros and cons of a possible course of action. After two minutes of this, Veton Dardani shook his head decisively. "Po," he muttered, and pushed himself to his feet; he stood for a moment. By the time I realized what he was planning, it was already too late. He called out, "Alo!"

The woods immediately went silent.

Veton Dardani raised his hands to surrender and stepped forward into the blackness.

"Eshtë! I mirë jam shqiptar…"

He took one short step, and then another before a shot rang out.

42

THE SACKCLOTH RUBBED my chin raw, Nexhmije Gjinushi. It had begun to hurt like shit, was a constant irritation, torturous. Even the slightest movement — the jiggling of my head as we drove over the rough roads, for example — and my chin would chafe against the inside of the burlap hood and disturb me some more. Sleep was out of the question. I was simply too uncomfortable, propped in what I assumed was the bed of a pickup truck, my hands tied tightly behind my back. There was no give and no conceivable way to get comfortable. Instead of sleep, I drifted in and out of a half-consciousness, never sure which was which, traipsing Kosovska *bitka* — the pleasant plain, site of the presumed battle — with Miloš Obilić and a regiment of hallucinatory martyrs or thumping along the invisible back roads that serpentined the Šar Mountains.

I assumed it was dawn. I had no way of knowing, of course, but the darkness which had blanketed me for the first — what? hours? days? — of my journey had given way to a dull light, a golden crepuscular insistence that permeated my hood. When I opened my eyes, I could now see the inside of the bag, the coarse lines of the fabric. This was my horizon, my sunrise. This was how I defined my world.

I tried to adjust my arms to relieve the pain in my shoulders and lower back. Nothing worked. I could not move my arms enough to make a difference, and ran the risk with every unnecessary motion of falling to one side or the other and making the situation worse.

More distressing than the pain in my back, though, was the wrenching of each breath. We are used to it, this automatic function, this breathing, that when we have to work at it, apply conscious effort, it brings about the most deadening hum to the soul. Within this hood, no breath came free. Everyone was bought and sold, was haggled over. There were no bargains to be had.

If my hands had been free, I could have at least pried my fingers through the bottom of the hood and pulled it back from the skin, just enough to capture an occasional fresh breath. But I had no such luxury. You had to hand it to these guys; they'd even found a way to squeeze the joy out of breathing.

Where I was, I could not say, although it seemed a safe bet that I was somewhere in the Šar Mountains. Where I was going, I couldn't even begin to speculate. They could have killed me right away (they had me defenceless, hunched down in the burnt-out pine) and thrown me onto the warehouse of corpses that had become Kosovo. Instead, they chose to spare me.

This was business as usual, wasn't it? Exodus and explosion ... again. For what *was* this captivity if not another kind of escape? Certainly, I'd avoided Death, and who knows, perhaps I was already on freedom's path. In any case, exodus is a process and not a specific outcome; it doesn't necessarily bring deliverance. Just ask the Jews.

As for the explosions, they were constant now. Mostly distant rumblings, like thunder growling at the door. Sometimes, though, a shell would land close enough to the truck that the driver would swerve to one side and come sliding to a stop, throwing me forward once again on my face. Thank goodness my nose was already beyond destruction, since that was what was regularly breaking my fall. These sudden stops were usually followed by the sound of a shell pounding into the ground nearby, as a rain of dirt and stones and leaves and other debris showered down on my back. Then I'd be stuck, my face plastered against the dented metal bed of the truck, squirming to right myself like an inverted turtle.

And throughout it all, my captors barely spoke to me. They had interrogated me briefly on the mountaintop, and I had answered their questions in the most basic Albanian, trying to avoid any phrases that would reveal telltale Serbian gutturals (and fully expecting, quite honestly, to be shot at any moment). Somehow — perhaps it was the thread-worn UÇK field jacket that threw them off? — they made a decision quite quickly to spare me. They'd given no such consideration to Veton Dardani. They'd shot the boy without hesitation as he crept toward them, his hands raised in surrender, cooing softly to them in perfect, pleasant Albanian. The bullet struck him in the chest and he spun when it hit him before falling to the ground. He landed on his hands and knees, shrieking in a most bestial and disturbing way, and then began gasping for breath, a sure sign that the bullet had punctured his lung.

He crawled forward on his hands and knees, his eyes wide with terror, desperately trying to recover his breath, as one of the UÇK guys marched up to him and held a pistol against the back of his head. A moment later, a bullet put Veton Dardani out of his misery.

I had not cried when Dobra Beba disappeared for good, or when Tristina and I were torn apart. When my mother wrote me to tell me that Brati had gone missing in Bosnia and was presumed dead, my eyes remained dry. In my short time, I'd seen such atrocities, such horrors — women raped and tortured, children slaughtered like pigs — things that would reduce more sober men to tears. For me, nothing. But when I saw Veton Dardani on his hands and knees, begging for one last gulp of air, asking God, in his Infinite Mercy, for one more crack at life, his eyes wide with innocence and death, I had to steel myself. There would be no tears for Veton Dardani — that would be suicide — but I must tell you: my heart broke for that boy.

Without a second thought, the ape that had killed Veton Dardani came toward me, barking orders in rough Albanian. He pushed me to the ground, alive with the smell of soil and rotting leaves, and as he pinned me down with a hard knee to my back, another guy bound my wrists and covered my head with this curious hood they seemed to have brought for the specific purpose of adding to my misery.

At least the walk was downhill. The ground itself was still wet from the rain, and without the benefit of my eyes and arms, it was difficult to keep my footing. But, as I quickly learned, falling down only earned me a kick to the head or ribs. I became a blind tightrope walker: cautious, determined, and completely at the mercy of Mother Luck.

43

"**LET US PRAY** to the glorious God who has delivered you."

I found myself drifting in and out, increasingly drawn to the Kosovo field of my imagination. By this time, I had been bundled up in the back of the truck for at least two days. I had not eaten or drunk the entire time, had not even been provided with an opportunity to use a toilet: I was swaddled in my own filth.

"I am sorry, Miloš Obilić, but I do not feel like praying today."

"Not feel like praying? One should always feel like praying. It is how you connect to God; it is how you connect to everything."

Miloš Obilić was kneeling before me, at the point where imagined reality and the darkness of my hood converged. His hands were upturned to the heavens and he spoke without anger. He never lost his temper, which made him, I suspect, an even more fearsome warrior.

"Oce nash, izhe jesi na nebesjeh, Da svjatitsja imja Tvoje…"

My Obilić was washed in an aurulent haze, the morning sun shining from his helmet and visor, his mail and breastplate, his gauntlets — all a certain shade of gold — that created the illusion (an illusion of an illusion) that he was both here and not here.

"Da pridet carstvije Tvoje; da budet volja Tvoja…"

If my delusions were to be believed, Kosovo fields were gentler, vastly more pastoral, than one might assume. You must understand, every Serbian child is brought up on stories of this place, fairy tales of mythic knights and black-hearted Turks. One comes to imagine a desolate place, a barren desert of stones and dirt, devoid of vegetation or any semblance of life.

"Jako na nebesi i na zemlji, Hleb nash nasushni dazd nam dnes…"

The field itself is almost in the geographic centre of the region called Kosovo and sits on the edge of the town of Kosovo Polje, a suburb (to use a Western term that may not exactly transfer to this context) of Priština. At the start of the Troubles, Kosovo Polje had been home to a large population of ethnic Serbs. Perhaps as many as a quarter of the townspeople claimed allegiance to the ancient House of Lazar. In the lead-up to the war, kidnappings and assassinations were common as Christians and Muslims strove to take control of this worthless little city.

"I ostavi nam dolgi nashja, Jakozhe i mi ostavljajem dolzhnikom nashim; I nevovedi nas vo iskushenije; No izbavi nas ot lukavago…"

Today, Nexhmije Gjinushi, a massive medieval rampart rises from the crest of the low hill that overlooks the battlefield. A picture of it hangs on the wall of every grade-school classroom in the country. Known as the Gazimestan Memorial — the word roughly translates to mean "the meeting place of heroes," and implies a point of transformation and ascension — the tower is a lasting monument to distrust and division, and both a challenge and a threat to anyone who looks upon it. It is here that Slobo gave his famous speech to commemorate the six-hundredth anniversary of the mythic battle between Lazar and Murad. He spoke of the "resolve, bravery, and sacrifice that was present here in the field of Kosovo in the days past" and called on Serbs everywhere to ensure that the memory of heroic sacrifice made in this field would live forever. His words were read as code by Serbs and Muslims alike: the battle was on again.

"Jako Tvoje jest Carstvo i sila i slava, Oca i Sina, i svjatoga Duha, ninje i prisno, i vo vjeki vjekov,

Amin."

Miloš Obilić pushed himself to his feet. He moved slowly, as befit a man who had lived on the edge of reality for almost seven hundred years. He took a deep breath and then executed a short series of deep knee bends. "Have I told you," he began, raising and lowering himself methodically, "the story, Young Knight, of the eve of the great battle, how I stood up to the boastings of that traitor Vuk Branković and vowed to personally slay Murat Hüdavendigâr or die in the attempt?"

"Most certainly. You have only four or five stories, and I've heard them each a dozen times or more."

"And so I've told you of how I lay on the fields of blood in wait for the Turkish Sultan, only to rise from the corpses and cut his head off with a single stroke of my sword?"

"Been there, done that, Obilić, a hundred times."

"And how Prinze Lazar himself commissioned me."

"Yes, yes, Miloš Obilić. You have the disadvantage of existing in only myth and song: the marrow of your life is indeed rich, but it would never make a feast for dogs."

Miloš Obilić stood upright and stretched his arms over his head. "We had a good fight here, Puppy. We fought for the Holy Golden Cross of God and Freedom. You know that. Certain, these hills are rich with minerals — lead, zinc, silver, chrome, nickel, andesite, basalt, granite, limestone, marble, and gold — and this point, Young Prince, this exact spot, marks the crossroads of the Balkans, the point where East meets West in brotherhood and battle. But we did not fight for material gain. We'd made a pact with God. We fought for honour and to secure for all Serbians a seat among the Sainted Martyrs of Heaven."

Obilić bent down and picked up a stone. He examined it closely, then stood up again and surveyed the sky. He pointed to a cluster of limestone boulders nestled in the green grass not five metres from where we stood.

"This is the spot where the battle began. Murad's *akıncı* came at us first, attacking a division of foot soldiers ten-thousand-strong under the leadership of Vlatko Vuko. A good man, Vuko, honourable in battle — but a devil with the ladies..."

Obilić smiled distinctly and threw the stone. It just missed a blackbird flitting through the morning air.

"They were crazy as shit, these *akıncı*, mounted horsemen who descended on us with no thought to their own safety or the safety of their steeds. Their aim was to terrify our troops and produce pandemonium. Vlatko Vuko stood strong, and his men followed suit. Although they outnumbered our division two to one, the *akıncı* were repulsed."

Obilić turned and pointed to a cluster of bushes at the mid-point of the field.

"Right there, Little Dog, that is the place where an archer's arrow felled Bayezid, Murad's eldest son, who sat on his father's right-hand side at the battle's outset. Bayezid had raised his visor momentarily to clear his head, and at that exact instant, the arrow struck him, piercing his eye. Could there be a clearer sign from God as to whom His chosen people were? Bayezid fell from his mount and, upon regaining his footing, grabbed the arrow in both fists and — I saw this myself, mind, or I would have never believed it — tore the arrow from his head, extracting it eyeball and all. Without another thought, he regained his mount and threw himself back into battle. I must confess, I was never fond of Bayezid, but he was an excellent soldier, I have to give him that, and he comported himself admirably in battle that day."

Obilić walked up the hill a short distance, then turned around, and walked back toward me.

"This is the exact spot, *the exact spot*, where John of Palisna fought both Savci Bey and his lover Andronicus, the son, no less, of the Byzantine emperor himself. The three stood hand-to-hand, armed with heavy swords and shields emblazoned with, alternately, the cross and the crescent, for over two hours — it exhausted me just to watch them struggle — without a decisive blow ever being struck. In the end, they all fell to the ground, beyond exhaustion, and had to be carried off: John, by a contingent of Knights Hospitallers; Savci Bey and Andronicus, by a harem of young and hairless eunuchs."

Quite suddenly, Miloš Obilić leaned his head back and roared to the sky, a sound halfway between terror and joy. He ran to me, his usually mad look risen to an even higher level of insanity, grabbed me by my shoulders, and shouted: "Look well upon Kosovo Polje, My Son; look well! History lives in this place. It reaches forwards and backwards and up and down and to one side and to the other. Kosovo is history, Little Prince, and History is nothing but Kosovo."

Then he calmed himself and begun to hum softly, a lilting, distressing melody perhaps Sephardic in origin, but certainly as ancient as these green hills. The humming grew in intensity, and presently he began to sing in a language I could identify as somewhat Serbic, yet neither the words nor even the sounds were completely recognizable.

He droned this way for several minutes before grabbing my hand.

"Come, Vida, do not be intimidated. The glory of ancestors should not prevent a man from winning glory for himself. Sing with me. Sing the Song of History. It is your song, Vida. It is the song, my son, of Kosovo."

"I'm too tired to sing, Miloš Obilić, and frankly, the music turns my stomach."

There is no Gazimestan Memorial in the Kosovo Field of my hallucinations. It is pristine and green and always captured in the morning light. There are farmhouses in the distance and, just beyond the hill, a grove of walnut and mulberry trees. A breeze is always wafting in from the west, disturbing slightly the hair and brightly coloured shawl of the Kosovo Maiden, who stands forever at the edge of my vision, her arms folded, her back towards me...

44

"IT'S YOUR LUCKY DAY."

"Not now, Miloš Obilić."

Deprived of sleep and food and water, of any real visual stimulation, I had lost my capacity to distinguish reality from hallucination. When I heard the voice, I assumed it was Obilić reaching out to me again from the void.

"Miloš Obilić?"

"Or whoever you are: Boshko Yugovich, Srdja Zlopogledja, the traitor Vuk Branković."

I was drifting further and further from reality. I could not guess how many days we had been travelling. I was hoarse from thirst and way past the point of hunger, reaching a kind of ascetic discomfort that brought with it a consciousness all its own.

The voice outside the hood continued to speak.

"Who I am doesn't matter to you, Lucky. I am the one who comes to tell you that we are not going to kill you. Yet."

"Thank you, sir. Can you possibly extend a further courtesy and untie my hands?"

The owner of the voice grunted by way of laughing.

"I don't want you to get too comfortable, Lucky. You won't be staying with us much longer."

By the smell of things, we had stopped to take on petrol. I assumed I was talking to the driver, who had decided to extend to me the minimum of human courtesies: small talk.

"Can you at least tell me where I am going?"

"You have been summoned, Lucky. You are going to places no Serb has gone before."

I thought of protesting, of proclaiming my pretend Albanian heritage, but realized it was of no use.

"There are many places where no Serb has been: Bangladesh, the Arctic Circle, paradise. Tell me then, good brother, where is this Serb going?"

"All in good time, friend; just know that Korbi Artë has taken an interest in you. That is either very good for you or very, very bad."

Korbi Artë! See how the threads of my testimony keep drawing together, Nexhmije Gjinushi. I knew of him, of course, through military briefings and Jadranko Kovač's ravings, which had the UÇK leader associated with everyone from al-Qaeda to the Bask Euskadi Ta Askatasuna. At a time when it seemed that anyone with a patriotic uniform and odd haircut could become, with the help of the right photographer, a military leader, Korbi Artë had distinguished himself as a man of some intelligence and acumen, who, in his interviews with the press, was just as inclined to quote Nietzsche and Sun Tzu as spout political rhetoric.

"Korbi Artë? What would he want with me? I'm less than insignificant. I am a fragment of a molecule…"

"You are insignificant, Lucky, that much is true, but useful nevertheless. Korbi Artë needs prisoners, and you'll do fine."

"Prisoners?"

"Trade-zies, Lucky. Some of theirs for some of ours. All in good sport. We're not animals, after all."

"I'll have to take your word for that, Brother, unless you are willing to take this damned hood off."

And there it was. The gods had changed their plans. That I was now to be part of a prisoner exchange seemed hardly just. I'd only been a captive for a matter of days. Surely there were others more worthy than I? It's a strange world, Nexhmije Gjinushi; it's a strange, sick, fucked-up world, my dear.

And so we continued, and by now the roads, which had never been good to begin with, were getting considerably worse. At times, it seemed we were traversing a collection of potholes rather than an actual road, and we now made regular stops as the driver and his passenger (I was almost sure by this time there were two of them) worked to dig the truck out of yet another mudbank.

Comfort was simply out of the question. I had given up trying to maintain my balance sitting up and had now allowed myself to flop to one side, where my head was left unprotected and was also the primary point of contact with the bed of the truck. After one particularly violent pothole, my head rose up impossibly high and slammed down again, my mouth smashing into the ledge of the flatbed. Immediately, a warm liquid flowed across my lips and I could taste my own blood. I savored the tang. It was the first sustenance I'd had in days.

We were for the most part going up, although steep inclines were often followed by shorter, steeper declines. Up, down, left, right — it was meaningless to me. I had drifted beyond almost all level of thought. Even Miloš Obilić had abandoned me. And that's why I cannot be certain when the first shell struck. It wasn't the sound of the bomb going off that hammered me into reality; it was the abrupt stop of the vehicle. I could hear the truck engine revving and felt the back end slide as the tires spun in the mud. Another shell landed even closer, and I felt the rush of debris around me and the sound of shrapnel slicing through the air. The driver and his comrade were yelling at one another inside the cab, and I heard the passenger door open. The engine revved again, and the tires screamed as they strove to get a grip. Finally the truck lurched forward, stopped briefly for the passenger to hop in, then took off quickly. The driver was racing madly now, as I slid around the flatbed like a load of garbage, and then — a thunderous howl that vibrated through my bones. The force of the blast lifted me clear out of the vehicle and deposited me on my backside in a thick pool of mud.

I listened carefully. I could no longer hear the truck engine and silent too were my captors. In fact, the silence only intensified the sense of dread that had overtaken me: surely another shell was on its way? It is the spaces between the moments that are the worst.

I did a quick inventory. Arms, legs, penis. In place and functioning as far as I could tell. My neck seemed intact, and I was able to turn it from one side to the other. All good. I rolled over onto my side, struggled to my feet, and crouching as low as possible, made my way forward. I was aware of the absurdity of my situation. For all I knew, I was skulking through an open plain, surrounded by hostile soldiers with guns at the ready. But I was compelled to move and was consumed with the belief that, if I could find the truck again, everything would be okay.

I continued creeping forward, feeling with my feet for any clue that might lead me back to the truck. A few steps forward and with my boots I felt a tire lying on its side. It's possible that this tire had come from another vehicle — of course, I could have been standing in the middle of a junkyard full of tires. I took a few more tentative steps and came upon a large piece of metal, which I soon ascertained was a vehicle door.

And in this manner I plodded forward, mentally reconstructing the truck a piece at a time. Eventually, I came across the flatbed, blown free from the chassis and lying half embedded in the mud. Just beyond that I found the head and partial torso of one of my captors. Whether it belonged to the driver or his passenger, I had neither the means nor the inclination to discover.

I made my way back toward the bed of the truck but must have listed off to one side, because try as I might, I could not rediscover it. The more I looked for it, the more disoriented I became. I had come to the edge of the road, as the sand and mud embankment gave way to stones and low shrubs, and tried to follow this natural line back to my starting point, but soon the road edge came to an abrupt halt. I almost walked into the trunk of a large tree and turned to make my way around it. As I seemed to circle it and circle it, without ever coming back to the road, dread descended. My only hope for survival was to be spotted by someone — anyone, friend or foe.

As I stumbled to regain the road, I felt I was wandering further into the labyrinthine forest. In my panic I called for Miloš Obilić, but being the most unreliable sort of delusion, he did not appear. Then I called for my mother and my father, I called for St. Sava, Prince of Zahumlje and founder of the Holy Orthodox church, and for Jesus and the Holy Martyrs. I called to Sventevith, the four-headed god of war and divinity, called to him in his many names — Svetovid and Suvid, Svantovít and Zvantevit, Vid — and implored St. Jude the Apostle to deliver me from my lost cause. I tried to slow my breathing and find a point of meditation, to summon the Buddha himself to deliver me to the Path of Enlightenment, or any path for that matter. I even prayed to the God of the Albanians, to Allah, conjuring as many of his attributes that would come to mind:

Ar-Rahmaan, the Compassionate One; Al-Muqaddim, the Expediter; Ar-Raheem, the Merciful; Ar-Rasheed, Guide to the Right Path; and on and on until my voice was raspy.

And still I crept forward into the woods, fighting like a ram through the thickets and brambles that clung to me like leeches, over fallen logs and rotting stumps, through fetid bogs that threatened to swallow me whole, and on until I took one hesitant step in the wrong direction. My foot seemed to come to rest on a strong log, but as I shifted my weight forward, the log cracked in half and I tumbled down a steep embankment. I rolled like an acrobat, careening first off a rocky finger and then off the hard stump of a tree. I came to rest in some nettled shrub, almost face down, with my legs and neck entangled in the branches. The more I struggled to free myself, the more imprisoned I became. I stopped for a moment to catch my breath. I intended to rest for a moment only, but I found myself instead beginning to weep. Perhaps it was out of frustration, perhaps desperation. For the record, Counsellor, a single tear soon gave way to another and another, and before I could catch myself I was wailing like an old woman, weeping and groaning in a most unseemly, self-pitying way, and calling out, between schoolgirl sobs, a single word which brought me a comfort of sorts, a single collection of syllables that both defined my misery and articulated my one slim hope for redemption.

Tristina!

The next thing I can remember, Nexhmije Gjinushi, is awaking under a mountain of comfort: a crisp linen sheet, three or four bright quilts, my head on a thick, goose-down pillow. It took me a moment to realize: I could see! And somehow I had made my way into a small, tidy bedroom. How I'd arrived here, I could not say.

I looked around the room. My guess was that it belonged to

a little girl. It was sparsely furnished. My legs from the knees down hung off the end of the bed, which seemed better suited for a fairy-tale dwarf than a man. Other than that, there was only a wooden chair in one corner and, in the other, a small dresser with a mirror propped up on it. Beside the mirror, an antique hairbrush with an ornate silver handle and a collection of toy ponies. The walls were bare except for two large posters of the Backstreet Boys.

I adjusted my position slightly and felt an intense pain shoot from my elbow to my shoulder and down right to my groin. I turned to my left and realized that my arm, from the wrist to the elbow, was secured in a makeshift splint.

"Water." The word came from me automatically. "Please someone, water."

I waited in silence. I spoke again, louder. "Hello? Someone? Please, water!"

A moment later, a primordial woman entered, her wrinkled skin absorbed inside a colourful kerchief. She looked at me sternly: "No Serb!" She ordered, in a thick Albanian accent. And first held her fingers to her lips and then shook her fists — suggesting to me some dire consequence if I continued speaking in this manner.

"*Ajo e gjyshes në rregull. I flasin shqip,*" I responded, assuring her that I could speak her language.

She carried with her a ceramic tray and placed it on the foot of the bed. She took a glass of water from the tray, and propping my head gently with one hand, she brought the water to my lips. I drank fully, deeply, the entire glass. The old woman let my head fall back to the pillow. She set the glass back on the tray and retrieved what appeared to be a small cylinder, but which I quickly came to realize was a hypodermic needle.

Placing one hand on my forehead to soothe me, she began to sing, using words that I could not understand but a melody that seemed at once foreign yet familiar. Gently, almost lovingly, the grandmother pulled up the right sleeve of my borrowed nightshirt and rubbed my arm to lift a vein. She continued rubbing intently for a moment, then pressed the needle into my arm. I felt nothing except a warmth that immediately emanated from my arm across the universe of my body. I had tried heroin only one time before, but knew enough that, when the brown dog came calling, you were wise to simply stand back and let it enter.

I doubt you've ever tried heroin, Nexhmije Gjinushi, but I can tell you the feeling is simply indescribable. A delicious, orgasmic presence that takes over your body and connects you with, perhaps for the only time outside of heaven, your soul. It's as if the volume on every pleasure centre you have is suddenly turned to high. It is like being planted in the most wondrous dream you've ever had and feeling as if you have always been there and always will be, and yet knowing completely that it is not a dream but a new reality that is exponentially greater than any dream world or any reality you have experienced or ever will. It's like glimpsing the face of God, realizing that you must cling to the memory forever, as you will never see His visage again.

And that's when you come down, which is not unlike descending to hell. Every fibre and molecule hurts, vibrating not just in physical pain, but in a genuine spiritual angst as you realize you will never feel such a glorious high again, outside of heaven.

And then you sleep, deep delta sleep, without dreams, your breathing slowing, your body as close to death as it can get.

And the only thing you recall when you wake up is the depth of the silence, and then the strains of a soft melody, rising in the distance like smoke from the darkest corner of the universe.

How long was I under? I could not tell. I know that, when I finally awoke, golden sunlight flowed through the tiny window. The cumbersome splint on my left arm had been replaced by two smaller bandages: one on my wrist and the other wrapped around my elbow. And, on the small wooden chair in the corner, sat a child. It was nine or ten, its mouse-brown hair clipped short. It had large Asiatic eyes that stared at me, deeply blinking every moment or so, as if it were watching an exotic pet snake or lizard in a terrarium. The child wore a rough, red sweater, with patches dutifully darned over the holes in the arms and collar, and a pair of yellow corduroy pants. I assumed it was a girl, because of the hairbrush and Backstreet Boys poster, but nothing about the child's appearance completely assured me of its sex. Was this one of the *virgjëresha* Boz had spoken of?

"*Mëngjes i mirë, motra e vogël*," I greeted her, as pleasantly as I could.

Immediately she leapt to her feet and ran from the room, screaming for her father.

A moment later, a sad-eyed man entered the room carrying a plastic plate with some bread and cheese on it, his curious daughter weaving between his legs, well out of my reach. The man placed the plate of food on the dresser, then spoke to me firmly but not without a certain warmth.

"I have welcomed you into my house as guest; I expect you to honour my courtesy."

He spoke in a most straightforward manner, and I responded in kind.

"I honour it and more, my brother. I owe you my life."

My host snorted and shook his head.

"We owe each other nothing beyond common courtesy."

His name, as I learned, was Fisnik Valboni. His daughter — indeed, little Didi was a girl — had discovered me while the two of them were searching for stray sheep in the woods that ran along the edge of their property. Not a tall man by any means but as broad as two Zavida Zankovićs, Fisnik carried me two kilometres on his back, and brought me to his modest farmhouse to tend to my wounds and pull me back from death's greedy arms. I was so severely dehydrated that my skin was dry as paper; my left elbow had become completely dislocated (whether from the fall in the woods or the explosion on the road, I had no way of telling) and was likely broken, as was the wrist; my stagnating shit and piss had burned deep holes into my skin, while the rope burns on my wrists, my split lip, and the sackcloth sore on my chin had all festered and were boiling with pus. A full seven days had passed since he pulled me from the nettles. Gjyshe (who was in fact one of Fisnik's maiden aunts) had nursed me back to health, dressing my wounds with a herbal poultice made of sheep's waste and *lule basani*, and spoon-feeding me an oat-mash pabulum commonly sold as feed for horses.

As to the heroin — I had not dreamt it. Gjyshe applied it at regular intervals to keep me in a semi-catatonic state and allow the healing process to work.

"But heroin, Fisnik? Excuse me, but I must say it hardly seems in keeping with the rustic image of the mountain farmer."

I was enjoying my first full meal in weeks — hard bread, herbed goats' cheese, wild greens, and boiled lamb — and slowly fermenting in the heat of the Valboni kitchen.

Fisnik shrugged. "These woods, they are full of many things. Some good, some bad, and most neither good nor bad."

"With all due respect, my host, that is not really an answer."

Fisnik dropped his head and looked at me with his sad eyes, a Balkanoid Buster Keaton. "Look, you are sitting in the midst of one of the most significant drug routes in Europe if not on Earth, Davidi. Drugs flow from the poppy fields of Afghanistan, Iran, and Pakistan through Turkey and into Kosovo. This is the heroin warehouse for central Europe. The sheep, they're nice to eat, and keep you warm with their wool and fat with their milk. But heroin, it's how we pay the bills."

Fisnik began to lay out for me his theory of Heroin Everything, how the Communist invasion of Afghanistan, the collapse of the Soviet Union, the dissolution of Yugoslavia, the wars in Slovenia, Croatia, Bosnia, Kosovo — everything — could be traced back to the heroin trade.

"It's a four-hundred-billion dollar business, Davidi. You can see why Clinton would want a piece of it. Forget about what you've heard about geopolitical ideologies in conflict, East versus West, Muslim versus Christian. The war here is about one thing, and mark my words, Davidi, the fighting across the region will continue for as long as heroin is produced and people need to find an escape."

And so, Nexhmije Gjinushi, that is how I came to stay with Fisnik Valboni and his small family. As I regained my strength and health, I was able to help Fisnik around his farm and learned many things in a short time.

Sheep, for example, have excellent hearing but, despite seeing in colour, bad eyesight. They suffer from a limited field of vision (often impeded by the wool on their face) and poor depth perception. For these reasons — combined with their timorous nature — sheep avoid shadows and high contrasts, and like the souls of the survivors of near-death experiences, they prefer to head toward the light. They are sensitive creatures too, and do not like the feel of water on their feet or of the wind at their backs. Given their druthers, sheep will always move into the wind and uphill, and Fisnik's dog had to forcibly drive them back down the mountain every night to get them safely into their paddocks. Sheep are also like turtles, in that if they fall on their backs they cannot right themselves. They will lie that way squirming until they die unless some helping hand comes along and rights them.

I also learned about my host, Fisnik. A man of quiet dignity, he made his living raising sheep and using every part of them as efficiently as he could: the wool, the milk, the meat, even the teeth and entrails and hooves — he had a market for all of them. On the side, he worked for the heroin traders and UÇK, acting as a guide and occasional driver, helping convoys of trucks make their way through overgrown roads and trails that ran like arteries just below the mountain canopy.

His wife, Mirjeta, had died from a bronchial infection while Didi was still an infant, and another daughter had contracted encephalitis from a tick bite. The infection was unusually severe, and she had succumbed to it after six agonizing days in the paediatric ward of the Priština University Hospital. Gjyshe (I never learned her real name) had moved in a short time later to help raise the daughter and care for the widowed Fisnik.

Fisnik was an ethnic Albanian and his people had shared these mountains with Serbs, Gorani, Roma, and Turks for centuries, while his grandfather on his mother's side was a full-blood Serb whose own great-great-great grandfather had forsaken the Patriarch Arsenije's Grand Migration, opting instead to stay put in Kosovo, a decision that six generations of ancestors had no reason to question. Since the Troubles began, Fisnik told me, his Serbian cousins had all been driven from their homes and fled north, to the refugee camps of Novi Pazar. The UÇK gunmen were one thing, but what really terrified Fisnik's cousins was the inevitable infiltration of KFOR troops — NATO's Kosovo land troops.

"As they saw it, the Albanians were a known commodity; but could my cousins really trust that a coalition that has bombed them relentlessly, killed their children as they slept, murdered their grandmothers as they cowered in their dark little rooms — could they really trust that these people would now march into Kosovo and protect them? No, America hates Serbs more than we Albanians do. My cousins had it right. They had to get while the getting was good."

When it came to religious practice, Fisnik was reluctant to go into much detail. He was not being diplomatic, mind, but simply felt that his faith was far too complicated to describe to an outsider.

"I could explain it to you, my friend, but that would entail me understanding it myself."

He explained that he was a Bektashizmi, a member of a mystical Islamic order somewhat related to (if not derived from) Sufism, yet vastly more subtle. The main tenet was the veneration of the Trinity made up of Allah, Muhammad, and Ali and a disposition that questioned existing authority and accepted the reality of other mystical experiences. Fisnik, for example, did not pray to Mecca, instead preferring to commune with his God before a small shrine in his sitting room, a shrine that included a plaster statue of Hajji Wali, the Persian saint who founded the Bektashi order, and a chipped ceramic mosaic, clearly Byzantine in origin, featuring the Holy Blessed Virgin, her hands outstretched in wonder.

"Personally, I must tell you, Fisnik, I have given up on religion. I studied for some time to become a pretend Buddhist, but now I am content being a closet atheist. Although, I'm also rather fond of football."

Fisnik nodded. "It's easy to give up on God. He is not evidently reliable. But then I've come to accept that, while faith in God makes all things possible, it makes nothing easy."

And so my health returned, and to bide my time, I set to work for Fisnik Valboni, Sufi mystic, sheep farmer, heroin runner. I repaired his fences, chopped his firewood, drew water from his well, tended his sheep. The last bit I particularly enjoyed, and quickly came to understand why the great monolithic religions of the world — Judaism, Christianity, and Islam — all emerged when shepherding was a legitimate career option. It was both rhythmic and unpredictable, like watching waves roll across a lake, and therefore highly meditative. I fancied that I could easily become used to this life. One needed only a pastoral disposition and enough intelligence to out-think your charges. It didn't take a lot of investment up front: some sheep (I'm sure Fisnik would have spotted me a couple, if I'd asked), a smart dog or two, a hooked staff (largely for effect; the dogs did most of the actual work keeping the sheep in line), and perhaps a cloak. It was a far lot easier than dealing drugs or working the black markets and vastly more productive than soldiering.

I spent more and more time in the hillocks and pastures just beyond Fisnik Valboni's farm, with Engjell, the cheerful and somewhat lazy mutt charged with marshalling and protecting Fisnik's herd. Part Qen Šar, an ancient breed of Albanian mountain dog, and part God-Knows-What, Engjell made for the best of all companions. As content to lie at my side, his head resting on my ankles, as to run about pointlessly, he nevertheless kept one sleepy eye on our charges and, being something of a bully at heart, enjoyed snapping them into line whenever he saw fit. Most of all, he was an excellent listener, glancing up at me every so often to reassure me he was paying attention, flunking his tail heavily once or twice whenever I used his name, and nuzzling his muzzle into the crook of my ankles when he sensed emotions rising in my voice.

"I am thinking of writing her again, Engjell, to bring her up to date on my curious adventure."

Engjell's tail instinctively slapped the dirt at the sound of his name.

"She must be sick with worry by now, wondering if I am ever going to come home. Be brave, my little flower — that's what I would tell her, Engjell. Be brave my little flower, I am thinking of you and longing to be in your arms again."

Engjell peered up at me.

"What, Engjell? What? A little sappy perhaps, but I am still young and allowed my romantic excesses. Besides, you've been in love before, my friend, I'm sure. You know that it reduces a man to a child, it unsexes him at the same time as it turns him into a complete sex machine."

Engjell yawned and I could see the black spackling on the pink skin inside his mouth. Qen Šar are big dogs, and unlike other herding dogs, which get by on their wits and a neurotic tenacity, Qen Šars have a vicious streak and a reputation as fierce brawlers (in fact, they were a favourite breed in the dog-fight clubs of Moscow, Bucharest, and Beograd). Although as much mutt as anything, Engjell had the Qen Šar size and colouring — thick reddish brown fur with black mottling — and a primitive glint at the back of his eyes that suggested the bestial power that lay just beneath his cosy surface.

"Do I bore you with my talk, Engjell? My Tristina doesn't interest you? I always thought that everyone liked a good love story, the sadder and more desperate the better. But it will end well, my friends, everyone is destined to find their soulmate, and no god is as cruel as to keep true lovers apart forever."

Engjell suddenly lifted his head. He sniffed the air intently.

"What is it, Engjell? a fox? wolves?"

Engjell continued sniffing, then lumbered to his feet, his ears forward, his tail alert. He began a low growl and pawed slowly toward our flock.

"What is it, boy? What's up?"

Engjell took a couple more delicate steps, then dropped to his belly, his lips pulled back, the hair on his spine and tail on edge.

"Go boy, go! Kill! Kill!"

Spurred by my words, Engjell took off and ran to the far edge of the flock, just at the point of the treeline. Already sensing Engjell's anxiety, the sheep were now in an accelerating frenzy, each one pushing towards the centre of the flock and the relative security the sea of wool brought them.

Engjell ran along the line of trees, barking furiously and stopping every few metres to lower his head, sniff and growl, before starting off again. I scoured the woods, but could see nothing, and decided it was most prudent to draw my service revolver.

"What is it, boy?" I climbed onto a rock to get a better look. "Who's out there?"

Engjell looked back at me, all business now. He hesitated for a moment, looking to the woods then back to me one more time. He cautiously penetrated the forest, his dark fur quickly blending into the shadows and trees. And then all was silent. In that moment of anticipation, I caught something out of the corner of my eye, and turning to my left, I saw her for the first time. She was positioned at the forest's edge, perhaps 150 metres from my vantage point, very close to where Engjell had hesitated only moments before. Although her back was turned toward me, I could see her elbows protruding from her side and could tell that she was standing with her arms folded across her chest. She wore a bright, old-fashioned cloak — festooned with intricate needlework — not unlike those you see on the Roma women Sunday mornings as they wander the streets of Beograd. The collar of the cloak went halfway up the back of her head, and strands of her hair spilled over the collar and down her back. From where I stood, it could have easily been Tristina (save for the raven-coloured hair) and I had an urge to call her name. But that would have been too foolish to consider.

"Miss?" I called hesitantly in Albanian. She did not budge. "Hello?" I tried in Serb. Nothing. Not a muscle moved.

I lowered my head and stepped off the rock. When I looked up again, she was gone and Engjell was lumbering toward me, his fat tongue drooling from his mouth, his expression now careless, his only concern that I would be pleased to see him.

"Engjell, where'd she go? The woman, Engjell, what has happened to her?"

45

I RETURNED TO that same spot every day for the rest of the week, Nexhmije Gjinushi, but saw nothing of my mysterious maiden. Fisnik was dubious from the start.

"I know we live simply, Davidi, but that does not mean we are simple people. We have TV and read books. Myself, I have a degree in organic chemistry from Universiteti i Prishtinës. We don't believe in spectres and wood nymphs. Baba Yaga doesn't chase me through the night."

"I understand completely, Fisnik, and I am not suggesting she is anything but a real woman —"

"Well that's the other part, Davidi. We don't normally have beautiful maidens hanging around in our forests. This isn't actually a hub of activity, my friend. There are no shopping malls or water parks."

"You seem to be questioning my . . . I don't know what. Sanity?"

"I am far beyond that, my friend, but that is beside the point. What I am suggesting is that you have been through a lot and are still recovering, and that both the heart and eyes are prone to play tricks on us at the best of times. You saw something, I am most certain, but a shadow or a light or a speck on your eye.

The thin mountain air, the hot sun, and the hypnotic bleating of those damn sheep did the rest."

I was prepared to give in; it was just a figment of my imagination. What else could it be? The fact that this Kosovo Maiden was an almost exact double of the Kosovo Maiden who haunted the edges of the hallucinatory Field of Blackbirds was proof enough. When confronted with the impossible, one could be certain that the heart was playing tricks.

And that was what I was entirely prepared to believe, as I set out to tend my flock in the early morning on the Sunday following St. Jovan Vladimir's feast day. It was hazy when I started off, but the warm June sun dissolved the low-lying clouds and left me with a clear and unobstructed view of the meadows, mountains, and woods. I was up in the high pastures, perhaps half a kilometre higher up than I had ever been before. The sheep settled into their ruminations quickly, while Engjell inspected the area, nose to the ground, revelling in a spectrum of scents that I could not even begin to imagine. I've heard it speculated that smells are like music to a dog, an endless fascination and captivating sensory experience that helps inform, define, and elevate canine existence. But from my own observations, I suspect that these olfactoral compositions are vastly richer than anything we humans can conjure up with a pinch of *Šaban Šaulić's novokomponovana* or a healthy dose of *Quatuor pour la fin du temps*. Deprive a human being of music and they would go about their life slightly less distracted but no worse for the wear. Deprive a dog of its sense of smell (as Pavlov's protégé Boris Babkin demonstrated in a series of experiments conducted in the waning days of the Russian Provisional Government) and it will lose interest in itself and its surroundings, and grow more and more despondent until it slips into a deep sleep. At that point, recovery is unthinkable; the dog is as good as dead.

And so Engjell swept the area, his tail held high, concentrating on the important job that lay before him. As he moved to a stand of immature pine trees on the far side of the pasture, he once again stopped and lifted his head, sniffing intently. I watched without speaking as Engjell walked toward the green pines.

Suddenly, Engjell stopped and whined. He made a circle, and then another in the opposite direction, before crouching down to slither away from the pines. After about ten metres, he turned back and examined the trees, his head now low, his tail dropped, an attitude of submission. He crouched in the tall grass and emitted a soft growl that can only be described as plaintive.

And that's when she appeared again. I saw her first through the trees, taking slow, weighted steps that ensured she remained just on the edge of my view. Then I lost sight of her, only to catch a glimpse out of the corner of my eye. She was looking at me (as near as I could ascertain in the moment my brain registered her presence), a puzzled expression on her face, as if she were trying to remember how she knew me. And then she was gone.

When I saw her again, it was far up on the edge of the trees, now standing with her back to me, her arms folded as in our first encounter. I rubbed my eyes once and then once more, but she remained in my sight. I looked around sharply, to see if there were any other Kosovo Maidens imposing themselves on the landscape. But no.

"Come," I called to Engjell. "We shall investigate." But the mutt was having none of it, and no matter how I chirped and whistled and cajoled, he would not follow me into the woods.

"Be a man, Dog! It's only an imaginary woman." Engjell dropped to his belly. I forged on without him.

Up and up I headed, always, it seemed, just missing her as she disappeared on the crest of another hillock. She had an eerie omnipresence, like one of those paintings of the Saviour where the eyes follow you wherever you go. If I lost sight of her or came to a fork in the trails, I could arbitrarily turn right or left, take a few steps, and emerge from the trees just in time to see her fade once again into the horizon.

I was fully aware of the futility of the exercise — and of the danger. These woods were full of UÇK men and drug runners. I had dodged the bullet, literally, so many times, why bother to tempt fate again? I also completely understood that in pursuing my Kosovo Maiden I was chasing a kind of madness. Every disappearance and sudden reappearance, every slow dissolve into yet another horizon, every step further into the dark and hostile woods — all of it was illusion of one kind or another. Why did I continue? We've all felt it, that compulsion that drives us forward, overtaking our willpower and undermining our judgment. Whether we're on the trail of pussy or chasing our next deal or sinking into the mud of a heroin undream or flushing out stragglers in an enemy village, every one of us sometimes shuts off our rational mind and allows ourselves to be swallowed by pure impulse. I would argue that it is an intensely meditative experience, as savoury as if one were praying on the lips of death.

And so I persevered. Eventually I lost sight of my Kosovo Maiden. I was in a shallow gully, with steep rises on all sides of me. I tried to take the path going up one slope, but the ground was too dry and crumbled as I stepped on it. I could not get traction. I tried the other direction and found the brambles simply too thick for me to pass. My one choice appeared to be a low trail, a rabbit warren really, overgrown with hawthorn and stinging nettles. I crouched down, then lay almost flat on my belly and, despite my tender elbow, pushed myself forward along the tight trail with my hands and knees, like a proper soldier. The nettles clung to me like history, and very quickly I was enveloped in a near darkness, although it was not yet midday.

A wave of panic washed over me, but I calmed myself and took stock. At this point, I had only two options: go back and try and retrace my steps (which seemed impossible, with the innumerable twists and turns my journey had taken) or forge ahead into the unknown. I was not ready to commit to either and wormed my way forward a few more centimetres. That was enough to bring a shard of light into view. I pushed forward a little more, and there was now an even larger break in the undergrowth some twenty-five metres away. I pushed forward, tearing my way through the nettles, as determined as a badger.

I emerged at the side of a dirt road. It was deserted as far as I could see, although the forest grew thick on both sides, threatening to swallow the road at any time. I walked around, studying the trees carefully for any sign of life. Then I looked down into the dust and scanned for tracks. The road was definitely in use: there were several lines of tire tracks running in both directions. I bent over a little and looked some more. There, near the side of the road, I saw what appeared to be small boot prints in the dust. I got down on my hands and knees to get a closer look and imagined myself Engjell for a moment, my muzzle to the earth, my ears and tail alert.

Yes. They were indeed boot prints! Much smaller than mine, and narrower, but boot prints nonetheless. Had I been an Indian tracker in some Karl May western, I might have been able to ascertain with confidence all sorts of valuable information. I was left to speculate: were these perhaps the prints of my elusive Kosovo Maiden?

"What are you doing, bumpkin?"

The sound of a man's voice ripped me from my investigation. I turned quickly to see two paramilitaries smirking down at me.

"Are you lost, *vella*?" the shorter of the two asked me. He had a broad flat forehead and looked vaguely like a cartoon caveman.

"In a manner of speaking."

"If you are missing some sheep, we passed some back on the road a ways." His friend was speaking now, the taller one with a perpetual smile emerging from below a moustache that would have done Stalin proud.

"Thank you, *vella*."

"Not much of a shepherd, if you get lost trying to find your strays." Happy Stalin smiled even more.

"It's not as easy as it looks, friends. I don't just sit around all day doing sit-ups and jerking off, like you army boys. I've got responsibilities."

The two men laughed, and one of them offered me a hand up.

"And why have you not joined the good fight?" Stalin was speaking now, without malice.

"First, I am a lover, not a fighter. Second, I have very carefully avoided being press-ganged and do not intend for it to happen now —" I looked from one to the other for any sudden sign of hostility. They only continued to smirk, perhaps believing they had stumbled upon a yokel simple enough to provide a few moments of diversion in their otherwise invisible day.

"And, third, I am a father, *vella*, and there is no one else to care for my daughter since my wife died . . ."

I silently apologized to Fisnik Valboni for stealing this

part of his life and then I turned away to suggest that I was experiencing a rush of emotion; curiously, as the words came out of my mouth I found myself tearing up.

The two men nodded compassionately, and my new friend Stalin put his arm on my shoulder. At first he seemed friendly, but he soon tightened his grip and forced himself directly into my view.

"Tell me, friend, do I detect a bit of a Beograd accent?" He smiled thinly.

I could do nothing but hold his look and smile back.

"Meaning?"

"Nothing friend, really. Just that there is a certain cadence to your speech, a rhythm that is rather not of here and not of us. Something more Serbian perhaps…"

Stalin's eyes narrowed as his talons dug deeper into my shoulder.

I paused for a moment, barely entertaining the thought that I had come too far to find my wandering angel to be struck down by a matter so trivial as the truth. I merely shrugged.

"Of course," I said. "*Ja sam srpski rođen i odrastao*! This coat" — I elegantly straightened the fraying lapels — "I found in a ditch. I took a wrong turn, you see, at Niš and have been wandering ever since, like the proverbial Jew. I've come to throw myself on your infinite mercy, Kosovo brother."

I tilted my head slightly and raised my eyebrows, pleading, softly I suppose, for my life.

Stalin stared me down, and suddenly exploded into laughter, little machine-gun bursts that left him and Alley Oop bent over double. I was indeed the amusing bumpkin. Eventually, Stalin threw his arm around my shoulder again.

"Come, Bo Peep. We'll walk you to your sheep. We'll share a joint. Do you have one?" He looked at me quizzically for a moment, then sounded another short laugh. He yanked a fat spliff from behind his ear.

"Yes," the Caveman piped in. "Walk with us, shepherd. We don't want to run the risk of you getting lost again. The road is only so wide, with hardly any signs at all."

And so we walked, Nexhmije Gjinushi, wary comrades in arms, united by our mutual humanity, some harsh grass and a deep-rooted desire not to get shot. Both men were from Novo Brdo, an antique city several hundred kilometres to our immediate east. They had grown up blocks from one another in the shadow of an extinct volcano and the decaying shell of a medieval Serbian fortress.

We talked of nothing. The boys recited some of the most recent jokes they'd heard, and we spent an inordinate amount of time discussing our favourite foods. They told a couple of amusing stories about one of their troop, Dita, a compulsive masturbator, who was renowned within the unit for collecting his stuff in plastic film canisters and mailing it off to his girlfriend in Priština once a month, like clockwork. What she did with it, we could only speculate.

Mostly we just got stoned and walked in relative silence.

We had walked maybe twenty-five minutes, smoking two of Stalin's harsh joints and drinking blackcurrant wine from a sheepskin flask, when we came to my new friends' base camp. I was a little apprehensive at first, concerned that I might run into someone who would recognize me from my earlier travails, but I'll save you the burden of false suspense: the men for the most part ignored me, going about their business without a second glance. Outside of a couple guys imitating sheep, I was left alone.

And there I might have parted with my new comrades, but as I set off on my own, a curious sound caught my attention.

Somewhere a radio was playing, and while it was too distant to make out the specific words — KFOR, maybe, and the optimistic use of "surrender" — something in the cadence of the voice caught my attention. I stepped off the road and walked toward a collection of tents bivouacked in a clearing by an ancient walnut tree. It seemed the voice had changed now. Gone was the singsong lilt, replaced by the perfect modulations of an Albanian news reader. The words were clearer, but I could still only make out the occasional one. And then, there it was again. That voice: slightly wheezy but measured and calming. I walked closer to the sound and came across an older recruit, perhaps in his mid-forties, sunning himself and flipping through what appeared to be collection of Paul Celan poems, a battered transistor radio at his side.

"Excuse me, brother. What are you listening to?"

"Who wants to know?"

"Only me, brother."

"And who the fuck are you?"

"No one, sir. A lost shepherd."

The reader thumbed through his book silently for a moment and then, having decided, I suppose, that I would not go away until he dealt with me, he looked up.

"It's the RTP news from Priština."

"And who, may I ask, is that speaking?"

"So many questions, nosy fellow. Be careful, or I will have you shot as a spy."

"Please, I am just curious."

The fellow paused and listened for a second.

"It's the news reader I suppose. Dževahira Koljenović or Sanela Bilalović perhaps."

"With all due respect, sir, I think it is neither Dževahira Koljenović nor Sanela Bilalović."

Then the fellow raised his eyebrows and dropped his book to his lap with a dismayed and studied sigh. He turned his head for a moment to listen to the radio, then looked at me, raising his hands in disbelief.

"Are you serious?"

I shrugged.

"Man, you've got to spend less time diddling your sheep and more time paying attention to the world around you."

"Please, sir, if you could just tell me. Who is it?"

"Why, it's Korbi Artë now, isn't it?"

"*That* is Korbi Artë?"

"Of course; any fool can tell. But you are obviously not just any fool. You've studied the art."

I paused, then pushed a little bit more.

"If you could, sir, do you have a picture?"

"Do I have a picture?"

"Yes."

"Of Korbi Artë?"

"Yes, if you don't mind."

"Why, of course, yes. I'm keeping a Korbi Artë scrapbook. I'll just get it from my dresser. It's right next to my pink diary and autographed picture of Ebru Gündes."

"Please sir, if you could. A newspaper photo, a magazine, anything."

The man sighed deeply and slammed his book on the ground.

"I will check the library." He got up out of his cot and began searching the area. A moment later, he came across a discarded *Koha Ditore*. He thumbed through the paper, scowling all the while, then finally stopped and folded it open.

"There," he said, thrusting the paper toward me. "Now if you don't mind…"

He lay back down on his cot and picked up his book.

I smiled and nodded my thanks, then looked down at the picture. Two men in ornate military uniforms, reviewing a field map and looking pensively off-camera, as if studying the future. The one man I recognized as Gjarpëri, the ferret-eyed leader of the UÇK. The other was even more familiar.

"Brother, please. One last question, if I could."

I held the photo up for him to see.

"This man, here, beside Gjarpëri — he is Korbi Artë?"

"No, that's Elsa Lila, Kosovo's entry in the 1999 Eurovision Song Contest. *Of course that's Korbi Artë!* Now, if you don't mind, I am trying to make the world a better place, one poem at a time."

The reader returned to his book, but I had to pester him still.

"Please forgive me friend, but I must ask another thing. Korbi Artë, do you know where to find him?"

"Do I know where to find my Commander-in-Chief? I suppose I could track him down."

"Then could you help me find him, sir? Could you contact him and ask him if I might speak to him?"

"Of course. And after he's finished shooting me and feasting on my brains, perhaps he'll give you a hand job as well."

"I rather suspect he won't be angry, sir. Please, could you contact your headquarters and tell them that someone wishes an audience with Korbi Artë."

"By all means. And whom shall I say is wishing to pop in and say 'Hi'? The Duke of Windsor? Bono? The Lord God Jesus Christ Himself?"

"Tell him that it is indeed a wonderful day! Tell him that his son Zavida is back from the dead."

46

I KNOW WHAT YOU'RE thinking, Nexhmije Gjinushi. Are you certain, Zavida Zanković? Korbi Artë, your father? It's almost too perfect to believe. And in truth, I didn't completely believe it myself. The man in the photo certainly looked like my father. He was stouter than when I had last seen him, and his hair, once salt and pepper, was fully grey. There were deep lines on his face, although I recall distinctly that the last time I had seen my father his face was smooth and pink. He stood there in his army fatigues, his head stuffed into a camouflage-coloured *qeleshe*, eyeing the future suspiciously, a strange severity to his aspect, a sharpness to his eyes, and a confidence to his manner that I had seen only once before, in the aftermath of the explosion at Crnilo.

But what great alchemy was this? From denigrated Serbian outcast to Albanian warlord? It's just my father's way, I suppose. If the lie is big enough, and you commit to it with your whole heart — anything can happen!

I continued to inspect the photograph in the newspaper, transfixed by this vision of my almost-father.

"Well?"

It was the reader, whose solitude I had disrupted with my questions.

"Shall we call your *father*, young prince? Or should I just go back to bed and pretend this nonsense never happened?"

I was hesitating, absently biting my finger as I considered my next course of action, when I heard a voice calling from by the road.

"Bo Peep! Come on now." I looked up. It was Stalin, holding a small lamb in the crook of his arm. "We found her, little Adelina Ismajli. Come take her before someone else makes their move."

I took a step toward Stalin and then another, then quickened my pace and met the soldier at the edge of the road. He handed me the lamb, which maaaed dutifully as it reached my arms, then he slapped me on the back.

"Follow this road just around this corner and down maybe half a kilometre. You'll come to a crossroads. Simply turn left and follow the road downhill; you'll be back to where you started soon enough."

I thanked the soldier and, holding the lamb firmly in my arms, began walking to the crossroads. I stopped a time or two, looking back to the encampment and trying to decide which direction I should choose. I thought of Korbi Artë and couldn't help but wonder if my father had done it again, working his absurd alchemy, turning base Dobroslav Zanković into pure Korbi Artë, who now stalked the Balkans like some wildcat, bringing the Serbian dogs to their knees.

A moment later I reached the main roadway and encountered a steady flow of people — civilians mostly, loaded like mules with anything they could carry — and hesitated a moment. I decided without any real thought to turn right and not left, because right, I reasoned, seemed to be taking me to a wider road, paved on both sides, and left would only take me back to where I had been.

But as I began my trek, holding my woolly charge close to my breast, a voice called to me from behind.

"Bo Peep, a moment if you will." I turned to see Stalin now standing with the reader and two heavily armed men whom I immediately took to be paramilitary police. They stood erect, their hands near their side arms, as Stalin smiled ever more broadly and gestured to me with open arms. "It's your lucky day, friend. Korbi Artë is anxious to see you! Won't you stay a while longer and enjoy our hospitality?"

47

THE REST OF THE STORY you know, Nexhmije Gjinushi. I suffered the long ride from the UÇK mountain base, seated on the back of an ancient Russian motor scooter, hanging on to Vasile Lupu with one hand, cradling little Adelina with the other.

We rode for four hours, along the rough, winding, and sometime treacherous roads of the Šar, to a housing compound where you find me now. I was held for three days under what could only be described as notional freedom before my subsequent arrest, at which point Adelina and I were immediately moved to a room across the hallway. It was almost identical to my previous room except that it had an iron bolt on the outside of the door and contained a wash basin in one corner and a tiny fridge in the other. The transfer took mere minutes.

And so, I was duly arraigned. I sat on the edge on my new bed as Vasile Lupu read the formal list of charges to me.

"Fomenting Treason. Conspiracy to Conspire. Impersonating a Prisoner of War. Impersonating an Officer of the Ushtria Çlirimtare e Kosovës…"

Et cetera.

Vasile Lupu processed me most thoroughly, detailing my name, rank, unit number, my father's name (Korbi Artë — he wrote it dutifully on the Register of Prisoners), my mother's maiden name, my date and place of birth, everything, recorded in a delicate and studied script.

At the end of my intake, Vasile Lupu slid the registration form over to me and offered his pen. I noticed that his hands were impossibly small, like those of a very young child. I suppose I could have easily grabbed the pen from Lupu's little fingers and plunged it through his sparrow ribcage, deep into his heart. Instead, I took the instrument and dutifully signed. He handed me a yellow receipt.

"Don't lose this. It includes an inventory of your personal effects, all of which will be returned to you pending your release."

"And what is to become of me, Vasile Lupu?"

"Personally, I cannot say. I have no influence on the future. My job is to ensure that the present is accounted for."

"But this father of mine — do you not perceive a certain..." I had to think carefully, and choose my words with diplomacy, "a certain imaginative energy at work?"

"I do not follow you, sir."

"It's just that my father —"

"You say he is your father, sir. I note, however, that you are currently facing charges of identity theft and fraud, with a civil suit pending in the high court, brought forward by Korbi Artë on a matter of defamation of character."

"Very well. My alleged father, don't you think he lacks a certain... consistency of manner?"

"I cannot speak to that, sir. I am not the sort given to speculation or the asking of questions that do not require answers."

And that brings me up to the here and now, Nexhmije Gjinushi. And I must say, I am feeling rather abandoned. Not a word from you now in three days, Counsellor; not a word from anyone. Beyond the twice-daily ministration of Imbrahim

Kaceli — to bring my simple meals and tend to my bedpan — I am left to myself.

I am determined to keep on writing, Nexhmije Gjinushi. That's a commitment I've made to you, and otherwise I spend my time lying on the bed in a half-sleep or stroking Adelina. Occasionally, I peek through the barred slit that passes as my window, seeing only the very tops of mountains in the distance or, closer, the garbage overflowing from a rusted green dumpster by the cinder-block wall.

Sometimes, I listen to the shells falling here and there, sometimes close, sometimes far away. I count the seconds between explosions. One could almost imagine it is thunder.

At other times I have long, imagined conversations with my father. We discuss trivial things mostly — the weather, family history, coal production in pre-industrial Wales — and he grills me on the details of the lives of the Holy Martyrs of the Serbian church.

I can hear Miloš Obilić prowling around the grounds beneath my window, tossing pebbles at the turret to get my attention and calling to me, inviting me to pray to God most high.

"I've given up praying," I tell him. "I am now a devout atheist, Miloš Obilić, and worship only those things unseen that have yet to happen."

I even held little Adelina up to the barred window as if to imply that I had my own sheep now, and would no doubt at any moment be founding my own religion.

48

AND SO, IT HAS COME to this, Nexhmije Gjinushi. The waiting game. Today, by my reckoning, we should be wrapping up our case, preparing our final arguments, practising, perhaps, the cross-examination — I was expected to speak in my own defence, was I not Counsellor? Instead, here I sit, my thumb up my ass, the pot of tea, brewed in anticipation of your arrival this morning, growing tepid.

I understand now my naiveté. You are a professional, after all, hardly one to be taken in — or frightened off — by my school-boy advances. There are larger forces at work, even in this tiny room. I forget that sometimes, Nexhmije Gjinushi. Does that endear me to you?

We Serbs have a saying (indulge me one last time, Counsellor): it is not at the table but in prison that you learn who your true friends are. By this measure, I have learned that Vasile Lupu is a true friend. He laid it all out for me this morning, Counsellor. The war, he said, is all but done. The trial, as you well know, has been postponed indefinitely now that NATO is running the show. No need to fan the flames further, I suppose. Besides, my understanding from Vasile Lupu is that judge and jury himself may not exactly be in any frame of mind to attend, let alone conduct, the proceedings.

I suppose these latest developments put your own position in flux, Counsellor. I assumed you were in the direct employ of the UÇK or some other agency of the Kosovo Provisional Government. But now that the war is almost over, NATO seems to have taken control. NATO likes to run a tight ship and already this compound is crawling with those KFOR people. A relentlessly cheery lot, these Western troops. Do they know there's a war going on? I was introduced to Captain Blum already this morning. I am hoping that he is just a temporary stand-in for you, but am beginning to fear that, with the prospects of a trial diminishing, you and I may be seeing less and less of one another. (Do not fret, my dear: I will continue to maintain these records, as I promised!)

My introduction to Captain Blum was rather lacking in formality. I was awoken by a soft hand, shaking me, and a strange, narrow face staring at me.

"Piss if you must. I've brought you some coffee."

His Albanian was rough and heavily accented. I rubbed my eyes and seemed to be staring into the face of a hairless badger. His nose was long and slender, with two black eyes set far back on the head and almost no cheeks or chin to speak of.

"Here."

He handed me a white mug. I stared at it for a moment, then blew on top. A curl of steam rose up.

"I'm trying to place the accent. Swiss? Swedish?"

The badger smiled, and for the first time I noticed he had a thin moustache. It was light, almost flesh-coloured.

"*Norsk*; Norwegian."

He smiled.

"Norwegian? Is that a country?"

"Norway, my friend. I know you've heard of it."

I had, of course, but that at that point, in that timeless

placeless place, my memory failed me. I stared blankly.

"You know, a-ha? Raga Rockers? Jokke & Valentinerne?"

I shook my head. The captain turned his head and smiled.

"Darkthrone? Burzum? Gorgoroth?"

"I fear you're playing with me now, friend."

"I am sorry, Zavida — may I call you that? — you are right. I've really come to ask you some questions."

I took a sip from my cup. Real coffee! A good roast too, with a thin cream on the top. What magic was this?

"First, may you be so kind as to tell me who you are and what the fuck you are doing here?"

His name was Reidar Blum and he was a captain with the Forsvarets Spesialkommando, a Norwegian special forces unit that was, he told me, cooperating with the UÇK as part of the NATO advance on the Serbian army. He had come to ask me about my father.

"Korbi Artë ?"

"No. Dobroslav Zanković."

"I see. What do you care to know?"

"Nothing too specific. Just tell me about him."

"Why?"

"Because I'm curious."

"I am curious as to why you are curious."

"Let's just say that we both have a vested interest in your answers."

I grunted and adjusted my blanket. I was sitting up by now, and very much in need of a toilet.

"He's just a normal fellow, I suppose, after a fashion."

"And his health, it is good?"

"I haven't seen him for months. You tell me."

"But normally, is he...sick?"

"In a manner of speaking. He suffers from a bad case of history. What is your real question?"

"Can he…is he someone to be trusted?"

"My father?"

"Yes, *your* father. Not, say, Korbi Artë."

"Is my father to be trusted?" I considered the question for a moment. "That's a tall order. He is a person better understood than trusted. He's an alchemist, you know, which, if I understand the science well enough, means he is something of a magician. Not a wizard — not supernatural — but hyper-natural, a studied conjuror pulling ever larger rabbits out of ever smaller hats. If you understand this, understand the limitations, you may not be able to trust him but you can perhaps trust yourself around him."

Captain Blum leaned back, took a pack of cigarettes out of his breast pocket, and offered it to me.

"Thank you," I said, helping myself to a half a dozen smokes. "Do you have any weed, Captain?"

The Norwegian shrugged. "I can get you some, Zavida, would you like that?"

I nodded, and leaned forward as he struck a match to light my smoke.

"I would kill for a bag of pot right now. And a shower. A bag of pot, a shower, a box of Kentucky Fried Chicken — I used to get it in Beograd, you know — and a crap. Those are my demands."

Blum laughed. "You're asking a lot, for a prisoner of war."

"Well, I'm beginning to suspect, Captain Blum, that you want something from me. And so I am taking the initiative. I always like to lead a negotiation. I feel that at strong opening position gives one the upper hand."

Captain Blum laughed again.

"Well, the shit is yours, I'll write that on paper if you like. The weed — the shower too, and I could probably throw in a run in the sack, if you like. We have a woman under contract for just such purposes. The chicken — that'll be a problem."

I folded my arms and pretended to be offended.

"You know my price, Captain. Now tell me yours. What is it you really need from me?"

The Norwegian took a moment to collect his thoughts, running his index finger across his invisible moustache. Finally, he folded his hands in his lap and looked me square in the eyes.

"Your father, is he mad?"

I took another long drag and blew a series of small smoke rings.

"Mad may be overstating the matter. Then again, it may not."

"Well, we need him to be sane. We're reaching a critical point in" — and here the captain struggled to find the right words — "negotiations. We need everybody on board."

"There are degrees of sanity, Captain, and while certain degrees are available to some of us, other degrees can be as elusive as my fried chicken. So let me put it this way. My father's problem is not with sanity or insanity; his problem is with truth. He is a man of honour, you see, and great intelligence, but hampered by an active mind that does not clearly delineate the boundaries between fiction and fact. He's not a liar — I would never say that about my own father — but he is a man, as I mentioned, of great integrity, and for men like that, a lie once uttered becomes fact. How could it be otherwise? He would not say these things if they were not true. And so I'll ask you again, Captain. What is it you want from me? What is on the table?"

"What's on the table, Zavida Zanković, is your freedom —"

It was my turn to laugh. "Freedom: that's like saying 'sanity' or 'truth.' Very relative indeed."

"Be that as it may, your relative freedom awaits you. All we need you to do is speak to your father, talk to him and tell him that the war is at its end. For the sake of Kosovo, for the sake of history, Korbi Artë needs to disappear and your father must rise once more."

49

VASILE LUPU ESCORTED ME there himself, Nexhmije Gjinushi. Down through a series of concrete corridors burrowed into the earth below the compound to a dank, lightless bunker that stunk of moisture and rat urine.

"He prefers the quiet," Lupu offered.

I shrugged, to let him know that no explanation was required.

"And the light . . . it hurts his eyes . . ."

Lupu led me to a doorway at the end of the bunker and quietly knocked. He waited a moment, then pushed the doorway open a crack. Immediately, the smell of shit hit me like a stone wall.

"Commander? Sir? You have a visitor. Your son is here to see you, sir."

Lupu fidgeted for a moment, then found the switch he was looking for. He turned on a dim light, humming on the far wall. I held my hand up to my face to protect my nose and peered in. I could make out the details of the cramped room: a small writing table in the far corner, surrounded and piled with white buckets of what I assumed was human waste, and a metal cot pressed against the far wall, straining under the weight of my father, in full military uniform, his head stuffed into a camouflage-coloured *qeleshe*, and a long row of medals, including, somewhat anachronistically, his Medal of Merit in Economy, Third Class, stretching from his breastbone to the edge of his arm.

"He hasn't been himself for weeks," Lupu whispered, with genuine concern in his voice.

I raised my eyebrows and responded. "He never was."

"Hmmm?"

"Himself. He never was."

Lupu nodded and gave a pained smile.

Indeed, Father did not look well. He was pasty and unshaven, and his flesh appeared bloated, like that of a corpse.

"Sir? Commander? You have a visitor."

Lupu stepped toward the bed and tugged on my father's toe.

Slowly, Father opened one eye and then the other. He squinted for a moment, as if trying to get me in focus, then closed his eyes again.

There was a long pause. "Who is it?"

"It's your son, sir. Zavida."

Slowly, Father opened his eyes again. He lay there for several moments in his army fatigues, staring at me like a fish, unblinking. I realized that I too had likely changed for the worse since the time he had last seen me. I'd always been thin, but now I had wasted away to nothing, and my poor beard had gone weeks without a trim or even proper cleaning. I rubbed my face self-consciously.

"What does he want?"

"I've come for you, Father. The war is over and I've come to take you home."

Father stared at me for a long time. A fly landed on his forehead and still he stared, never bothering to flick it off. At one point, he opened his mouth as if to speak, but soon shut it again. Several minutes passed before he closed his eyes again.

"Tell him to go away, Vasile Lupu. Tell him Korbi Artë is indisposed and not receiving visitors."

50

HOW LONG DID I STAND there in the stinking darkness, Nexhmije Gjinushi? minutes? hours? days?

I cannot be certain, the hum of the light, the weight of my father's breaths, the dim shadows...these are the sorts of things that have a negative effect on one's perception of time.

Eventually, Father opened his eyes again. By now, Vasile Lupu had excused himself. It was just my father and I.

Finally, I took the initiative.

"You've been well, Father?"

He snorted and tried to raise himself up on one arm.

"What time is it?"

I shook my head.

"Day?"

"I haven't been keeping track, Father."

He dropped back down on the bed.

"What good are you then?"

"Not much, Father. Not much good at all, I'm afraid."

There was an uncomfortable silence, broken only by my father's laboured wheezing.

"Mother sends her love..."

Father spat a ball of air. "Ha! You obviously haven't spoken to her."

I recoiled for a moment with the realization that not only was he quite correct, but I hadn't actually spoken to her for months.

"Of course I am lying, Father. Mother sends no one her love. That's not her style."

Father smiled, briefly. I now managed to convince Father to take a sip of the soup Vasile Lupu had left for him. He leant on one elbow and took one short draw from the spoon I held out for him.

"She's a cold pot of porridge, your mother." Father almost sounded wistful.

"We should go visit her, Father. Come."

I offered him my hand. He slapped it away.

"I'm not going anywhere, son. My country needs me."

"Your country?"

Father slid back down on the bed and, turning to his side, closed his eyes.

"You know. This place, these people. You get the picture."

51

"WHAT IS THIS LATEST MADNESS, Father?"

The soup, Counsellor, had given him a little energy. He had pushed himself up into a sitting position, allowing me to adjust his pillows for him.

"Father?"

"What is it now?"

"I'm asking you, what illusion are you providing? And for the benefit of whom?"

Father closed his eyes. His breath became laboured.

"Vida, Vida, Vida…" His eyes suddenly sprung open. "You want there to be a simple answer for everything. I am Korbi Artë. What else do you need to know?"

"Well, that tells me nothing, Father. I'm owed, I think, at the very least an explanation of what you are doing here and what plan you have, if any, for me."

"You're a big boy now, son, I am assuming you can take care of yourself?"

"Are you serious, Father? As I recall, you are the one who had me arrested. You ordered a trial for me. You are the one who has imprisoned me and put my liberty and very life at risk."

Father closed his eyes again. After a moment he shrugged and mumbled something.

"Pardon, Father?"

"I said, it's just business."

"It's just — what's that supposed to mean?"

"It's just business, son. You can't take it personally."

I stared at Father, still not comprehending.

"Look Vida, Korbi Artë can't very well have someone out there claiming to be his son."

"But I am your son!"

"More so the requirement for your silence."

By now, I found myself growing angry. I threw my hands up and turned to the door, taking a few paces back, then turning again to face my father. He had slid back down on the bed and, rolling to his side, closed his eyes, a shallow frown on his face that landed him somewhere in the range between indifference and self-pity. I considered walking out on him but remembered my purpose.

"Look at you, Princess. Lying about in your bed, crying for yourself."

"Do not measure the wolf's tail, my son, before the wolf is dead."

"Your folk wisdom will not help you now, Father. I am expecting a lot more from you; we all are. Is this how a Serb behaves?"

"I am not a Serb, Vida."

"Or a Turk? Or a man, for that matter, Father."

"I'll warn you, Son, you do not want to make my blood boil."

"Or what? The great Korbi Artë will rise from his bed like a wet dog from its bath and shake with fury? You're past that, old man. You are a dry seed, a slack cock. You're a former person, Father, you've blurred the boundaries to become something less than nothing, a stain, a reeking memory…"

This was becoming too much for Father. He did indeed

push himself from the bed, righting himself like a capsized boat, slowly at first, weighed down by gravity and history, but then springing forward with such energy that he had to take a moment to stabilize himself and find his balance. We fell together, two dry sticks, each trying to grip the other's collar and get the upper hand. It was a sad fight indeed. Neither of us had any spirit left, and any passion we may have felt was simply a shadow of our former passions. Still, Father was deft in his way. He managed to get one hand around my throat and pressed his thumb into my Adam's apple with enough force to bring me to my knees. I grabbed his arm with both my hands and dug my dirty nails into his skin. If he felt any pain, it did not register on his face.

I was panicking now, flailing at him with both hands, and managed to catch on his beak with enough strength that he loosened his grip. I fell forward holding my neck, gasping.

"There's a...nastiness to you...now, Father." I spoke between breaths. "I'm not sure...being an...Albanian warlord brings out...the best in you. Besides, Father, I am a lover, not a fighter."

"That's the problem, though, isn't it? You're neither a lover nor a fighter. You're a lamb, my son, a vassal of history. I expect —demand—a lot more from you."

Father had made his way back to the cot.

"There it is again, the nastiness, Father. It is very unbecoming. In any case, I respectfully disagree with you. I am by nature, a lover. Why, look at my relationship with Tristina —"

"Relationship? What the fuck does that mean? Relationship!"

"I think it speaks for itself."

"Your *relationship* consisted of scurrying around in her shadows, worshipping from a distance. Even when you were with her, you were not with her. She's a convenient excuse, for you, son; that's all. A thing that provides you with the illusion of greatness without actually having to get in there and do the dirty work."

"The dirty work of love, Father? You are talking nonsense."

He was sitting on the edge of the bed now; I kept drawing myself back an inch at a time, moving closer to the door.

"Love, real love, is all dirty work, Vida. It is an act of constant sacrifice and therefore constant destruction. You are bound to get a little grime on your hands."

"Love is sacrifice, is it Father?

"Everything is sacrifice, my son, or at least a gradual unwinding. We must, all of us, fight for something, must, all of us, seek to uncover the truth beyond the superficial…".

"You're a champion of the Truth, are you now Father? This from a man whose entire existence depends on convincing people he's something he isn't."

"You are focusing, Vida, on the uniform and the little hat and all the trappings of Korbi Artë." My father smoothed the lapel of his officers' uniform. "But these trappings are exactly what I am talking about. Was I born Serb? a Turk? a Croat? a Brahmin outcast? a circus clown? What does it matter? These people, all they care about is that they've found someone who'll stand up to history. Not ignore, not defy it, not worship it like some timorous lover, but grab history by the balls and spit in its face."

"And that is you, Father?"

"That is me."

"The Big-History-Ball-Grabbing-Face-Spitting-Son-of-a-Gun."

"At your service," Father smiled, and lowered his voice.

"You see, Vida. I've never asked a lot of you but have expected much. It is my wish, my firm desire, to see you make

314

something of yourself, to stand up to the forces of this world, to embrace Death as wholly as you have scurried away from Life, to join the Pantheon of Heroes and Martyrs. A lofty ambition, to be sure, but a father can dream, can't he?"

"The days for heroes have come and gone —"

The shelling had begun again, and even in this grave, the walls growled and shook. Milošević's army was launching one mad, final assault before the inevitable defeat.

"You have to understand, Father: I don't want to join the Pantheon of Heroes. I don't want to live or die for the Greater Good of This or That. I want to slither away, Father, to sleep off the rest of my natural life in the arms of My Sweet Angel of the Dogs, dissolving a molecule at a time while my love fixes my supper and scavenges my back for blackheads. I am done with war, Father. I am done with history. I am done with Eternity and Enlightenment and Politics, I am done with the myriad of ways we insignificant many try to distinguish ourselves. I am ready to move on, Father, to live out the rest of my life in useless joy."

Father grew silent again. The combined effect of the thin broth and insults was already wearing off. The light that had danced through his eyes for a moment or two had begun to fade again.

"How did we wind up here, Father?" I asked, after a long silence.

He shrugged.

"Me? I found a uniform at the side of the road. It happened to fit. The rest, as they say..."

"No. I mean here, in this place, this Kosovo, so far from where we started?"

"Son, this is exactly where we started. We haven't moved an inch."

Father put his head down and pulled the thin blanket up from his feet.

"You should go now, Vida."

"Come with me, Father. We'll go — somewhere. America, I think, or Buenos Aires."

"Goodbye, Vida."

"The war is over, Dobroslav Zanković. You are no longer needed here."

"Wars are like buses: there'll be another one coming soon. I'll wait it out."

I hesitated, and then leaned forward to embrace him. Father ignored me. He rolled to his side and pulled the blanket over his head.

"Goodbye, Zavida Zanković. Turn the light out when you leave, please, and tell your mother that I love her."

Was he joking? I could not tell. But I did as I was asked and shut the door softly behind me.

52

THEY HAVE TAKEN AWAY my lovely iBook, Nexhmije Gjinushi. It seems they're going out of business. But I managed to squirrel away a pencil and paper to scribble these last lines and bring my sorry story to a proper end. Shall I mail it to you, my dear?

To: Nexhmije Gjinushi, c/o the Priština School of Law and Cosmeticological Sciences?

Let the record show, my Kosovo Muse, that Adelina and I got a ride in a Norwegian transport truck to the edge of a paved road. The driver left us there to make our way on foot. We were once again in the human river, even larger than before, swelling with people coming from every direction, emerging from the woods and fields, old men in muddy caps, women in ill-fitting overcoats, children, and, more and more, younger men in tattered uniforms or ill-fitting suits, no doubt pilfered at the last minute. It dawned on me that perhaps this war was really over.

"Excuse me, brother," I called to an older man limping along the side of the road carrying a small motor scooter in his arms like a sleeping baby. He turned when I spoke to him and looked at me with sunken eyes that, while not filled with hope, reflected a certain certainty of purpose that I can only characterize as determination. "Where does this road take us?"

The man shrugged. "Somewhere, I suppose. The camps perhaps."

Somewhere. Well, that was better than every other place I had been, I thought, and a good deal more promising than anywhere else I might go. And following the flow I continued walking for several more kilometres until I encountered another intersection, this one splitting off onto a major highway with concrete embankments on either side. There were private cars and UN transport trucks and the occasional Red Crescent ambulance, not to mention a constant stream of pedestrians, each of them carrying what was left of their lives on their backs or in plastic shopping bags or inside bulging suitcases held shut with thick rubber cords. I clutched my lamb even more tightly. *One sheep*, I thought; *not much, but a beginning at least, and halfway to starting my own herd.*

I looked as far up the highway as I could. There were thousands of people before me, their heads undulating like plum blossoms in a spring breeze. I parsed each one searching for a familiar sign. My mother? No. My brothers, Jovo, Djordje? No sight of any of them. Miloš Obilić, in the guise of some mendicant Turk? No sight of those other heroes, Boshko Yugovich, Srdja Zlopogledja, or Yug Bogdan? And the martyrs, Father Stefan Puric, Hariton Lukic, Gavrilo Gabriel...

I saw none of them. Only fellow refugees and scores of children, darting back and forth within the throng, playing tag, saddling up to the Dutch and Norwegian soldiers in their blue UN vests and helmets, angling for a piece of candy or perhaps a slice of apple.

And so I walked and walked and walked and walked, clinging to my lamb with both hands I continued on, past a first checkpoint and then a second, eventually arriving at an enormous processing station, where my fellow travellers and I were asked to form single-file queues that seemed to go on for miles, queues so long, in fact, that they transcended any sense of inconvenience or annoyance and became things simply to be marvelled at, like an enormous stack of dishes balanced on an acrobat's head.

It was some time past two in the morning when I finally took my place at a rusting metal desk. An official sat there, holding a single clipboard on his lap.

"Name? he asked in broken Albanian, barely looking up.

I thought for a moment, then smiled.

"Amerika," I said.

"Amerika? That's it?"

I nodded.

"One word, like 'Cher'?"

I nodded again.

"Place of birth?"

I paused. "In all honesty, I can't remember. I was just a baby, you see."

"Occupation?"

I held up my little charge. "Shepherd."

He shrugged, then turned his attention to a yellow form. He ticked all the right boxes and wrote down whatever responses I gave him. Then he scribbled on the form for a moment, stamped it triplicate, and handed me a copy.

"Here you go, buddy. Welcome to No Man's Land."

I took a couple of steps forward and for a moment marvelled that at some point, over a distance no thicker than a blade of grass, I had stepped out of Kosovo, beyond the once and future Serbia, stepped clear of history and family, and now stood outside of it all.

I surveyed the scene. Row on row of identical white tents, as far as the eye could see, like the reflection of a reflection of a reflection. I placed Adelina on the ground and, taking off my belt, fashioned a leash and secured her firmly. Together, we set out to find an empty tent and a place where we could rest our heads and sleep. And later still, as I lay on the soft ground contemplating the stars and a future without a real name or a family or a place or a history, I heard music wafting down from the hills like smoke. Some insomniac refugee, perhaps, already pining for his ancestral lands. It was a soft simple melody, played on a *guzal* or *kaval*, that rose and curled and tried to wrap itself around me like a snake. I rolled to my side, blocked my ears with my arms, and found that, if I concentrated on my breathing hard enough, I could almost completely blot the music out. I closed my eyes tightly and thought of Tristina for what would be, as I had already decided, the very last time. Already, I was starting to forget the details of her face and could not remember at that moment the exact colour of her eyes. I thought to ask for her forgiveness. But there would be plenty of time for forgiveness and I decided instead to sleep. When the daylight came again, I would have forgotten her, forgotten everything I had seen and heard in my short life. I would find a place and speak to certain people, acquire a visa to Canada or Luxembourg or Panama, and be done with it. And, Tristina, I decided, if she really loved me, would dream of me at night sometimes and would eventually, sooner rather than later, I prayed, forget me, too.

Excerpts from the *Rig Veda* are from Charles F. Horne's classic translation.

The details of the "incident" at the Kalabria Restaurant are taken in large measure from Rod Nordland's chilling account, "Daddy, they're trying to kill us," published in the June 27, 1999, issue of *Newsweek* magazine.

Special thanks to:
Greg Stephenson and Nick Picard, for their editorial insight and generous reviews of the book;

John Pearce and Bruce Westwood and everyone at Westwood Creative Artists, for their collective wisdom and determination;

all of my friends who read the book and provided thoughtful feedback; Bethany, Susanne, Corey, Julie, Colleen, and all the hardworking people at Goose Lane Editions, who, in the face of overwhelming odds, remain ridiculously committed to Canadian literature;

Hope, Hannah, Charlie, Tavish, and Keating for their love during these difficult times.